D0021927

AFTERMATH

ALSO BY KELLEY ARMSTRONG

THE DARKEST POWERS TRILOGY

The Summoning

The Awakening

The Reckoning

THE DARKNESS RISING TRILOGY

The Gathering

The Calling

The Rising

THE AGE OF LEGENDS TRILOGY

Sea of Shadows

Empire of Night

Forest of Ruin

The Masked Truth

Missing

AFTERMATH

Kelley Armstrong

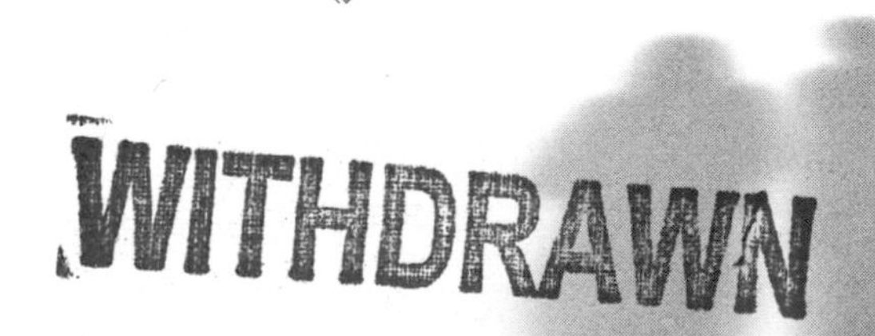

CROWN *New York*

This is a work of fiction. Names, characters, places, and incidents either are the product of the author's imagination or are used fictitiously. Any resemblance to actual persons, living or dead, events, or locales is entirely coincidental.

 Published in the United States by Crown Books for Young Readers, an imprint of Random House Children's Books, a division of Penguin Random House LLC, New York.

Crown and the colophon are registered trademarks of Penguin Random House LLC.

Visit us on the Web! GetUnderlined.com

Educators and librarians, for a variety of teaching tools, visit us at RHTeachersLibrarians.com

Library of Congress Cataloging-in-Publication Data is available upon request.
ISBN 978-0-399-55036-2 (trade) — ISBN 978-0-399-55038-6 (ebook)

Printed in the United States of America
10 9 8 7 6 5 4 3 2
First Edition

Random House Children's Books supports the First Amendment and celebrates the right to read.

For Julia

PROLOGUE

Three Years Earlier

I will not say that the day Jesse Mandal asked me out was the best of my life. That's silly, trite, foolish. But I was thirteen, which means I was all of those things. After school, I would have danced home, humming "Best Day Ever." I'd have tweeted cryptic emojis of hearts and endless exclamation marks. I'd have lain in bed listening to All-Time Five sing about love, glorious love.

I was thirteen. I was that girl. But I didn't dance home at the end of the day. I didn't send any tweets. I never listened to ATF again. Because after that day, I'd never be that girl again.

That day started as mine had for the past year, with me no longer rising to my mom singing whatever song she could mangle my name into—"Good morning, Skye-shine," or "The Skye will come up tomorrow." I'd groan and bury my head under the pillow until she went off to do the same to my brother, Luka—who got Suzanne Vega's "Luka," having been named after the song.

It was only when those wake-ups stopped that I realized how much I'd secretly loved them. Just like I'd loved her hot breakfasts, even when I complained that I could sleep in an extra twenty minutes if she'd let me grab a juice box and granola bar, like all my friends did.

That day I rise to the alarm moments before Luka raps on my door with, "Skye? You up?" He showers first—he's sixteen and needs it more, and sometimes there's no hot water anyway, if Mom forgot to pay the bill again. We both try to be quiet and not wake her. When Dad is away on business she's rarely out of bed before noon, and in the past six months he's been gone more than he's been home.

I'm grabbing a juice box and granola bar when Luka says, "That is not a proper breakfast."

"So you've said. Every morning."

"That isn't even real juice. You might as well drink soda."

"Well, then . . ." I take a Coke from the fridge.

He plucks the can from my hand. "Sit. I'm making you scrambled eggs and toast."

"You don't have time."

"I do. Isaac's picking me up today. He's borrowing his mom's car and—"

A horn sounds outside. I arch my brows.

Luka's cell pings with a text. He reads it and says, "Seriously?"

"That's Isaac, isn't it?"

"Yeah. He's early. Something's up. *So* important." He rolls his eyes. "It always is with him." He starts to type a response. "I'll walk to school."

"Then you'll be late. And if we fight about it, we'll wake Mom."

He hesitates before saying, "Tomorrow, okay? I'll cook for you tomorrow."

"And I'll drink real juice today. Just for you."

He comes over and squeezes my shoulder. "You're a good kid, Skye. Even when you try not to be."

I stick out my tongue. He grins, grabs his backpack and jogs to the door.

In math class, Jesse passes me a note asking me to meet him at afternoon recess. Of course, it doesn't actually say that. It gives GPS coordinates.

I tap his back with my pencil and lean forward to whisper, "I don't think this is the answer to *any* of the questions."

He shakes his head without turning.

"Do *you* need an answer?" I whisper. "I can help you out, you know, if you're having trouble."

I get a flashed middle finger for that. At the front of the class, Ms. Cooper's eyes widen. Then she shakes her head sharply, as if telling herself she saw wrong, because Jesse Mandal is "not that kind of boy."

"Skye?" she says. "Are you bothering Jesse?"

"She keeps asking me for the answer to 3A," Jesse says. "I know math is hard for her, but she needs to figure it out for herself."

A snicker ripples through the class. Ms. Cooper knows there's no chance I'm cheating—Jesse and I have been competing for the top grade all year. She does, however, give me a stern look, warning me to stop making trouble, because Skye Gilchrist *is* "that kind of girl." When you've gone to the same school since kindergarten, you earn your labels early, and they stick long after you've outgrown them. Well, mostly outgrown them.

When recess comes, I zip along the hall, after waving to tell my friends I won't be joining them. I plan to sneak through the front door, but the principal and two teachers are in a whisper-huddle outside the office. They're talking to Ms. Molina, head of the PTA, and not one of my biggest fans, ever since fifth grade, when I called her daughter a bratty bitch. In the middle of an assembly. While standing onstage. Next to the microphone.

I duck down a side hall and see Mr. Garside moving fast in my direction. I backpedal, but he only nods, as if distracted. I zoom past him and out the side door.

Until this past September, Jesse and I had been what Mom calls school pals, meaning we'd say hi if we passed in the shopping mall or talk if we were in the cafeteria line together. Then came two hours assigned to a shared bus seat on a school trip, during which Jesse Mandal became more than a nice guy from school. He became someone interesting.

We've played the coordinates game enough that I can guess where his latest set leads: the recessed janitorial door. I race around the corner and . . .

No one's there.

As I pull out my phone to check my GPS, hands slide over my eyes.

"Tell me what you see," Jesse says, and I grin, because this, too, is our game.

"A mountain cave," I say. "It's dark, but something's moving inside."

"What do you hear?"

"A scratching, like claws on rock."

"Smell?"

I inhale. "Musk. Like a dog when its fur gets wet."

"So what do you do?"

"Sneak closer to see what it is, of course."

He laughs. He's endlessly fascinated by how quickly I can make up a story. If I do the same to him, he sees fingers in front of his eyes, and he can't imagine anything else. That's not how his brain works.

His hands withdraw, but my vision stays blocked by what looks like a cardboard rectangle.

"What do you see now?" he asks.

I make out a few printed words. "Are these—? All-Time Five tickets?" I spin to face him. "For real?"

"I hope so, considering I spent my *dida*'s birthday money on them."

I breathe so hard I swear I'm going to hyperventilate. "Oh my God, oh my God." I inhale and say, "So you're going to the concert with one of the guys?"

He rolls his dark eyes. "Do you think I'd show these to you and then take one of them?"

I smile. "Maybe your brother likes ATF."

"My brother's a jerk. I want to go to the concert with someone I actually like. That's you, Gilchrist. And you'd better say yes, 'cause if I get turned down the first time I ask a girl out, I may never get over it."

"You're asking me . . . ? You mean . . . ? Like a date?"

He goes still. Then he shoves the tickets into his pocket, saying, "No, no . . . well, yeah. Kind of. But it's up to you. We could just go as friends if you want."

"Or a date, if I want?"

He catches my grin, and his eyes light up, and he opens his mouth, but a voice says "Skye?" and we both jump. It's Mr. Garside. He looks from me to my companion. "Jesse?"

"We were talking," I say.

Jesse nods.

"You're both needed at the office." Mr. Garside sounds as distracted as he looked earlier. "Follow me."

"If we're in trouble for sneaking out, I'll tell them it was my idea," Jesse whispers as we follow Mr. Garside.

I shake my head, but Jesse says, "Hey, I actually did something wrong for a change. I want to take credit. Boost my rep."

I've started to answer when I catch the sound of a radio coming from the office.

"—events at North Hampton High School this afternoon. One shooter has reportedly been killed. Another has been taken into custody—"

I stop so fast my shoes squeak. Everyone in the office turns and sees us. Someone says, "Turn that off!" and Principal Salas rushes out, her arms blocking the office doorway as if she can block the sound, too.

Jesse has stopped beside me.

"Did they say . . . ?" he starts.

"The high school. Luka." I can barely form the words. "My brother goes to North Hampton."

"Lots of kids do," Jesse says as he moves up behind me, and there's this weird hollow tone in his voice, and I spin on him, ready to snap that I don't care how many kids go there, I'm talking about my brother.

That's when I see the wall photos of graduates. Over the frames hangs a North Hampton Wildcat banner, because that's where we go. Dozens of kids here have an older sibling there. And yet Jesse and I are the only ones who've been summoned to the office. That's what he means.

"We're having an assembly, right?" I say. "You're getting all the kids in the auditorium to tell them what's happening?"

Mr. Garside nods, too emphatically, and my heart pounds.

"No," I say. "You just wanted us. Me and Jesse."

"Your parents will explain," Principal Salas says. "Jesse? Yours are on their way now. Skye? Mr. Garside will drive you to your mom."

"My parents can take Skye," Jesse says.

There's a sound, like a harrumph. Ms. Molina stands behind the counter, and she's looking straight at me. Glaring. I'm wondering what I did when the principal says, "That's . . . not a good idea."

My heart's pounding, blood rushing in my ears, and I can barely hear what he says, barely hear what I say when I whisper, "Tell me what's going on."

The principal shakes her head. "Your parents will—"

"Tell me what's going on! Now!"

"Skye!" Ms. Molina snaps. "Enough of that."

"No, Skye's right." Jesse steps forward to stand beside me. "We know something's wrong. The radio said . . ." He swallows. "They've been shot, haven't they? Our brothers."

"Your parents will—"

"No!" I say.

Jesse lays his hand on my arm and says to the others, "You don't want to tell us what's happened? Fine. Tell us they're okay."

Silence. I look from face to face, searching for a sign, any sign, *please give me a sign . . .*

"Are they—?" My voice hitches. "Alive? Tell us they're alive."

No one says a word. No one will even look at me.

I see their expressions, and I crumple to the floor. I hear this scream, this terrible scream, and I realize it's coming from me. Jesse's crouching, his arm around me as he pulls me against his shoulder.

Jesse helps me to my feet, and I can feel him shaking, but his voice is calm when he says, "Skye is coming with me. With my parents."

"No, Jesse," the principal says. "I'm sorry, but that really isn't a good idea."

"Our brothers are . . ." Jesse's voice wavers, and he swallows. "They were both . . . both victims of . . ." Another swallow. "We're going together."

"No, you're not." Ms. Molina comes out from behind the desk, her gaze fixed on me. "Skye's brother wasn't a victim. He was one of the shooters."

Skye

Forty-four hours after I heard those words, I was in the backseat of my grandmother's car, with all the belongings I could stuff into a duffel. Anything I'd left behind, I'd never see again. We were running. Running as fast as we could, and the only reason we hadn't left sooner was because my aunt Mae had insisted Mom stand firm. Except my mother was, at that point in her life—as at any point thereafter—barely able to stand at all.

That was three years ago.

I'm skipping those three years. I have to. The aftermath of that day . . . Even thinking about it makes me feel like I'm back there, caught in the eye of a tornado, hanging on for dear life.

My father is long gone. He called my mother that night to say he wasn't coming home. That whatever happened with Luka, it was her fault. Which was exactly what she needed at that moment. *Sorry, but this one's yours, babe, I'm outta here.*

When the divorce went through, he married the business

partner who'd been with him on all his trips. What happened with Luka just gave him an excuse to dump us for her, and I'll never forgive him for that.

Three years.

I can break it down from there, like a prisoner tracking time on her cell wall. I keep everything about that first month confined to its place—don't let it out, even when it pounds at the back of my head, sometimes a dull throb I can ignore, other times a gut-twisting migraine.

One nightmare month followed by six of mere hell. A period of shame and guilt, the feeling that I'd failed Luka. Or that I'd failed to stop Luka.

There's grief, too, but I bury that even faster. You aren't allowed to grieve for someone like Luka. It doesn't matter if he was an amazing brother. Luka Gilchrist was a monster. Write it on the board a hundred times and don't ever forget it.

There's doubt and curiosity, too, which must be doused as quickly as the grief. I want to understand what happened. I want to know how my brother—my kind and thoughtful brother—joined his friends in a school shooting.

How my brother killed four kids.

Except Luka didn't kill four kids. He didn't kill anyone.

No, see, that's an excuse. You aren't allowed to make excuses for him, Skye. He participated in a horrible tragedy, and he would *have killed someone, if he hadn't been shot by police. Making excuses for him belittles what he did and belittles the value of the lives lost.*

Judgment. That's the big one. Being judged. Sister of a school shooter.

My early curiosity led me places I shouldn't have gone, into online news articles, where I got just enough details to give me nightmares. Then into the comments sections, which was even worse as I discovered total strangers who thought I should die for my brother's sins and said it so offhandedly, like it was the most obvious thing. *Hey, I hear one of those bastards has a sister. Maybe someone should take a gun to her school. Or maybe someone should take her and—*

I won't finish that sentence. I see the words, though. Thirteen years old, reading what some troll thinks should be done to me and wondering how *that* would help anything.

Then came anger and resentment and feeling like maybe, just maybe, I didn't deserve the petition that went around my new school saying I shouldn't be allowed to attend, for the safety of others. But on the heels of that anger and resentment I would slingshot back to shame and guilt, thinking about the kids who died and how dare I whine about whispers and snubs and having DIE, BITCH written on my locker and yes, the janitor will paint that over the next time he does repair work and no, I'm sorry, Mrs. Benassi, but there are no other lockers for your granddaughter at this time.

Six months of that. Then Gran moved us, and I registered under her surname. That blessed anonymity only lasted a few months before someone found out. Then it was homeschooling and moving again and that time the new surname worked. By then two years had passed, and when kids did find out, I lost a few friends, but otherwise, compared to those first six months, it was fine.

Now, three years later, I'm going back.

Back to Riverside, where they have definitely not forgotten

who I am. Back to Riverside, where I will live two miles from my old house. Back to Riverside, where I will go to school alongside kids I grew up with.

I'm returning to the only place I ever truly called home. And there's nothing I can do to stop it.

My aunt Mae picks me up. It's a tiny airport—Riverside is a city of three hundred thousand—and I scuttle through the terminal, my head down, praying I'm not recognized, and knowing that even if I succeed, I've only dodged one bullet.

I have to deal with this. That's what Mae says, just like she said to my mother three years ago.

"You did nothing wrong, Skye," Mae insisted when I asked—no, begged—for some other solution to our predicament. "Your mother should never have left Riverside. Your gran wanted to make things easier on you two, and I get that—I really do—but it didn't help your mom."

I'm not sure anything could have helped my mother, spiraling into depression even before the shooting, drifting from us as our father drifted from their marriage.

Mae continued, "You're going to come home, and you're going to look people in the eye and lift your chin and say, 'I'm sorry for what my brother did, but it has nothing to do with me.'"

Fine words. Strong, sensible words. But Mae was only the aunt of a school shooter, and while I'm sure she got her share of whispers and glares, I bet no one said they thought *she* should be sterilized so she didn't pass on her tainted genes.

When I walk into the baggage claim, she's there, looking as if she's stepped off a magazine cover. Mae runs her own firm, one of those vaguely named businesses conducted in hushed offices full of very busy people. She's never married. She's had one live-in girlfriend, but it didn't last long. I'm her only niece. Luka was her only nephew.

When Mae sees me, she smiles and calls, "Skye!" as she strides over and envelops me in a hug that smells of cherry blossoms. "Welcome home."

I want to say this isn't my home anymore, and I'm certainly not welcome here. But I'm too busy cringing as my name rings through the tiny terminal. People look over. I tell myself it means nothing. Skye is only a moderately unusual name, and I'm even less unusual-looking—straight dark-blond hair in a ponytail, average height, average build. Stick me in any high school classroom and at least two girls could pass for my sisters. It's that kind of look.

We're waiting for my luggage. Mae's talking to me, and all I can hear is her appending my name to every sentence, as if she needs to remind herself who she's talking to. Each time she says it, I swear more people look over. I tell myself I'm being paranoid. Then a college-age girl whispers to her mother, whose gaze swings on me.

I'm imagining things.

Except I'm probably not. The shooting at North Hampton hit front pages across the country. While that may have faded elsewhere, the people here will not have forgotten. They will not have forgiven.

We have my luggage, and we're heading out and that mother's gaze is glued to me, her face gathered in that look I know well, the one that asks what right I have to be walking around like a normal teenage girl.

"I thought we'd eat at Frenchy's," Mae says as we walk out. "I remember how much you guys loved that place."

You guys. She means me and Luka. He hated Frenchy's almost as much as Mae did. Greasy food served halfheartedly, as if by a mother who's really tired of cooking for her ungrateful offspring. Luka never let on how much he hated it because I loved it, and that's the kind of brother he was. The kind of person he was. Except he wasn't, was he?

I used to have nightmares where Luka wasn't involved in the shooting. Where they investigate again and discover it was all a mistake. Those were wonderful dreams . . . until I woke and remembered that wasn't how it happened, and the recollection would twist them into nightmare.

I want to say that whatever happened that day, Luka would *never* have fired a gun. Not the guy who wouldn't go hunting with our dad, couldn't even stomach shooting lessons. I'd taken those lessons instead, so our father would leave him alone.

A guy like that *couldn't* be part of a school shooting.

But if I even think this, I'm making excuses. Refusing to face reality. Downplaying Luka's role. Disrespecting the dead.

But he *is* one of the dead. No one ever says that, though. The North Hampton shooting claimed the life of *four* kids—four *real* victims. My dead brother exists in another place, beyond where I can speak to him, speak *for* him, mourn him. He's just gone.

"I don't really feel like Frenchy's," I say as Mae waits for an answer.

Relief floods her face. "All right. Well, if you still like burgers, I know a little shop that does gourmet."

"Can we just pick something up? I'd rather not go out."

There's a heartbeat of silence, and in it, I hear disappointment. I am not the girl she hoped I'd be.

Maybe I should feel a surge of inner strength at that, should be shamed into saying that the burger place sounds good, and then she'll smile and be proud of me. But I can't form the words.

"We'll get takeout," she says finally, and we continue through the sliding doors.

I'm supposed to go to school the next day. I consider skipping. But it's not like I can avoid it forever, and my pleas for a day of rest fell on deaf ears. It's Monday, an excellent day to start, and the school is expecting me. Chin up. Get on with it.

Mae insists I take a cab. I have it drop me off a few blocks away. As I walk, I call Gran. She had a stroke two weeks ago. Last Tuesday I was at the hospital with her late into the night, and then Mom took a turn for the worse the next morning, so I faked a sick call to school. Big mistake. Child services had been hovering ever since Gran's first stroke. When a teacher called with her concerns, they swooped. No one cared that I could take care of myself *and* make up my schoolwork. Which is why I'm with Mae.

Talking to Gran isn't a two-way conversation—the stroke affected her vocal cords—but she listens. She always listens.

"Mae's new condo is worse than the last one," I say. "All steel and glass, and I swear she sets the temperature at sixty. It's like a walk-in freezer."

Gran makes this noise that I know is a laugh.

"My bedroom is white," I say. "White with more steel and

more glass. I'm telling myself it's good practice for when I'm an astronaut."

I'm not really going to be an astronaut. I said that when I was five, and Gran never forgot. For years, I thought it was an actual possibility, well past the stage where most kids realize it's like saying you want to become a rock star.

I keep the joke with Gran, though I'm not sure she realizes it's a joke. Like Mae, Gran's one of those "you can do anything you put your mind to" people. I used to believe that. Now, when people ask what I want to be when I grow up, I want to say that just growing up seems like an accomplishment. Not everyone gets that far.

"I see the school," I say. "I'll let you go and call Mom before dinner."

I put my cell phone into my backpack. There's no reason to keep it handy. The friends I left behind were "school pals," and I doubt I'll hear from them again.

Sometimes I'd see kids in the corners of school cafeterias, perfectly content with their own company, and I'd wish I could be like that. For me, my own company can be noisier than a table full of football players.

I'm walking up to the school. It is not North Hampton High. NHH had already been slated to close, so after the shooting, they shut it down early. This is Riverside Collegiate, one of the two places the NHH kids ended up. One of the two places my old classmates ended up.

I wanted to go to another school, whatever the travel time. Mae thought RivCol was best—face my fears. I understand her reasoning, but there's a point where her encouragement starts to feel like a punishment.

I have to meet my vice-principal—Mr. Vaughn—before class. I follow a few other early birds, and right inside the doors, there's a metal detector. My heart starts thudding, and all I can think is that there were never metal detectors at schools in Riverside before. Now there is one, and it might as well have a plaque on the side: BROUGHT TO YOU BY ISAAC WICKHAM, HARLEY STEWART AND LUKA GILCHRIST.

When I stop at the detector, a girl behind me says, "What? Never seen one of those before, Skye?"

It takes a moment to recognize her. Lana Brighton. We'd been classmates since kindergarten. Lana was the kind of girl you know well enough to invite to your birthday when your mom says you can have twelve kids and you really only count eight, maybe nine, as good friends, but you want your full allotment, so you add kids who don't get asked that often. It's the right thing to do. I'd invited Lana to a few of those parties, and she used to sit with us sometimes at lunch.

"Lana," I say, hoping my voice isn't shaking. "Good to see—"

"Just walk through the damned metal detector, Skye," she says. "In fact, I think you should walk through it twice, to be sure we're all safe." She turns to the kids waiting. "For those who don't know, this is Skye Gilchrist. Luka Gilchrist's sister."

Blood pounds in my ears and my vision clouds, and I stand there, unable to move, until Lana gives me a push, saying, "Go or get out of the way."

I'm turning to walk through, and I catch a glimpse of a boy rounding the corner. For a split second, my brain sees Jesse and screams no, it can't be, that Mae swore he went to Southfield.

The last time I saw Jesse was the night after the shooting. I'd been in my room, sitting on the floor, shaking so hard, unable to cry. I heard stones at my window and looked down to see Jesse below.

I still remember the relief I felt seeing him—the one person I could talk to, maybe even cry with. Then I saw his face, the anger, the rage, and I remembered what had happened, that his brother was dead and mine was to blame. One look at his face, and I shut that blind as fast as I could and curled up on the floor, and cried, finally cried.

Now, as I catch a glimpse of this boy, I think it's Jesse. But then he's gone, and I realize I was mistaken. This boy is tall; Jesse was an inch shorter than me. This boy has wild, curly dark hair; Jesse always kept his short and neat. Even the face isn't right, too angular, too hard for the boy I knew. I'm left with the feeling that the only reason I even jumped to that conclusion was that the boy has brown skin and Jesse's grandparents came from Bangladesh, and that just makes me feel worse, that I jumped to such a stereotyped conclusion.

I push through the metal detector and hurry to find the office.

Jesse

Skye Gilchrist.

Jesse leans against the wall, out of sight of the school doors. When he spotted her, he backpedaled so fast he nearly fell on his ass.

It isn't Skye. Cannot be Skye. She left three years ago and never looked back. Never reached out. Never contacted him. Never even said goodbye.

The last time he saw her, he was standing under her window. He escaped the hell of that day and went to the only person he could talk to. He ran all the way to Skye's house and stood under her window, seeing the light on, knowing she was in there, tossing pebbles at her window, getting no response, and growing more and more frustrated, the stones getting larger until finally she looked down. Looked down . . . and shut the blind.

It took him a day to calm down. A day for the turmoil in his head and in his home to settle, just a bit, and let him realize, well, he'd kinda been an ass. Skye had lost her brother, too, and he'd only been thinking of himself, *his* anguish, *his* confusion.

Skye had been hurting, and she just hadn't felt like talking. He needed to understand that. So a few days later, he went to try again . . . and she was gone. Left Riverside without a goodbye, and that hurt—hurt like hell—but he told himself it was temporary. She knew where to find him. She would text. She'd email. She'd do something.

She did nothing.

Three years of silence.

He thought they were friends. *Good* friends. Maybe even becoming more. He liked her. No, let's be honest, he fell for Skye the way only a thirteen-year-old kid can fall. The first girl he couldn't stop thinking about, couldn't wait to see again, to talk to again.

Now, at sixteen, he looks back and wants to roll his eyes at that. Silly kid stuff. Only it didn't feel like silly kid stuff. And when he caught a glimpse today of someone who looked like her, what he felt . . .

One spark of heart-in-throat joy, followed by a gut-twisting crash, the pain of her rejection and her betrayal coming fast and hard.

Not kid stuff. Damn it. Not kid stuff at all.

But it isn't her. Can't be. Jesse takes a few deep breaths. Then he heads back to the door and walks inside, and there she is, up ahead, turning down a side hall. He sees her, and there is no question. Absolutely no question that this is Skye Gilchrist.

He backs up fast, bumping into a kid who mutters, "Watch it!" Then he breaks into a jog and gets out of the school as fast as he can.

He makes it two blocks before a silver minivan pulls over. It's his chem teacher, Ms. Blake.

"Going the wrong way, aren't you, Jasser?" she says.

He tenses at the name. It's his, and he's fine with it, but no one uses it at school, not since first grade, when a kid called him Jesse by mistake, and he declared that was what he wanted to be called. He feels silly about that now, being so eager to jump at a name that made him fit in better, but by sixteen, he *is* Jesse, and no one outside his family uses Jasser . . . except Ms. Blake, when she's annoyed with him.

"I forgot something at home," he says.

"Well, you'd better hop in, and I'll drive you. You have that makeup quiz with me this morning, and I'm not rescheduling if you skip it, too."

"I was home sick Friday. My dad called in."

"Your dad. That's right. He's phoned in sick for you a few times this term . . . and it's only October. I've started to wonder if we should follow up with your mom. I know she's a doctor, and I'm sure she's concerned about your health."

Jesse wants to shrug and say whatever and continue walking home. If he does, though, his parents will get a call, and they don't deserve it.

"Climb in," she says. "Let's go pick up what you left at home."

He mutters that it's not important and jogs back to school.

Skye

I eat lunch in a bathroom stall. I've been in there awhile and the initial rush has passed, and I think I'm alone. Then I hear two girls talking.

"What's she even doing back here? Isn't there a law against that?"

"There should be."

"Lana Brighton started a petition, saying it's disrespectful to the families and friends of the dead kids to have her here."

"Where is it? I'll sign."

I should confront them. Three years ago, I would have done exactly that. Walk out, chin up, and say, "Oh, hey, I heard you talking about a petition. Tell me more." That's the old Skye. The new one stays in the bathroom stall, stuffs her half-eaten sandwich into her bag and waits for the bell.

○○○

I have survived my first day at school. Well, almost. One period to go. I'm feeling okay. I've had looks in the hall. Whispers trail after me. But I've had kindness, too, particularly in my second-to-last class—senior physics—and maybe it's because the kids are older, college-bound and focused on their studies. Instead of glares, I get sympathetic smiles. Instead of whispers, I get the same questions every new kid gets, like asking where I moved from. At the end, a girl who looks familiar offers to walk me to my next class.

"You probably don't remember me," she says. "I'm Tiffany Gold."

I stiffen. I don't mean to, but I remember her now. Isaac's girlfriend. Isaac Wickham, ringleader of the North Hampton shooting.

"Yep," she says with a wry smile. "*That* Tiffany Gold."

Shame floods me. "I'm sorry. I didn't mean—"

"No, it's okay. It's got to be a shock, seeing me here. I should be in college."

"You were younger than . . ." I trail off.

"I was a year younger than Isaac and Luka. I'm doing a victory lap this term. Which means I'm the only student at RivCol who was there that day, and you don't need to worry about bumping into others. If that helps."

"It does, thanks." I take another step. "How are you doing?"

"Fine. People have pretty much forgotten my connection by now. Even in the beginning, they cut me slack. I was just the poor girl who got mixed up with the wrong guy." She makes a face. "I'm not handling this very well. I wanted to say hello."

"Thank you."

She smiles and relaxes. "Anytime you want to talk, I'm here. If you'd rather not, I get that, too. No hard feelings."

I thank her again, and she helps me find my last class.

I have math now. I'm not top of my class anymore. Far from it. One therapist said that's because I learned about the shooting right after math class. Loathing by association. I don't always buy my therapists' theories, but that one was spot-on with this. Math used to be my favorite subject, and now the only reason I still take it is that I'll never get into a science program otherwise.

The teacher directs me to a seat. The girl behind me promptly moves. I ignore that. I can get through this.

I *will* get through it.

Class is about to begin. The teacher—Ms. Distaff—is turning on the SMART Board when the door opens. And it's him.

It's the boy I saw this morning.

And the boy I saw this morning?

Jesse.

For three years, I've tried to banish this face from my memory. When I thought I misidentified some random guy earlier, I was actually relieved. It proved that I no longer remembered what Jesse Mandal looked like.

Then I see him, and it doesn't matter if he's wearing his hair longer. It doesn't matter if his face has matured, soft cheeks hollowing, the last traces of baby fat gone. It doesn't matter if this guy looks like he rolled out of bed in yesterday's clothes while *my* Jesse was so perfectly groomed I used to tease him about ironing his T-shirts. Even his expression is unfamiliar. I remember a boy who was thoughtfully serious but ready to smile at any provocation. This guy shuffles in like math class is court-ordered and he'd be elsewhere if his parole officer wasn't watching.

This boy is nothing like my Jesse. Yet he is unmistakably Jesse Mandal.

Jesse walks in. He sees me. He stops short. He looks around and realizes the only open chair is the one the girl vacated behind me.

"Well, hello, Jesse," Ms. Distaff says. "Are you actually joining us today? Or just coming to see if anything's changed since the last time you showed up?"

She must be kidding. My Jesse never skipped class. I did, if only a couple of times, curious to see if I could get away with it. Once, Jesse wanted to give it a try, and we planned to fake a sick call and go hiking, but at two a.m. I got a text, Jesse about to be genuinely sick with anxiety.

Yet today, Jesse just says, "My seat's taken."

"Which is what happens when you skip an entire week. There's an empty seat behind our new student, Skye. I doubt she bites."

My cheeks flame, and a girl titters behind me.

"I know who she is," Jesse says.

"Lovely, then you can skip the formal greetings and put your butt in that chair so I can start."

"I can't sit there."

"Put your—"

"He's right," says a guy in the back. "Her brother was Luka Gilchrist. The guy who killed Jesse's brother. She shouldn't even be in the same class as him. It's disrespectful."

Silence. Five long seconds as I pray for release. For someone to point out that Luka didn't shoot Jamil Mandal, and maybe, yes, maybe, I hope that someone will be Jesse.

No one says a word.

"I—I can switch seats," I say, getting to my feet.

"Or," the boy in the back says, "you could just leave."

Now Jesse will speak up. One thing we had in common was our sense of right and wrong, the first kids to be outraged by injustice.

Jesse silently walks to the back of the class, slides to the floor, and sits there, knees up, gaze fixed on the SMART Board.

The next thing I know, I'm running down the hall, and I don't stop until I'm out the front doors.

Skye

My wild flight from school is cut short by the sight of a security officer. The old Skye would have flown past, not caring about the tornado of consequences that would follow. Sure, I'd earn detention the next day. Sure, my parents would get a call. Sure, Luka would sigh and explain why I shouldn't do things like that. But I'm upset, damn it, and I'm entitled to a little drama.

When I stop on seeing the guard, it isn't maturity. It's shame.

I slink back into the school and revisit my new bestie: the girls' bathroom. I stand in the stall and take out my phone to text Mae.

You told me Jesse wouldn't be here.

There's a whine in my words, and I rewrite the text.

Jesse's here. I thought he wouldn't be.

That's better. More mature. An implied request for information rather than an outright accusation. Yet I still don't send it. I read the words, and I want to erase them and write *Hey, Mae? You knew Jesse was here, didn't you? You lied to force me to face him. You know what I have to say to that?* Insert appropriate emoji.

I turn off my phone and stare at the screen and wish I could call someone. I think of Gran. I think of Mom, before her problems. I think of Luka, and I know I'm not supposed to, but sometimes I can't help it. My defensive wall doesn't fly up fast enough.

I think of Jesse, too. Because, once upon a time, that was him. It was only a blip—six months of my now sixteen years, but it was exactly the right time for a friend like Jesse. Mom was getting sick, and Luka was struggling to keep the household running, and Gran was so far away and, let's face it, at thirteen, I didn't want to complain to any of them. I wanted to text the guy who'd send back "That sucks" and "Wanna talk?" along with whatever cute animal gif he found to cheer me up. I remember that, and then I think of the guy I just saw in math class, and I want to cry. I just want to cry.

Instead, I sit on the toilet and do my physics homework. When anyone comes in, I stop, so they don't hear my pen scratching against paper.

I hang out in the restroom until I hear the bell. As I walk, I mentally picture my route, like an invisible GPS display.

For the quickest route, turn left at the next intersection and continue fifty feet—

"Miss Gilchrist?"

I stop midstep and turn. My VP—Mr. Vaughn—is bearing down on me.

"A word, please, Miss Gilchrist," he says.

Then he walks right past me. I could play dumb, but I know I'm meant to walk with him. Mr. Vaughn is well over six feet tall, with gangly giraffe legs, and I need to jog to keep up, my shoes slapping the linoleum. The sound echoes like a drum roll, and everything slows as kids turn to watch me being escorted by the VP.

I'm trying to look straight ahead, but the crash of something hitting a locker makes me jump. It's just a guy goofing off. Behind him, though, I catch a glimpse of Jesse. He's taking something out of his locker, but I know he's seen me. He shuts the locker and turns the other way, careful to keep his back to me. He starts cutting through a cluster of kids.

"Mr. Mandal," Mr. Vaughn calls.

Jesse keeps moving.

"Mr. Mandal," Mr. Vaughn says, louder.

Jesse slowly pivots. Doesn't say a word. Just turns.

"Would you like to join us, Mr. Mandal?"

"Nah, I'm good."

A few kids snicker.

Mr. Vaughn's color rises. "That wasn't an invitation."

Jesse shrugs, says, "Sounded like one."

More kids snicker. Mr. Vaughn glowers, beckons Jesse over, and then resumes walking.

I want to tell Jesse that I'm sorry. Not about his brother. The time for that has passed. I'm sorry if I've gotten Jesse in trouble. I get the sense that's nothing new, and I'm still trying to wrap my head around that. How could he have changed so much?

Well, it starts with having his brother murdered in a school shooting . . .

Jesse's walking on the opposite side of Mr. Vaughn. Deliberately staying on the other side. I hope he'll sneak a glance my way so I can mouth an apology. He doesn't.

We pass the Wall of Fame outside the office—a corridor of

photos and trophies. There's a section for North Hampton, stuff moved here after the school shut down. Mr. Vaughn knuckle-taps the glass as we pass, and he says, "Fine boy. An all-around fine boy." Jesse tenses, and the look that passes through his eyes is one I do recognize from my Jesse, and I know who Mr. Vaughn is referring to even before I glance over.

Inside the display is a photo of Jesse's brother, Jamil, surrounded by athletic awards. A memory flashes. I'm walking past the park with Jesse, and Jamil's shooting hoops. The ball slams into Jesse hard enough to knock him to one knee.

I grab the ball, and Jamil strolls over, saying, "Still can't catch, bro?" Then he looks me up and down, in a way that makes me want to hug the ball to my chest. "Your friend here doesn't have that problem. Maybe she could teach you, in exchange for helping her with her homework."

Jesse says, "Skye doesn't need homework help," and Jamil smirks and says, "Then why's she hanging out with you?" and I whip the ball back, knocking him off-balance when he catches it, but he only grins and winks at me as he saunters back to the court.

No, Jamil Mandal was not *a fine boy*. I shouldn't say that about the dead, but it's true.

I try again to catch Jesse's eye, to offer some sympathy. Then I realize that's entirely the wrong response from entirely the wrong person.

We get to the main office, and Mr. Vaughn waves me into a side room. It's not much bigger than a broom closet, with a single chair, like a movie interrogation chamber, and as I sit, I expect him to follow and loom over me, saying, *We have ways to make you talk.*

Instead, he stays in the main office, leaving the door between us half open as he says, "I hear you refused to sit near Miss Gilchrist."

"I asked to be allowed to sit elsewhere."

It takes me a moment to realize it's Jesse speaking. Until now, I've only heard a few words from him, more grunts than sentences. His voice is deep, unfamiliar.

"Ms. Distaff tells me it was a little more forceful than asking to be seated elsewhere. You disrupted the class. You caused Miss Gilchrist to run out, and now I need to discipline her for that."

I'm at the doorway before I can stop myself. "It's not Jesse's fault. Ms. Distaff didn't know our history. It was awkward, and I've had a long first day, and I overreacted. I take responsibility."

"No one is asking you to, Miss Gilchrist. I am well aware of the *history*, as you put it, and my advice to Mr. Mandal?" He turns to Jesse. "Get over it. Miss Gilchrist had nothing to do with what happened to your brother, and by reacting the way you did, you give fodder to all those students who want to be outraged for no reason other than that they enjoy the adrenaline rush. I would like you to lead by example, Mr. Mandal. I know that isn't your natural bent. Your brother was the leader."

Jesse tenses.

Mr. Vaughn plows on. "But I am going to ask you to lead in *this* by not treating Miss Gilchrist like she was the one holding that gun."

I cringe. I understand what Mr. Vaughn's saying, but the way he says it . . .

I back up quickly, close the door and sit down to wait my turn.

Skye

Five minutes later, Mr. Vaughn comes in.

"As you overheard, Miss Gilchrist, I have no choice but to discipline you for leaving class. I am not unsympathetic to your situation, but if I exempt you from the usual punishment, students will complain that you have received special treatment. You will remain in here, on detention, until I return. You may contact your aunt to tell her you'll be delayed by approximately thirty minutes."

There's no need for that. Mae won't be home until five. So I pull out my homework, finish physics and move to English. When I'm done, I realize it's gone silent outside. I check my watch. Nearly an hour has passed, and Mr. Vaughn hasn't returned.

I push open the door to ask the secretary if I can leave. Her desk is deserted. The whole office is deserted.

I slip out carefully. If I'm in trouble for fleeing class, then fleeing detention sure isn't going to help, but there's no one here.

I walk to the main office door and turn the knob and . . . it doesn't open. I keep twisting as panic sets in. Heart-pounding, can't-catch-my-breath panic. That pisses me off. I used to be the girl who'd find herself locked in the main office and think, *Cool. Never had this happen before,* and then snoop around before looking for a solution. Afterward, I'd go home and write it as an even more interesting scene for a story. Not just locked in the office, but locked in on a Friday . . . right before the school is due to be demolished!

I'd started working my way back to being that girl. And now, one accidentally locked door reignites all my anxieties, and I'm hyperventilating as if I am indeed locked in a building about to be demolished. As if I don't have a cell phone with a full battery and full service.

I will not be that girl. I won't even be the girl who telephones for help. That's just embarrassing.

I examine the knob. It's a double-sided keyed lock. After a few minutes of searching, I find a key in the secretary's desk.

I congratulate myself on my keen detective work as I put the key in and . . .

Nothing. The key turns, but the door won't open.

I bend and look through as I turn the knob. The plunger withdraws, and I see nothing else to stop the door from opening. But it won't.

When I push, the door gives a little. Okay, it's not locked—just sticking. By pressing various parts of the doorframe, I determine that the bottom is jammed somehow. The door opens outward, meaning something external must be blocking it. A prank, then, kids figuring they were locking in the VPs.

I push and pull and jiggle until the door's open an inch. Then two. Crouching, I squeeze my hand through and find a doorstop, one of those brown rubber ones. I wiggle it out, and the door swings open.

The hall is empty. Silent, too, except for the distant clomp of footsteps. Was someone trying to prevent *me* from leaving? That seems like paranoia, and it's too easy to fall down that hole. For the sake of my mental health, I'm going to presume that whoever put the doorstop in was just playing a prank on whoever happened to be in the office.

As I walk, I hear the swish of a broom. I turn the corner to see the custodian. It's a young guy, college age, tall and muscular. He looks familiar. When I walk over, he stops and watches me, his face expressionless.

"Hi, I'm—"

"Skye," he says. "I know."

"Right. Um, so—"

"I helped coached your Little League team about five years ago."

It clicks then. "Owen," I say with a smile. "I remember."

He doesn't smile in return, and as I process his name, I remember we have another connection. His cousin Vicki was injured in the shooting. No, not "injured." That sounds like she tripped and twisted her ankle. Vicki is in a wheelchair now. Will be in a wheelchair for life.

"So, I, uh . . ." I resist the urge to take a slow step back. "I . . . was in detention and Mr. Vaughn seemed to forget me so I'm . . . I'm just going to leave now."

I start to go, and Owen says, "He does that."

I glance over my shoulder, and Owen is leaning on his broom.

He says, "I swear you're the third kid Vaughn has forgotten

this term already. He just split with his wife. He has a lot on his mind."

"Oh. Okay. Thanks. And, um, I don't want to get anyone in trouble, but when I tried to leave the office, someone had stuck in a doorstop. I'm sure it was just a prank. But if Mr. Vaughn is known for forgetting kids on detention, it might be something to watch."

Owen's brows knit. "A doorstop?"

"One of those brown rubber ones. I can show you."

He follows me. We round the corner to the office, and I say, "It's right there on the . . ."

It's *not* there. I pick up my pace, until I'm at the office, looking around.

"It was right here," I say. "Brown rubber. Like they use in classrooms."

"We don't use doorstops."

"Then someone brought it in."

His frown deepens. "Brought a *doorstop* from home?"

I'm breathing harder now, anxiety rising. I want to say I know what I saw, but I hear myself saying, "M-maybe I made a mistake."

"All right."

He's studying me, and I hurry on to say, "I'm sorry. I had a long day. I didn't mean to bother you," and then I start toward the front doors.

"Those are locked," Owen says. "You'll need to use the rear ones."

I nod and head for the back doors. Or I hope that's where I'm heading. The school isn't laid out in a simple rectangle. I don't dare ask Owen for directions—I've pestered him enough. I passed the rear doors earlier today. Now if I can remember how to get there from here . . .

Down one hall. Around a corner.

I hear footsteps. I stop. They stop.

I continue on. So do the footfalls.

"Owen?" I call.

No answer. Again the footsteps stop when I do.

Maybe because they're actually mine, echoing through the empty building?

Speaking of paranoid . . .

I shake my head and keep going. Around another corner, and I'm certain the exit is right ahead. It's not.

I turn, and my shoes squeak, and under that squeak, I hear a voice.

"Hello?" I say.

No answer. I head toward the voice. When I can make out words, the hairs on my neck rise.

"What's she even doing back here? Isn't there a law against that?"

"There should be."

"Lana Brighton is starting a petition, saying it's disrespectful to the families and friends of the dead kids to have her here."

"Where is it? I'll sign."

It's the same thing the girls said in the bathroom. Word for word.

It even sounds like their voices.

That's not possible. It must be different girls talking about the same petition.

I keep moving toward the voices, but they've stopped now. So have the footfalls. Then, as I'm about to go, I hear them again . . . coming from the opposite direction.

"What's she even doing back here? Isn't there a law against that?"

"There should be."

I squeeze my eyes shut and take deep breaths.

I'm stressed and imagining things. I must be. I never have before, but I don't know of any other explanation.

And the doorstop?

When I think of that, I start trembling. I can accept that I imagined voices, but to imagine that I was locked in the office? That I hallucinated a doorstop that I'd held in my hand?

I break into a jog, my shoes echoing through the corridors.

Jesse

Jesse stands outside the school doors, waiting for Skye. He's going to talk to her. He needs to, even if he has no idea what to say. He stands slumped against the wall, hood pulled over his eyes, hands in his pockets.

He never used to be able to stand around doing nothing. When he was little, his parents would buy him math puzzle books for even short car rides.

"You know that's weird, right?" Jamil would say when their parents couldn't hear. "No one does math for fun. Only freaks."

"That's not no one, then, is it?" he'd say, and Jamil would scowl and mutter "Freak," and Jesse would ignore him, because if being a freak meant he wasn't like his brother, that was fine by him.

Skye used to sit and stare at nothing. Except she was *doing* something. She was thinking. Imagining. Creating. Jesse would sit and watch her, and that was as close as he ever came to doing nothing. Except he was doing something, too. Waiting and wondering what she was thinking, marveling at the fact that she could be so busy while sitting so still, her face lighting in a smile or falling in a frown, both too faint to notice if you didn't know her. Jesse knew her.

The moment she snapped from her reverie, he'd be ready with a casual "What were you thinking about?" and she would smile at him—that smile that made his heart beat faster—and she'd tell him. Whatever crazy, wild story she'd been creating for her own amusement, passing downtime like he did with his puzzles. She would share it with him.

Jesse rubs his face. Skye isn't that girl now. She probably never was, except in his head.

But whatever Skye was—or is—she doesn't deserve what she got at school today. He saw her face when she ran from class, and he realized *he'd* done that and felt like crap. That's what he'll tell her now. Apologize for making her feel bad . . . and then get the hell out of here.

Which will be a whole lot easier if she actually shows up. He checks his watch. Her detention should have ended a while ago. Did she leave through the back?

Or did she see him and *duck* through the back?

"Yo, Mandal," a voice calls.

Jesse hunkers down, shoulders raised, one heel against the brickwork. Between the stance and the lowered hood, the message should be clear. *Leave me alone.*

Three guys stop in front of him. Seniors. That's all he knows—he hasn't been at RivCol long enough to put names to faces, and it's not like he wants to anyway. He's just putting in time until he graduates, and then . . .

Damned if he knows what happens then. It used to be so clear, his life laid out in perfect order. He's blown that all to hell, and he doesn't care. Hasn't cared in a very long time.

"Yo, Mandal, you hear us talking to you?"

He lifts his hood, just enough so he doesn't provoke them into a fight. He can't afford that. His parents might pretend they sent him to RivCol for a "fresh start," but it wasn't like they had a choice. They were only grateful that Southfield agreed to go along with the fiction, keeping his expulsion a secret "out of consideration for his family's tragedy."

You can get a lotta mileage from a family tragedy, if it's big enough and public enough. It's the public part that does it—Southfield didn't want the drama of expelling Jesse Mandal, the understandably troubled younger brother of poor Jamil.

"Mandal, I asked you—"

"Hey," he says. And he nods. Because even being that troubled kid doesn't erase who he was. He imagines Jamil sneering and saying, *You can't even be a proper badass, can you, freak?*

Jesse's greeting throws the seniors off-balance, but the biggest one bounces back with "Heard you won the track meet last week. Big track star, huh? Like your brother?"

Jamil didn't do track. He thought it was for losers who couldn't throw or catch or hit a ball. But Jesse doesn't correct them. He just waits to see where this is going.

"My brother played football with yours," the big guys says. "Want to know what he thought of him?"

Jesse remembers Vaughn tapping the trophy glass.

Fine boy. An all-around fine boy.

"Ben thought Jamil was an asshole," the big guy says.

Then Ben was a fine boy himself, a fine judge of character.

Shame washes through Jesse as he thinks that.

When Jesse doesn't respond, the big senior leans in. "He thought your dead brother was an asshole."

"Okay."

The senior glances at his friends for help. The red-haired one says, "Someone told me you're Indian. If you want to pull that off, tell your mother to stop wearing a head scarf."

"Bengali," Jesse mutters, and he hates correcting them, but there's still that kid inside him, who must patiently explain, as if people actually gave a damn.

"Bengali," he says again. "My grandparents are from Bangladesh, which is beside India. I'm American. I was born here."

"I've seen your mom's head scarf, Mandal," the big guy says. "You gonna tell me she's just cold?"

"Half of Bengal is Muslim. My mother chooses to wear the hijab."

"So you admit you're Muslim?"

"I've never denied it."

They look at each other. This conversation clearly isn't going the way they expected. Jesse is new at RivCol, and he came with a rep for fighting, so they want to put him in his place. But they need to provoke him into throwing the first punch. That's how it works. Whoever hits first is the instigator.

A few months ago, they might have gotten what they want. But Jesse has learned his lesson. When he hefts his backpack, the big guy steps in front of him.

"We want the new girl's number," Red Hair says.

Jesse tenses. "What?"

"The new girl. Raine or Sleet or Skye or whatever her hippie parents named her. We heard you and her go way back."

The big guy snickers.

"No, I don't have her number," Jesse says.

"Then get it for us. She's hot. Seriously hot."

Now Jesse's temper does twitch. He hears Jamil, as he watches thirteen-year-old Skye saunter off, his gaze glued to her ass. *Mmm, she's gonna be hot someday, little brother. I'm gonna be thanking you then, for keeping her around.*

The big guy has that same leer on his face, and Jesse has to shove his fists into his pockets to keep from grabbing him by the collar, telling him he'd better not even *think* of bothering Skye, that she's got enough to worry about without this.

Instead, Jesse says, as evenly as he can, "I can't help you," and then ducks out. He continues to the other side of the school. When he glances around, there's no sign of the seniors. He swings around the corner and listens. After a moment, he hears voices and footsteps. The seniors are heading to the basketball court.

He should leave. He has practice in an hour, and he can't skip it—private lessons from the very expensive trainer hired by his parents. The same trainer who made him a track star. Jesse cringes again.

Fake. Phony. Poseur.

Oh, that's a good one, Jesse. Poseur. Showing off your vocab, smartass?

You're dead, Jamil. Stay dead. Please.

Wow. Did you just say that? About your own brother?

Jesse hunches his shoulders against an imaginary wind. He hears the creak of doors and, a moment later, Skye steps out the side exit.

He steps around the corner fast.

He can't speak to her. Not now. He isn't ready. But . . .

He looks over his shoulder, to where he can hear the distant voices of the three seniors. Skye's heading their way. Jesse needs to keep an eye on her.

Really? Does he honestly think they'll bother her? They were trying to rile him up, using everything they could think of—take a jab at his brother, his mother, his heritage, a girl he'd been friends with . . .

Maybe that's all it was, but he can't be too careful. Skye doesn't need their crap.

He lopes across the road, tucking behind a parked SUV and following until she gets on her bus safely.

Skye

Mae isn't home yet. She won't be for hours, despite what she said this morning.

"I'm taking off early to be home after your first big day."

"You don't need to do that."

"But I will. I'll be home by four."

Before lunch, she texted to say she wouldn't make it as early as she hoped. But definitely by five. Then as I'm heading up to the condo, she texts again.

Her: Stuck in a meeting. Home by 6.
Me: np.

Silence as I let myself into the apartment.

Then she sends: I have to stay, Skye. I'm sorry.

Me: np=no problem.
Her: Whoops! Gotta learn the lingo, huh?

I roll my eyes at that. I'd think she'd already *know* the "lingo." Gran did. I guess that just goes to prove what I already suspected: there aren't many—or any—teens in Mae's life.

I'm in the living room when she sends: Might be more like 7. Takeout?

Me: Sure.
Her: Thai or Korean?

I type: whatev. Then I erase it.

Make the effort, Skye. And it does take actual effort, like answering an exam question on a subject I've never taken.

Me: Thai.
Her: Excellent! See you at 7. Maybe 7:30. Snacks in fridge!

I head for the kitchen and open the fridge. It's this massive stainless steel locker so big I have to brace the door or I'm afraid I'll be knocked inside and freeze to death.

I might also starve.

There are four glistening glass shelves, containing a sum total of seven objects. Three are condiments. I take out what looks like yogurt. It's fat-free, sugar-free and, I'm sure, flavor-free. It's also labeled gluten-free for those who don't know where gluten actually comes from. I turn the yogurt container over in my hands, looking for the symbol that indicates that the milk comes from yaks, hand-raised and bottle-fed by the distant descendants of Attila the Hun. Sadly, it makes no such claim.

I can buy my own snacks. As I left, Gran pushed ten hundred-dollar bills into my hand, having mutely convinced some poor candy striper to access her ATM account. She handed them to me and made a spooning motion, and I laughed at the joke—that she was giving me money so I could eat. After seeing Mae's fridge, I'm not sure it was a joke.

I passed a little grocery on the walk from the bus stop. While the exterior suggested it may be where Mae buys her hell-yogurt, it must carry something edible. Even overpriced organic, fair-trade chocolate bars still contain chocolate.

I should go. I could use the exercise. My grumbling stomach says I could use the food, too. But when I look down from the window, the street seems an impossible distance away.

I take my laptop and settle onto the ice-cold leather sofa. I spend the next two hours surfing between YouTube and homework, with an emphasis on the former. I don't know what I watch. It really is surfing, skimming over the waves of prank videos and teen vlogs. I'm not sure which I find more incomprehensible.

As I watch some YouTube celeb giving eyeliner tips, I think maybe I could start my own vlog.

Hey, I'm Skye, and I'm here to teach you . . .

I'd need to be accomplished at something to actually talk about it.

Hey, I'm a very accomplished sister-of-school-shooter. Wanna hear tips on dealing with that? Er, on second thought, got *any tips on dealing with that?*

I turn on my laptop camera and see myself reflected back, a pale-faced blonde who could definitely use eyeliner tips. Or any tips beyond "How to make it look like you brushed your hair before putting it into a ponytail."

Stare. Stare some more. Hit Record.

Hey, I'm Skye Gilchrist. You may know me from such national tragedies as the school shooting in—

Uh, no.

Hey, I'm Skye Gilchrist, and I'm here to tell you . . .

I'm here to tell you . . .

I recall my sixth-grade teacher, coaching us on a personal video project, one we did "for posterity"—in other words, so we could store it and look at it again every five years, laughing more each time we saw it.

Say what you want from life. Where you see yourself in five years.

Five years . . .

Can I fast-forward through them? That's what I really want. To hyper-sleep to adulthood, because right now, I can't even find the motivation to get off this sofa. I'm staring at this girl in the screen, and I hate her.

She's weak and she's useless, and I really kinda hate her.

By the time Mae brings dinner, it's nearly nine, and I wolf it down, making her say, "Didn't you have a snack?"

I consider pointing out that Dijon mustard is not a food group, but I just say, "I was doing my homework and lost track of time."

"So how did your day go?"

That's the requisite question for anyone dining with a school-age kid. Gran never asked it, though. It's too easily answered with a grunted "Fine."

I consider saying exactly that. But I'm not sure I could do it with a straight face. I'm also reasonably sure it's the answer Mae actually expects.

So, how was the first day back in Riverside? With kids who know your brother was a school shooter? With friends who never once contacted you to see how you were doing?

Tell me, Skye, how did that go?

"You said Jesse was at Southfield."

She stops, the fork at her lips. Lowers it. Says, "What?"

"You said that Jesse was going to Southfield. Not Riverside Collegiate."

"Jesse Mandal?"

"Yes," I say. "He's in my math class."

"He went to Southfield last year, Skye."

"Well, he's at RivCol now."

"Did you talk?"

"No."

She takes her bite. Chews slowly. Swallows. "You won't want to hear this, but having him at Riverside Collegiate may not be such a bad thing. I remember Jesse. He was such a sweet kid. Did I tell you his family reached out after the shooting?"

I shake my head.

"I'd . . . I'd sent them a note. I had to. I couldn't just ignore what happened. I fully expected they'd tear it up. Instead, Dr. Mandal called. She wanted to know how you were doing, and to express *their* condolences for Luka. I remember clutching the phone, waiting for the other shoe to drop, for her to say something . . . else. I don't think I could have been that generous, if things were the other way around."

She takes a sip of wine. "Jesse's a good kid, from a good family, and I bet if he didn't speak to you, it's because he didn't know what to say. Tonight, think of what *you* can say, for an opener, and then catch him on his own, out of class. See what happens. You might be surprised."

Just talk to him. You might be surprised.

"He refused to sit near me."

"What?"

I shake my head. "It's not important."

"Yes, actually it is, Skye." She sets down her fork. "I suspect you've misinterpreted something."

I want to stick to my decision and drop it, but there's no way I can after that. So I tell her what happened, ending with, "I ran out before I burst into tears and humiliated myself in front of the entire class." Then I meet her gaze and say, "Does that sound like a misunderstanding?"

She stares. Then she takes out her phone.

"What are you doing?" I ask.

"Calling his mother."

"What?"

"I am telephoning Jesse's mother. This is unacceptable. Completely unacceptable."

I lunge, tablecloth sliding under my hand, plates clattering as I snatch the phone.

Mae jerks back in surprise. "Skye! What—?"

"Calling Jesse's *mother*? Seriously? We aren't in middle school anymore."

She reaches for her phone, but I keep my hand on it and she says, calmly, "I'm not calling to accuse her son of schoolyard bullying. I'm trying to enlist her aid in handling a delicate situation."

"No."

"I only want—"

"I'm sixteen. I handle my own *delicate situations*. What happened with Jesse today caught me off guard. I know where we stand now. I'll deal with it."

"You shouldn't have to. At least let me get you into a different math class."

"No."

"You shouldn't need to deal with—"

I cut her short by meeting her gaze. "You're the one who insisted I go to RivCol. So I *have* to deal with it."

I take my plate into the kitchen, drop it off and stalk to my room.

Skye

I survive the next morning at school. I put up my shields, and every whisper and sneer and scowl only powers that force field. I absorb the snark and the contempt and the fear, as I keep repeating my mantra.

I can do this. I will do this. I won't let them make me feel like crap.

I won't let Jesse make me feel like crap.

I carry that shield into battle . . . otherwise known as math class. Then I plunk my ass into the seat *he* should have taken. The seat he rejected.

Yep, this is the old Skye. The one you used to know, Jesse. I'm not hiding in the back of this classroom. I'm not pretending yesterday didn't happen. I'm sitting right here, where you wouldn't. Deal with it.

He's early. I almost smile when I see him come through the door. It wouldn't be a nice and friendly smile, either. It would be a smile that says I know why he's early, that he's making sure he has a choice of seats, as far from me as possible without making a scene.

That's it, Jesse. Just slide in and circle around, like you don't even see—

He walks right down my aisle. He's not looking at me. He has his hood up, headphones plugged in, and I can hear the thump of the music as he comes closer, closer . . .

He's staring straight ahead and doesn't see me.

He stops. Right beside my seat, as if ready to slide into it. He sees me there. Looks at the empty chair in front of me—my spot from yesterday. Frowns slightly, as if he can't quite figure out why I'm in the wrong seat. Then he turns around and . . .

And sits in the empty seat. Right in front of me.

I'm sitting behind Jesse Mandal. In math. Just like I used to. Just like I did that last day, when he passed me that note and I teased him and . . .

I try to forget that.

I cannot forget that.

Class ends. The bell rings. Jesse is out of his seat before it finishes, and he's gone, having never acknowledged I was there.

I'm at my locker when a guy says, "Hey," and there's this split second where I think it's Jesse. I turn, and it's just a guy. A cute one, though, seriously cute, with blond hair and a wide grin and freckles over his nose.

"Skye," he says.

"Uh-huh."

I brace. I've had this lesson often enough to learn it—some guy or girl comes over, acting cool, like they just want to say hello, and then they hit me with a zinger that makes everyone nearby laugh. This guy seems the type. A little too cute. A little too confident.

"You don't remember me, do you?"

"Uh . . ." I search his face, still knowing this could be a trick.

You don't know me, but I knew your brother. And I'm glad he's dead. I hope he's rotting in hell.

"Chris Landry," he says.

"Chris . . ." I blink. Then I see it, mostly in the freckles. Chris Landry—a boy I asked to dance a couple of times in middle school, mainly because no one else did, and he deserved better. Quiet and gangly, with freckles and crooked teeth and glasses and . . .

"I've changed that much?" he says, grin widening, orthodontically straightened teeth flashing. "Well, that's not a bad thing, huh?"

"I didn't recognize you. How are you doing? I . . ." I trail off as I remember exactly who he is.

Chris Landry. Cousin of Nella Landry. One of the victims. One of the dead.

"Oh," I say, and I want to flee before that grin changes to something ugly, something accusatory.

I lock my knees and say sincerely, "I'm sorry about your cousin."

"Yeah." He shrugs. "That makes this kinda awkward. But what happened doesn't have anything to do with you, which is why I wanted to say hi. Can I walk you out?" He smiles. "I know a shortcut."

"Uh, sure." I pack my books, and we set off, and yes, I'm still braced for trouble. After Jesse, I'm not letting my guard down.

When someone calls, "Hey, Christopher!" I tense. But I swear he does, too, and I flash back to middle school, the older boys taunting him.

When he turns, though, he relaxes and calls, "Hey. I'll be there in five." Then he says to me, "Yearbook committee."

"Is that the secret exit up there?" I say, pointing.

"It is."

"Then I can take it from here. Thanks. This *is* a faster way."

"Okay, then. I'll see you in English tomorrow."

"You're in my class?"

"Yep, hiding at the rear, where I won't be asked to answer any questions. Oh, and . . ." He lowers his voice. "Don't let the assholes get you down. What happened at North Hampton had nothing to do with you, and most of us know that. So ignore them."

"Thanks."

"Hey, you helped me, back when I needed it. And I mighta kinda had a crush on you. You were cool." He makes a face. "That sounded lame. I'm sure you still are. Anyway, English. Tomorrow. Take care."

I say goodbye, and he's gone, weaving through kids, hightailing it to his meeting. I'm motoring down the hall, zipping around clusters of students, when Lana Brighton steps into my path.

"Was it you?" she says.

"Was *what* me?" I say.

"Tattling to Vaughn. Telling him I started a petition."

A hand grabs my arm. "Skye. I've been looking for you all day. We need to talk about the newspaper club."

It's Tiffany. She looks at Lana. "Oh, Lana. I'm sorry. Were you talking—?"

"Figures," Lana says. "You two better be careful. Someone might think you're plotting to carry on Luka and Isaac's work."

Tiffany holds up a middle finger. Just holds it, silently, and waits. Lana mutters something and stalks off.

"Newspaper club?" I say when Lana's gone.

"That was just an excuse. I heard she's being a bitch to you." We start walking and she says, "But we *would* love to have you on the paper. I remember Luka used to brag about your stories."

I tense at that, and she says, "Sorry. I wasn't sure . . ." She pushes her hands into her pockets. "I wasn't sure how you are about that. Remembering him. So, uh, the newspaper?"

"I don't write these days. But thank you for the invitation."

"Well, it's an open one, so keep it in mind. Oh, and did I see you walking with Neville?"

"Neville?"

"Chris Landry. Neville's a nickname, and not one most people use to his face, though I'm sure he's heard it. Did you see the Harry Potter movies?"

I nod.

"Then you might remember the guy who played Neville. In the first films, he's what my gram would call unfortunate-looking. By the last ones, though? Totally hot. Amazing what contacts, braces and overcoming puberty can do for a guy. But, uh, a word of warning . . ." She lowers her voice. "Chris is a player."

"Okay."

"I know you guys went to school together. I'd like to think he'd never take advantage of that, but I don't know him by much more than his rep."

"Got it. Thanks. I appreciate the warning."

"Anytime."

She seems ready to go when I blurt, "What can you tell me about Jesse?"

Tiffany slows, glancing around.

"Sorry, I—" I begin.

"No, it's cool. I'm just . . . I don't mind being overheard talking about Chris. He's earned his rep. Jesse? Jesse's . . ." She exhales. "Most times, when I meet the survivors—the families of the victims—I feel sorry for their loss. That's all I owe them. Jesse?"

She adjusts her load of books. "I feel bad about Jesse. I feel guilty, like I had something to do with what happened. He's just . . . he's a mess, Skye. I remember him being at your house when I was there with Isaac, and I thought you two were so cute together, and he was such a sweet kid."

She adjusts the books again. "I remember thinking I wished I'd known a boy like that when I was your age. A really nice guy. A little nerdy, but that's not a bad thing. After his brother died, though, he just . . . changed. Rumor is that he got kicked out of Southfield for fighting."

"Jesse?"

"Don't quote me on that. I just know he's not the boy with his nose in a book anymore. He barely comes to class. The only reason RivCol doesn't suspend him is because they need him on the track team."

"Jesse?" I say again, in equal disbelief.

"I know his brother was quite the jock, and Jesse seems to have taken up the mantle."

The Jesse I knew hated sports. Well, not really hated them—we'd goof around with a ball, but he avoided organized games. He immersed himself in academics instead, where he could shine as brightly as his brother without competing with him.

When we were on Owen's softball team together, there was a running joke that Jesse got hit *by* the ball more than he hit it. While he *could* run fast, that wasn't much use when he never left the plate.

"But that's good, right?" Tiffany says. "It's not like he's started robbing gas stations or shooting up on the street corner. He's a track star. It's just . . . not what it used to be."

No, it isn't. Not at all.

I'm stepping out the school door when my phone chirps with an incoming message. I called Gran earlier, but the nurse was over, so I said I'd phone after school. I presume this is her and take out my phone. Instead, I see a message from a number I don't recognize. The text reads, Hey Skye, gr8 seeing u @ RivCol! Welcome home! There's a video clip attached, with a still shot of a kitten midleap.

I see that, and think of Jesse, and all the times he sent animal gifs to cheer me up and, yes, that message doesn't sound like him, but maybe like Mae said, we're both struggling here, trying to find a path through the quicksand. Even if it's not Jesse, someone is being kind to me. An old friend reaching out.

I hit Play.

The kitten leaps . . . and the screen flickers. I'm checking my connection when I hear a scream, and I jump, looking around. But it's coming from my phone. A girl screaming, and a boy saying, "Oh my God, oh my God," and then the screen clears, and the camera is zooming everywhere, and I can't make out what I'm seeing—

A desk. There's a desk. A girl cowers under it, and she's got one arm over her head, and she's typing frantically on her cell phone, and I hear screaming. Then the camera zooms away again as the screen goes black.

Words scroll across the dark screen.

Leanna Tsosie.

She was texting to tell her mother there was a shooter in the school, but she was fine.

It was the last thing she ever wrote.

The screen fills with another image. The girl, under her desk, sprawled, and there's blood . . .

I jab the Stop button. Leanna lies there, frozen, her dead eyes staring.

A girl jostles me from behind, and I turn fast, but she only mutters, "If you're texting, move out of the damned doorway first."

I step aside. My back to the wall, I stare at the final image of Leanna.

I remember you.

I remember Leanna came over to work on a project with Luka, and after she left, I said, *I think she likes you* and *She seems nice* and *You should ask her out,* and Luka turned bright red and shook his head and said I got it all wrong, that Leanna was nice, and she was just *being* nice to him, nothing more.

"Skye?"

It's a deep male voice and, again—I can't help myself—I think of Jesse.

Are you okay, Skye?

No, I'm not. I'm really not.

It's Mr. Mueller, my English teacher.

"Are you okay, Skye?" he asks, the exact words I imagined from Jesse.

Tears spring to my eyes. I blink them back fast as I nod, and then I take off.

Jesse

Jesse sees Skye running for the bus stop, and his first thought is *She's upset.*

His second thought? *I should do something.*

At dinner last night, his parents were asking him about track, and he struggled to answer their questions before blurting, "Skye Gilchrist is back. She's at RivCol. Living with her aunt, someone said."

His mom and dad looked at each other. Then his mom laid down her fork and said, "I hope you've reached out to her, Jesse. It won't be easy being here again, but you can set the tone. If you're kind to her, others will have no reason not to be."

He muttered something, and his mom started to pursue it, but his dad made this noise, the one that suggested they give Jesse a few days before they pushed. They were so careful with him. Their delicate, troubled boy.

It's a phase.

He'll grow out of it.

At least he has track.

Yes, at least there's that.

Now he sees Skye jogging for the bus stop, and he feels that initial surge of worry, and then realizes he's being ridiculous. She's running for a *bus* stop. To make sure she catches the bus. She's fine.

But still . . . He remembers what those seniors said yesterday. Skye is new here, and she's vulnerable, and therefore Jesse must keep an eye on her.

To do what? Defend her against guys who think she's hot? If they try that crap, she'll tell them where to go. That's the Skye he knows. One who doesn't need his help.

Following Skye like this is dangerously close to stalking.

He should speak to her.

Today, in math, she took the empty seat he refused yesterday. When he noticed the vacant desk in front of her, he sat there. As if the last three years hadn't happened, and he was walking into middle school math class and sitting in front of Skye, as he always did. And then he wrote notes to her.

Sorry about yesterday.

How're you holding up?

Can we talk?

That seemed to be the way to do it. A note. A little bit nostalgic. A little bit lighthearted.

Hey, remember when we used to do this? See, nothing's changed.

Except it has.

Everything has.

He still has those notes, balled in his pocket, heavy as rocks.

The bus rolls to the curb, and Jesse's leg muscles tense, ready to kick it up to a run. Run and swing on the bus and sit beside her and say, "Hey."

Just that.

Hey.

The bus stops. Skye gets on. The doors close, and the bus rolls away.

Skye

Mae has been delayed again, and tonight, I really am okay with that.

I've rewatched the video clip. The whole clip. I had to, in case there's a message I need to see, a threat or a hint about who sent it. That's my rationalization. The truth is that I watch because I feel, in some perverse way, that I owe it to the victims of the tragedy.

In the days after the shooting, I read the early news articles to understand what had happened, but the only thing they gave me was nightmares. I know the basics. The police received an anonymous report of a gun at North Hampton. They arrived just as Luka walked out of the boys' bathroom . . . holding a gun. They told him to drop it. He didn't. They shot him.

With that the police thought they'd averted the threat. That's when Isaac and Harley opened fire elsewhere in the school. When it was over, four kids were dead, ten injured. Harley was arrested. Isaac had fled. He was found two days later—dead, having saved the last bullet for himself.

This is what I know. Any later details, though, I consciously avoided, after those nightmares. It doesn't matter exactly what happened, only that four kids died, ten were hurt and hundreds more have to live with the memory of that day. A day my brother started. That is what counts.

Yet with each therapist, I asked whether I should know more. Whether I need those details, so I can truly understand what my brother did. They said no. To seek out more is self-torture.

I know they're right, and it's not as if those details are right there in front of me and I'm covering my eyes. Refusing to dig isn't actual avoidance. Or that's what I can tell myself . . . until someone sends me a video clip of the shooting.

This is the truth of what my brother was involved in. Not cold facts on a page. A girl lying dead under her desk.

I huddle on Mae's icy leather sofa, and I watch that video until tears soak my shirt. I think of Leanna with Luka, and then I imagine her sending that text, convinced she was safe.

Did her mother get the text before she knew Leanna was dead?

Or after?

Which is worse?

There isn't much more to the video, but what there is . . .

I wish I hadn't finished watching it.

And then I feel like a coward for thinking that, this voice in the back of my head saying I need to see what my brother started.

The still shot of Leanna's body stays on the screen for at least five long seconds. Then it disappears. The video flickers, and a room appears. An ordinary living room. The camera pans up to a bouquet of helium balloons and there's a squeal, and I tense at that, ready for more screams. Instead, a chubby toddler runs into the room, and someone says "Over here!" and she turns and looks right at the screen, her face in a wide grin as a chorus of voices shout "Happy birthday, Leanna!"

I watch it. Over and over, I watch it as I cry.

"Skye?" The clicks of Mae's heels cross the hardwood floor. They stop in the kitchen. The suction pop of the fridge door opening. More footsteps, her voice alarmed now, "Skye?"

"In here," I say.

Her heels click along the hall. "Why are you sitting in the dark?"

"Just doing homework." I grab my laptop as she appears in the doorway.

"Did you get my note about ordering takeout?"

"I, uh, didn't see it. Sorry." I head from the room, keeping my head ducked so she won't spot the tear tracks. "I'm not actually hungry. I'm just going to bed."

"It's barely eight."

"I'm leaving early tomorrow. I'm . . . I'm joining the school newspaper."

Her eyes light. "You are?"

Why did I say that? Backpedal, Skye.

I shrug. "I figured I should. Maybe start writing again."

That is *not* backpedaling. Damn it.

"I'll get up and make you breakfast," she says. "Do you like yogurt and granola?"

I mumble, "Sure," and hurry past her as fast as I can.

ooo

I dream of Leanna Tsosie. I dream of her under that desk, hitting Send on the text to her mother, then hearing a noise, and turning to see Luka in the classroom doorway. I dream that she's begging for her life, and he just keeps bearing down on her. I dream that he shoots her in the head. And then I dream that it isn't Luka holding the gun.

It's me.

I wake, as I lie there, shaking, I want to go home. I just want to go home.

Except I don't know where that is anymore.

Riverside was the only place I ever really considered home, and now it's not. It can never be again.

This is where I grew up. Where I had a family and friends and a future. Now it's a place where people hate me enough to send me videos of dead girls.

Go away, Skye Gilchrist.

Go, and don't ever come back.

There is, of course, no newspaper meeting before school. But since I told Mae there was, I have to go in early, so I hang out in my office—the girls' bathroom—waiting for the bell. Maybe I'll talk to Tiffany later and join the paper. I can edit or something. I still know the difference between *there, their* and *they're*, and that sadly gives me an advantage over most high school kids.

Speaking of English, I see Chris Landry in class. There's an empty seat beside him, and I wouldn't have taken it—I don't want to give the wrong impression—but he waves me to it, so I kinda have to. He's being nice; therefore, I cannot be rude. He talks to me before class and again after, and he walks out with me, and then we go our separate ways. All cool.

Gran has texted. I missed my morning call. Missed last night's too. I just couldn't manage it. I send back a Sorry! School stuff. Call tonight? and she replies with a thumbs-up emoji, one that makes me smile and makes me hurt, too, wishing I could be there, with her and Mom.

I eat lunch in the girls' bathroom. I plan to talk to Tiffany in physics but don't get the chance. Jesse doesn't show up for math. I'm making my beeline for the side exit when I hear "Skye Gilchrist to the office. Skye Gilchrist to the office."

I slow as every eye in the hall turns my way. Then I pick up speed, as if I misheard, until someone says, "The office is *that* way, Gilchrist."

I arrive to find Mr. Vaughn waiting. He waves me into his office and closes the door behind me. Then he takes a piece of paper from his desk and holds it against his chest, like it's the answer to a scholarship-winning quiz.

"I understand it isn't easy being here, Skye. It's high school. Hormones and stress lead to harassment and bullying."

"Uh, okay."

"The problem is that, when kids have gone through years of bullying and harassing, they can develop a sensitivity to it. They see insult where none is intended. They can get a little . . ." His lips purse.

"Paranoid?"

He makes a face. "I was looking for another word."

"Okay." *Is there a point here?*

"I've seen your record from other schools. You've had a difficult time. Coming here, you expect things to be even worse. How will you be treated by kids who knew your brother? Who were affected by his actions? How many kids at this school have some connection to that day?"

Yeah, thanks for pointing that out. Because, you know, I hadn't considered it until now.

"The point, Skye, is that I understand your sensitivity. But *this* doesn't help matters." He sets the paper on his desk. It's an email. An anonymous one reporting Lana Brighton for circulating a petition to get me kicked out of RivCol.

He continues, "The person who sent this was careful to use a dummy email account and a school computer. But to access those computers, you need to log in. This email was sent from a terminal logged into your account."

"My account?"

He looks at me like I've donated brain cells recently. "Your school account. Used to access the school computers."

I wave my backpack. "I have a laptop. I didn't even know I *had* an account here, so I've never logged into it."

He eyes me, saddened by my pathetic attempts to defend myself.

"I'm sure I can prove I didn't use that terminal," I say. "When was it accessed? And where? I—"

He drops the page into a file folder. "It's fine, Skye."

"No, it's not. I want to straighten this out. Either it's a mistake or someone intentionally sent it from my account."

"Yes, maybe you're right," he says, in a tone that makes it clear he doesn't want to continue this conversation. "There is no petition, by the way. I questioned Lana yesterday."

"Uh, yeah, there is. I overheard kids talking about signing it."

"We also searched her locker today. Normally, I wouldn't have gone that far, but I understand how difficult this must be, and I wanted to be thorough. There is no petition."

"Are you accusing me of lying?"

"Lana may have made an angry offhand comment, saying someone *should* start a petition. Others may have taken that to mean she was. But there is no petition. Lana knows that would be pointless. You have as much right to be here as anyone."

He says it as if I need to be reassured that I'm welcome. As if I'd been charged in the shooting and found not guilty.

"Have you considered getting more involved in school life?" Mr. Vaughn asks.

"What?"

"Once you're settled. Join a club or two. That will help."

Because, really, if I feel tormented, it's my own fault for not trying harder to fit in. I remember in grade school, sitting in detention hall and overhearing a teacher tell a boy that when he complained of being bullied. Not saying it was his fault, per se, but like Mr. Vaughn, suggesting he put himself out there more, let kids get to know the *real* him.

I flash back to seeing the boy leave that room, head bowed with shame, cheeks flaring as he realized it'd been overheard. I remember mouthing "She's an idiot," with appropriate gestures, and he smiled. That boy? Chris Landry.

I was never bullied as a kid. I would like to think I never bullied anyone, either, but having now been in these shoes, I'm not always so sure. I tried to be kind. But were there other kids, less likable than Chris, who may have been a target of my clever jabs? I hope not. I really do.

"Skye?"

I nod for Mr. Vaughn. It's that or tell him where to shove his patronizing suggestion, and I'm really not keen on another detention. Even thinking about it makes my stomach twist.

I *was* locked in here on Monday. I know that. Just like I know I didn't send this email. Like I know I heard those girls say they signed that petition.

But I also heard them again . . . when there'd been no one around.

"Your middle school record says you were on the softball team, volleyball and the debating club. It's volleyball season, and I know our girls' team could use extra players. Why don't I tell Coach Greene to expect you for tryouts—"

"I'm joining the school paper."

"Oh?" He smiles. "That is an excellent idea. I saw that you won a city writing competition in Riverside. The paper would be thrilled to have you. In fact, I think this is their meeting day. Do you know where their office is?"

"No, but—"

"Go down this hall and make a left. Then a right. It's a tiny room—blink and you'll miss it. A former janitorial closet, actually." He chuckles. "But most schools don't even get a dedicated newspaper office, so the club's quite pleased with it. I'll talk to you tomorrow and see how it went."

Skye

Apparently I'm joining the newspaper. I text Mae to say I'll be late—I was wrong about the meeting time. Then I follow Mr. Vaughn's directions . . . and spend the next ten minutes hunting for the office. Seems he can't tell his left from his right. He's correct, too, that it's easy to miss the office. It's just a printed sign posted beside the door, announcing HOME OF THE RIVCOL TIMES!

I knock. Knock louder. Look around, and then crouch to peer under the door. It's dark inside. I try the knob, to be sure, but it's locked from the outside.

I look at the sign and see, in faded print, JOIN US! WEEKLY MEETINGS THURSDAY 3:30 P.M. LEADS WELCOME.

Today is Wednesday. I sigh, heft my bag and head down the hall. As I walk, a text comes in from Mae.

Her: Pizza night? You like pizza, right? Silly question. You're a teen, right? LOL

I wince at that, but I *do* like pizza, and I know she's trying.

Me: sounds good
Her: How about a movie rental? I'll stop by the store.
Me: they still have those?

Pause. Pause.

Me: I usually rent online, but if u'd rather pick up . . .
Her: No, we'll rent online. You'll just need to show me how. :) Do you like romantic comedies?
Me: they still make those?

"It's a lie, you know," a girl says down a side hall.

My gaze shoots up, away from my screen.

The girl continues. "Her brother shot *all* those kids, but her family has money. They bought off the cops. Made them blame the other guys. That's what I heard."

"And her mom's crazy. Everyone knew that. The whole family's got problems. Even Luka."

"*Especially* Luka. I went to summer drama school, just to get to know him. And I *did* get to know him . . . I got to know he was weird. Seriously weird. When I heard he was the one who shot those kids, I knew it was true."

I'm frozen in place. Frozen on the outside—boiling on the inside.

My brother didn't shoot anyone. And buying off the cops? Seriously? We aren't rich. We just have enough money that we could pick up and get the hell away from people like this. People who call a woman who's clinically depressed "crazy." People who call an amazing, quirky guy "weird."

My phone dings with an incoming text, and I look down to see two from Mae. I sign off fast and start walking.

I'm not going to stand here and pretend I don't hear. Not this time.

As I march toward the voices, they fall to whispers, as if the girls hear someone coming. They're right around the next corner. I wheel past the lockers and—

The hall is empty.

"I hear she got kicked out of her last school." The voice comes from around the next corner. "They found her with a gun."

I march toward the voices. Around the corner and . . .

The hall is empty.

"Are you serious?" The voice comes from farther down. I've misjudged. It's so quiet that they sound closer than they are.

I keep walking, quieter now, muffling my footfalls as the other girl says, "Totally serious. She said it was for self-defense but, yeah, right. She's planning something. We need to get the petition filled, fast. Lana says if we take it to the media—"

I spin around the next corner while she's still talking and . . .

I'm staring down a short corridor of lockers with no doors or exits. A dead end.

I look around, searching for where the voices could have come from. A hidden recording? That's the only answer.

The *only* answer?

I didn't imagine those voices. I know I didn't.

I spin around, run down the hall, and turn—

I bash into a guy standing around the corner. I send him staggering back, me stumbling, and I'm waiting for the inevitable "Watch where you're going!" Instead, there's silence.

I look up and—

"Jesse?"

He gives a gruff "Hey" without making eye contact.

"I'm sorry. I was . . . I was running late. For the next bus. And I got turned around."

He nods.

"Are you okay? I hit you pretty hard." I didn't, but it's an excuse to keep talking.

"I'm fine," he mumbles. He stands there, hands stuffed in his pockets, hood raised, expression unreadable. I want to flee. Flee as fast as I can. But I dig in my heels and say, "I'm sorry if this is awkward. Having me here."

A shrug and a mumbled, "It's fine."

"Someone should have warned you. I would have insisted on it if I knew you were here, but I was told you'd gone to Southfield. That's why I chose RivCol."

He stiffens, as if insulted.

I hurry on. "I didn't want it to be awkward for you. You've been through a lot—"

"I said I'm fine." A split-second pause. "Don't you have a bus to catch?"

Isn't there somewhere you need to be, Gilchrist?

"I just wanted to say—"

"You said it. I'm fine. I have a meeting."

He walks away.

I'm outside the doors, and I'm shaking, and it's partly embarrassment but partly anger, too. I didn't linger. Didn't pester him or, God forbid, ask him to go grab a soda. I said exactly the right things, and he was a jerk about it.

Now I'm outside catching my breath and remembering where Jesse was when I crashed into him. Standing in a hall that ultimately led nowhere . . . except to me.

I head back inside. When I hear footfalls, I duck around a corner, but it's just Owen. I circle around, and then I hear more footfalls. Not the deliberate slaps of Owen's work boots but the scuffling walk of someone not going anywhere in a hurry.

I peek around the corner to see Jesse. He's moving at a stroll. Keeping my distance, I follow as he heads down one hall, then another . . . and eventually ends up back where he started. There he glances at his phone, as if checking the time. He nods, satisfied, and makes a quick left, toward the rear exit.

Here for a meeting, you said?

He's been killing time. I could take offense at that, presume the "meeting" was a lie to get rid of me, and that he then wandered around to ensure he didn't bump into me again. But that raises the question of what he was doing here in the first place, hanging around where the only thing nearby was me.

I keep thinking about that anonymous email. Jesse's interest in school has obviously dropped, but I remember him as the math whiz who planned a career in software engineering. A kid who was a genius with a keyboard.

I hear my voice, from a distant memory. "Hey, Jesse, question for you. Purely hypothetical."

We're sitting on a wall outside the playground. Sun setting, children playing, parents shouting "One last time" before they herd their kids home to dinner. Jesse and me, on the wall, our heels kicking it, impatiently waiting for the moment when the park will be ours.

The parents and kids will leave, and the sun will set, and I'll jump from the wall and hop onto a swing. Jesse will smile and shake his head, but he'll follow eventually, and we'll swing and talk, and later—if it's dark enough—I can even coax him onto the twisting slide, hear him laugh as he forgets he's thirteen, supposed to be past all this.

"Hey, Jesse, question for you. Purely hypothetical."

"Uh-huh."

"Let's say one wanted to access the school computers. Maybe . . . fix a few things."

"Uh-huh."

"Not grades. That'd be wrong. But, you know, erase some comments on a student record. Where a student might have done some things that got totally blown out of proportion but could look bad on a college application."

He slants a look at me. "No one's going to check a middle school record for college."

"I was thinking of high school. Could you hack *those* records?"

"You don't have a high school record yet, Skye."

"I'm planning ahead."

He laughs, startling a babysitter, who squints over, as if thinking that laugh couldn't possibly have come from the somber boy at my side.

"You *could* just stop getting in trouble," he says.

"Yeah . . . so, hacking the school system?"

He smiles and shakes his head. "Theoretically, yes. But ethically, no. Sorry. Not even for you."

But you could, right, Jesse? You could crack my school account and send an email to Mr. Vaughn.

And those voices I was chasing—you could do that, too, couldn't you?

Another kind of technology. Throw prerecorded voices, and when I don't find the source, I'll think I'm losing my mind.

What about the other day, when I got locked in the office? You knew I was in detention. You're the only kid who did.

According to Owen, I'm not the first student Mr. Vaughn has forgotten there.

Did you know that, Jesse? Did you find a way to distract Mr. Vaughn, help him to forget about me?

And then there's the video clip.

My shoulders tense, as if throwing off the very thought. *That* wasn't Jesse. Could not be Jesse.

Am I sure?

Earlier, I searched the phone number and discovered it was fake. Spoofed. Something a guy with tech skills could do.

I remember the opening shot on the clip. The kitten. Like real videos Jesse used to send me. A way to guarantee I would hit Play.

No. I don't care how much he's changed. I cannot believe the boy I know would compile that video, much less send it to me.

What about the voices I heard Monday? The ones replaying that conversation from the girls' bathroom. I was alone in that bathroom. So how could anyone have recorded them?

That should suggest it's not Jesse.

It should also suggest it wasn't anyone. That none of this is happening.

Isn't there a better answer? A more obvious one?

That I am losing it.

Just like Mom.

Just like Luka.

Skye

The next day, Jesse is back in math class. He sits in front of me again. He says nothing. Does not acknowledge me when he walks in or out. There are other empty seats, but he takes that one.

I said it was awkward for him, having me at RivCol. Does he know it's the same for me having him here? Is that why he makes a point of taking that seat? Forcing me to stare at his back for an hour?

I spoke to Tiffany in physics and confirmed that the newspaper meeting is after school. When I arrive, three others are there. Tiffany introduces me, and it's only then that I discover she's the editor in chief.

I don't know any of the other three kids. Two know me . . . by rep, at least. The guy—Alberto—tenses when I walk in. The girl—Melanie—offers a too-bright welcome. I'm not sure which is worse.

No, what's worse is the other staff member trying to figure out what all the fuss is about, until Melanie "discreetly" texts him, and then I have to watch his eyes widen, his gaze turn on me, that moment of silence where everyone knows exactly what's happened and they're all pretending they don't.

"So first order of business—" Tiffany begins.

"What exactly does she do?" Alberto says. "Is she looking to write or what?"

"*She* is sitting right there," Tiffany says.

"I think we should have discussed this before she came."

"Why?" Melanie says. "Doesn't our sign say anyone can join?"

"I just think—"

"Did we discuss you before you arrived?" Tiffany says. "Did anyone discuss *me*?"

Alberto shifts on his chair. "I just think we should have."

"I'm happy to take on whatever you need done," I say.

"Normally the newcomers are put on the leads box," Tiffany says with a smile. "But I won't do that to you."

"Why not?" Alberto says. "Does she get special treatment?"

"I know you can't mean lead stories," I say. "Oh, wait. I saw something on the sign about 'leads welcome.'"

"Leads *not* welcome," the other guy says. "Really, really not welcome."

"It's a joke," Tiffany says. "Years ago, the newspaper team decided to solicit anonymous leads from students. They got crap. But when they tried to say they didn't want anonymous leads anymore, the school stepped in and said they had to take them, that it was proper investigative journalism."

"Like any of us are going to be investigative journalists," Alberto says. "Or journalists at all. Well, unless we've got a trust fund, and can work for an online media site and not bother with that whole getting-paid nonsense."

"We're here because it looks good on a college application," Melanie says. "But the point is that no one wants to handle the leads box. If Tiff says you can skip it, take her up on that. Trust me."

I shake my head. "The newest person *should* take the crap job. Just show me what to do."

Everyone's gone. It's just me and the lead box. Apparently, no one has touched the box in a few weeks—just got busy, so busy—so I've volunteered to clear it out after the others leave.

I fish a lead from the bottom. It's a page that's been folded at least ten times. When I get it half open, I see a line that appears to have been written in crayon: top secret. It's been taped shut. I open it. Inside, more crayon: i hear tricia myers likes girls. please investigate. photo/video evidence required.

I roll my eyes, ball it up and toss it in the trash. Then I take a lead from the middle of the pile, a sheet printed from a computer, which seems promising.

> I would like the paper to investigate the cafeteria meatloaf. I've heard it's made from mealworms and that the school is serving it as part of a secret government experiment—

Ball up. Toss out.

Let's try the top of the box. The most recent stuff.

I pull out a sheet of lined paper and unfold it . . .

Someone needs to write an article about Skye Gilchrist. There are new kids here who don't know what her brother did. Kids who don't know who she is. That's wrong. It's like when a kiddie molester moves into a new neighborhood and everyone gets warned. She's the sister of a school shooter . . . in a new school.

I start to ball it up. Then I stop. Fold it. Smooth it. Set it aside. The last thing I need is for someone to discover that I discarded messages about myself. Let Tiffany handle it.

I start to reach back to the bottom of the box. I can't, though. I see those folded papers on the top, and I have to know. I have to reassure myself that this was the only one about me.

It is not the only one about me.

For five minutes, I sit there, reading note after note. I open ten from the top of the box . . . and six are about me.

SOMEONE NEEDS TO DO SOMETHING
ABOUT SKY GILKRIST.

Did they make that Skye girl take
a psych test before she came here?

I heard Sky Gilchrist took a gun to her old school,
and that's why she had to leave.

Luka Gilchrist murdered four kids!
And they let his sister come to our school?

I hope someone puts a bullet through Skye Gilchrist's head. And you can quote me on that.

That Skye bitch should be . . .

I won't finish the last. Somehow it's worse than the one about putting a bullet through my head. It's the kind of stuff I saw in those online comments sections three years ago.

All of it is like that. The sort of thing I have not seen in years, and I sit there, staring at the slips, shaking.

This is not one person badmouthing me. I leaf through different types of paper. Different handwriting. Different spellings of my name.

I've kept thinking that everything happening to me here—the petition rumors, the voices in the hall, the video clip, being locked in the office—is clearly all the same person. One persecutor. Otherwise, I've had it relatively easy. While I hear whispers and catch glares, actual hostility—like Lana's—has been rare, so I've made the mistake of thinking that means most kids are okay with me being here.

There *are* other kids who feel like Lana. Many more. They just know better than to complain aloud. Like online commenters, they vent their true feelings under the cloak of anonymity, and they have filled this box with their mistrust and their fear and their hate.

This is what kids really think of me being at Riverside Collegiate.

I'm still staring at those notes when there's a rap on the door. A single rap, the kind that makes you pause and wonder if you actually heard it. I swivel in my chair and spot a piece of paper on the floor.

It's blank.

I'm taking a closer look—invisible ink?—when another sheet slides under the door. It's also blank. I pick it up as yet another whispers across the linoleum. I see words on this one, in fifty-point font.

I KNOW WHAT YOU DID.

Then another, also faceup.

YOU'VE FOOLED THEM.
YOU DON'T FOOL ME.

A third, this one a newspaper headline, blown to full-page size.

FOUR KILLED IN TRAGEDY
AT NORTH HAMPTON HIGH

I lunge for the door and twist the knob.

It's locked.

Another whoosh, then another, more blank papers shoved under the door, and I'm whaling on the knob like I have super-hero strength and can snap it if I try hard enough. And I feel like I *could*, with my adrenaline pounding. My tormenter is on the other side of this door, and all I need to do is get it open and catch him in the act.

Another whisper. Then another. These sound different. Not

the whoosh of sliding paper but more of a chattering. I look down and . . .

They're sticks. Tiny sticks with red ends. At least a half dozen of them, zooming across the floor, and I should know what these are but my brain is stuck on the pages and—

A sizzle. One of the pages bursts into flames, and I realize what those sticks are. Matches. Lit wooden matches.

Another sheet sails across the floor, and this time I smell something sharp and astringent, like lighter fluid. The page hits a match and bursts into flame, pieces flying up, igniting others, and I stare, sure I can't be seeing what I am.

The room is on fire.

Someone is outside that door—right outside it—trapping me in a room and lighting it on fire.

Awesome, Nellie Bly. Are you going to do something about it? Or write your first RivCol Times *investigative article, complete with your own obit?*

I stamp on one page and then another, but there are so many, all ablaze now, and then the spark catches my stack of leads, and I'm stomping as fast as I can while I shout for help.

A box of paper catches fire, and I can't believe how fast it's spreading. I yank off my sweater and smack the flames, but that only seems to fan them, the fire spreading to the discarded leads. I toss my sweater aside. Smoke fills the room. Thick black smoke, and I cough and try to shout for help again, but I end up doubled over, hacking my lungs out.

Stop, drop and roll.

Uh, I'm not actually on fire.

As soon as I think that, I feel heat on my leg and look down to see sparks scorching through my jeans. I smack them out and stay down.

I crawl toward the door, reach up to grab the metal handle and fall back, hissing in pain. Grab my discarded sweater, put it over my hand—

My sweater's on fire!

Drop sweater. Grab handle. Grit teeth against pain. Bang on door with one hand while twisting the knob as hard as I can and . . .

The door flies open, and I stumble out. I hesitate, unable to believe I'm actually free. Then I spin. There's no one around. No one at all.

I break into a run, smoke filling the hall. I spot a fire alarm. I race toward it, and then there's a shout behind me.

"You!"

I wheel. It's Owen, running down a side hall.

"The newspaper room," I say quickly. "It's on fire."

He swears and shouts, "Pull—"

I'm already there, already pulling it, and the siren starts. I turn back to Owen, and as I do, I catch a glimpse of someone walking fast down the hallway behind him. I see who it is, and I tell myself I'm wrong.

Don't jump to conclusions. It's a guy in a hoodie. Lots of kids wear them.

As the guy veers down the next hall, I get a look at his face, and there's no doubt who I'm seeing. Who is fleeing the scene of the crime.

Jesse.

Jesse

As Jesse walks to school the next morning he can't recall the last Friday he actually attended. Other kids skip to start their weekend early. He just skips. Today he even has a good reason to not go. He couldn't sleep last night, so he took something because he needed to rest up for the track meet. Then he woke up groggy, which meant two cups of coffee, and now he's on edge, his stomach roiling.

He could say he's here because of the track meet, but it's not like anyone's going to say "Hey, Mandal, you didn't show up for class—cool your heels on the bench." He *is* the star, after all.

It's possible a teacher could mention his absence when his parents come to watch. Sure, let's go with that. He's here to avoid disappointing his parents and not because, with Skye at school, he feels some weird compulsion to shape up, a fear of her discovering how far he's fallen.

He barely gets through the doors when he hears "Jesse Mandal to the office, Jesse Mandal to the office."

Good thing he didn't skip. As for why he's being called to the office, he has no idea. Cutting class really is the extent of his rebelling.

No, that's not exactly true.

But *that* isn't rebellion, is it? It's not like he's doing it for himself.

Still, it'd get him into a lot worse trouble than skipping class. He'd be expelled for sure, and then his parents would find out, and they'd be crushed.

That'd be irony, wouldn't it? He starts doing something to make his parents proud, to distract them from his brother's death, and that same thing could hurt them even worse.

The secretary ushers Jesse into Vaughn's office, and the VP motions for him to shut the door.

"There was a fire last night," Vaughn says as Jesse takes a seat.

Jesse lifts his brows, as if he's surprised by this. He doesn't dare do more. He sucks at lying. He heard the alarms yesterday. Before that, he'd been outside running laps, working through some stuff, which mostly meant resisting the urge to follow Skye from school. That crap was getting weird, and all his self-talk about watching over her and worrying about her didn't erase the fact that if anyone caught him, it'd look like stalking.

Um, because it is?

So he ran instead. In books, he's read about love/hate relationships, and he never knew what that meant until he started running. He loved how it made him feel when the endorphins kicked in, and he loved the freedom of being in an empty field, just running, knowing no one would bother him.

But he hated running for competition, for praise, for awards. Especially when he hadn't earned it.

Yesterday, no matter how fast he ran, he couldn't escape the feeling that he should be with Skye. Looking after her.

Talking to her?

Yeah, there's an idea.

Once he decided Skye would be long gone, he came into school to change his clothes, and he found himself walking behind Tiffany and another kid. He heard them talking about Skye, which made him eavesdrop. It seemed Skye had been at their newspaper meeting, and they'd left her doing some kind of research.

He wandered a bit, but finally he couldn't resist circling past the newspaper office. Just . . . you know, checking on her.

The door was closed, with a light shining under it. When Jesse heard footsteps, he took off but didn't actually leave. He wandered the halls, working up the courage to go talk to Skye.

Then the alarm sounded. The fire alarm. Some idiot pulling it for fun, which meant Jesse got the hell out before anyone started asking why he was hanging around.

Now Vaughn is saying there was a fire. A real fire. And all Jesse can think is—

"Skye?"

Vaughn pulls back. "Interesting word association, Mr. Mandal."

"I just . . . I heard . . . I heard she joined the newspaper club, and I know they meet on Thursdays."

He waits for Vaughn's eyebrows to lift. For the VP to wonder why Jesse is taking such an interest in Skye Gilchrist's schedule.

He's ready with an excuse, but Vaughn just steeples his fingers and says, "Yes, Skye was here. That's actually where the fire started. In the newspaper office."

"What?" Jesse jerks forward.

He should have stayed. Should have made sure there wasn't a real fire. Made sure she was okay.

"Is Skye all right?" he asks.

Vaughn just sits there, his fingers still steepled. It's a stupid gesture, and Jesse wants to smack his hands down.

Instead, he repeats, "Is Skye all right?"

"She claims someone locked her in that office and pushed papers and lit matches under the door."

"What?"

"Someone also claims to have seen you take off after Skye escaped."

"She got out, then. So she's okay?"

"Did you hear what I said, Mr. Mandal?"

Sure, but it's true. He *was* there.

Then it clicks. He was seen hanging around Skye. After school. Following her.

"I was out running laps. Then I came back to change."

"Did anyone see you doing that, Mr. Mandal?"

There's a moment of panic as he scrambles for an alibi.

"You understand this is a very serious charge, don't you, Mr. Mandal?"

Stop calling me that, you pretentious ass.

"Okay," he says. "So someone saw me after Skye was . . ."

After Skye was trapped in a fire.

Vaughn isn't accusing him of being a little too interested in a fellow student.

"You think . . . You think I locked her in there? Set the fire? *No*. I'd never hurt—"

Never hurt anyone? That's what he used to say, wasn't it? What everyone said about him. He remembers in fourth grade, some kid shoved him on the steps. When Jesse fell and twisted his ankle, the kid tried to say Jesse kicked him.

Jesse? Seriously? You're accusing Jesse of hurting you? Try again, loser.

He might forget the name of the kid who pushed him, but he remembers the one who came to his defense, who helped him up and put his arm over her shoulders and got him to the office. The one who, years later, wouldn't even remember she did it because that was just second nature for her.

Skye.

And how did he help when *she* needed it? Led the charge by rejecting her in math class, and then told himself that following her around was "protecting" her. Like that earned him a gold medal for bravery.

"Mr. Mandal?"

"I would never hurt Skye. Ever."

Vaughn purses his lips, as if he's assessing Jesse's reaction. No, he's *pretending* to assess it. He's already made up his mind.

"I know you can't be happy about having Miss Gilchrist here," Vaughn says finally.

"Sure, it caught me off guard that first day, but I'm fine with it. I was a jerk. I keep meaning to apologize."

"So you haven't done or said anything to her since that first day?"

He shakes his head. "I've been sitting in front of her in math, to show I'm okay with her being there."

"Is it possible you've done something to make Miss Gilchrist *feel* you don't want her here?"

Besides being a jerk on Wednesday when she tried to talk to me?

"I don't think so." He pauses. "Is she the one who saw me taking off when the alarm went?"

"What do you think of her story, Mr. Mandal?"

"Story?"

"About the fire. Being locked in. Someone shoving paper and lit matches under the door. Seems a bit farfetched, don't you think? Her records suggest she does have a penchant for fiction . . . and for causing trouble."

"Sure. Skye . . ." Jesse sees where this is going. "You think she made it up?"

"It's a very odd story. Very creative."

"Skye pulled pranks as a kid. That's all they were. Pranks and sometimes mouthing off. She's not going to lock herself in a room and start a fire. That's nuts. And I'm pretty sure you shouldn't be discussing this with me anyway. Isn't that a violation of her privacy?"

Vaughn's lips compress. "That will be all, Mr. Mandal. Thank you for your assistance."

Skye

That morning, I arrive to hear Jesse being paged. Good. Vaughn will tell him that I reported seeing him at the time of the fire, and Jesse will confront me over it. That's what I want—to see his face when he denies it.

But the morning passes with no sign of Jesse.

After English, Chris asks me to lunch.

"Don't worry," he says when I'm startled. "I'm not pulling that shit."

I arch my brows.

He continues, "Cute new girl, having a rough time of it. Guy takes advantage and acts all friendly when really, he's just hoping to score."

"Score? No one told me there's a game."

He chuckles. "There's always a game, unfortunately. But I'm not playing it."

"Are you sure? I hear you *are* something of a player."

A sharp laugh, as if he's surprised I'd come right out and say that.

"Depends on your definition," he says. "Do I like girls? Guilty. Lots of girls? Also guilty. Do I lie to get them? Treat them like crap? No. If you're worried, ask around. I'm cool with that. I know my rep. Earned it, too. But I'm not angling for a date. I get the feeling you aren't looking for that right now."

"I'm not."

"Which is why I'm offering to take you to Mickey D's, where I can use my employee discount. I'd hope I could do better than that on an actual date. I just figured . . ." He shrugs. "I haven't seen you in the cafeteria at lunch. It can be awkward if you don't have anyone to sit with yet."

My cheeks heat. "I've been in the library. Working."

"Good idea. You know what I used to do when the guys were giving me a rough time?" He lowers his voice. "Eat in a bathroom stall."

My cheeks go redder, but he just continues walking and says, "I've got my mom's car today, and the McDonald's I work at isn't the one closest to the school, so it'll be nice and quiet. My treat. Discount and all."

I shake my head. "Your treat is driving. Lunch is on me. But I will take your discount."

"Sounds like a plan."

Jesse shows up for math. He comes in late, and as soon as the bell rings, he's gone without ever looking my way. I head to my locker. When I open it, a sheet flutters out. A folded piece of paper with typed words on it.

I think of the leads. Of the sheets pushed under the door. I want to shove this back into my locker and go get Mr. Vaughn.

See? Do you see what's happening?

I see that there's a note in your locker, Skye . . . and the only person with the combination is you.

I check the locker door. There are vents in the top. The note has been shoved through them. That won't matter to Vaughn. He'll only see that the most likely culprit is the girl who owns this locker.

I take a deep breath and open the note.

THERE'S MORE TO THE STORY.

I stare at it. Read it again.

It's the same stuff pushed under the door of the newspaper office.

I KNOW WHAT YOU DID.
YOU'VE FOOLED THEM.
YOU DON'T FOOL ME.

Random nonsense meant to get my attention. There's no point even racking my brain to think of what I could have done. I've only been here a week. Give me time.

The fact that the other notes came along with a newspaper headline from the shooting seems to suggest *that* was the accusation: I played a role in the shooting. But I don't even know where to start with that. It's just too bizarre.

THERE'S MORE TO THE STORY.

More to the shooting? Something this person believes I did? Or is this a different person accusing me?

Do kids here think I knew what my brother had planned? I heard that at my other schools.

She must have known something.

He was her brother. She lived with him. Of course she knew something.

Everyone has secrets. Luka more than others, it seems, as much as it hurts to realize I didn't even know him well enough to suspect he was angry.

Put that back in the trunk. Close the lid. Add padlocks.

I crumple the note into my pocket. I have no idea who's doing this, but I do know who I saw in the hall last night. I can solve *that* mystery.

Jesse isn't coming to me, but I know where to find *him:* at the track meet.

Skye

When I reach the stands, I hear the pound of running feet and the cheers of the crowd, and I hesitate. I want to linger in the back. Wait for him to finish.

I don't want to watch Jesse run.

I'm afraid I'll look out on that field, and I won't see any of my Jesse left. Instead, I'll see Jamil.

This is what I've feared since our first encounter at RivCol. My first time seeing the Jesse who was not *my* Jesse. The Jesse who shunned me. Who drove me off when I tried to apologize. The Jesse who has become an asshole.

Like his brother.

I've told myself that's silly. That first day in math, Jamil would have curled his lip and fired a devastating insult. But what Jesse did felt the same. Maybe even worse. If he'd insulted me, I might have found enough of the old Skye to fire back a volley and save my dignity.

But just because Jesse has taken up track doesn't make him a jock like his brother. Jamil was all about the sexy sports, the ones where the girls waved pom-poms and drooled over his biceps and six-pack. Football, mainly, but in the off-season, he'd grace other teams with his talent, if they showed proper admiration for it.

After the shooting, it was Jamil's photo on every article, one of him hoisting his latest MVP trophy, accompanied by the mournful line that the city's best football prospect was among those slain. Forget the other three victims. Forget Leanna, the state science fair winner with the Ivy League scholarship. Forget Nella Landry, who'd gotten an internship at the governor's office for her advocacy work. Forget Brandon Locklear, who'd been holding down two after-school jobs to support his baby. We lost a *football* star. That's the takeaway here.

It was as if Jamil's egotism reached beyond the grave and swiped aside anyone who might steal his thunder. Just like he did in life, even with his own brother. Particularly with his own brother.

The Jesse I knew—the quiet, sweet, studious boy—is gone. In his place is a star athlete who doesn't give a crap about school, who'll shun a former friend in front of the entire class, who'll sneer and send her on her way when she apologizes to him. All of which perfectly sums up another boy. One I loathed for how he treated his little brother.

If Jesse has become another Jamil, I can't hide from that.

So as they announce the hundred-meter dash, I screw up my courage, walk from under the bleachers and head toward the side, where I see a bunch of people, mostly adults. I pass three seniors talking loudly about how the competitors all suck, and I make the mistake of glancing their way. The ginger-haired one grins and gives me a once-over, like he caught me checking him out. I roll my eyes and keep walking.

The competitors are on their mark. I spot Jesse easily. I will always spot Jesse easily.

He's wearing shorts and a school tank top, and when I see him from the rear, I see his brother. I see Jamil Mandal in the long, muscled brown legs and arms. I see him in the glistening black wavy hair. I see him even in the sliver of jaw I can spot from this angle, set and determined.

The shot fires, and they're off. I'm staring at Jesse, forcing myself to watch as he breaks into a run and . . .

"Race ya."

Jesse's voice rises from my memory. We're in a field, and he's grinning at me as he walks backward.

"Race ya."

My competitive streak wants to refuse. Or at least demand a head start, so I have a chance. But I agree, and we take off, and Jesse outstrips me in a few paces, and I don't care. I just want to watch him run.

He can beat me easily, but he hunkers down and gives it his all, and I wonder whether that's for my benefit. If the guy who never shows off does it now, just for me. I like the thought of that. I'm not sure why. I just do.

Mostly, though, I just like to watch him run. Run and turn at the end, wiping away sweat as he says, "Beat ya." And then he grins. Grins the way he doesn't when he beats me on a math quiz. That one's a quiet smile that says he's pleased by the accomplishment but doesn't want to rub in his victory. This is a real grin, not about beating me but about succeeding at something that isn't usually his strength.

Now, as Jesse takes off from the starting line, that's who I see. Not Jamil. Not even the Jesse I've met in the past week. I'm standing behind him, where I've always been when he runs. And I see that old Jesse in the way he hunkers forward, in the way he runs, the flow of his muscles, the set of his shoulders.

He reaches the finish line, and I'm not even sure where he placed—I haven't noticed the other runners. Then a voice reverberates from a substandard PA system and announces that Jesse Mandal takes first place. He turns toward the stands, and he doesn't grin. Doesn't even smile. He just nods, almost a courteous thank-you, like he used to give when he won an academic competition. Tears prickle behind my eyelids.

Hey, Jesse. Missed you.

"Skye?" It's a woman's voice, and I tense hearing it. As I walked over here, I caught the looks, the whispers, from the adults.

That's her. Skye Gilchrist. *His* sister.

I did what I've been doing since I arrived. The mental equivalent of sticking my fingers in my ears and singing "La-la-la, I can't hear you."

If I can't hear you, you can't hurt me.

What complete and utter bullshit.

"Skye?" the voice says again.

I turn. It's Jesse's mother. I recognize her immediately. When I was thirteen, she was already a half inch shorter than me. She seems tiny now, but she walks with a purposeful stride that makes everyone give way. She's dressed in casual wear, with a wool coat, killer boots and a hijab.

I've lived in cities where the hijab is more common, but it was rare enough in Riverside that when I first went to Jesse's house, I tried very hard not to stare. I'm embarrassed by that memory now, but Dr. Mandal only smiled and later said I could ask her anything. I didn't, not then, but as Jesse and I became friends, I *did* ask, haltingly, and I got my answers, with patience and kindness.

"Dr. Mandal," I say. "It's good—"

She pulls me into a tight hug with a whispered "It's so good to see you," as fierce and sincere as the hug. When I step back, Jesse's dad is right there, with a hand on my shoulder and a "Welcome home, Skye."

I should have known they'd be here. They always went to Jamil's games. Jesse's dad is an engineer and his mom's a doctor, so getting time off isn't easy, but they would make it work, whether it was for Jesse's math competitions or Jamil's football games.

"Come over here where it's quieter," Dr. Mandal says as another cheer goes up. Then she leans in and whispers, "Jasser's finished, so we don't need to pay quite so much attention."

I smile, and she steers me toward the end of the stands. I ask how they've been, and then I wave at the track field and say, "That's new. For Jesse, I mean. He's doing awesome."

"Yes, he's doing well in track."

The "in track" part speaks volumes, as does the cloud that passes behind her eyes and the twitch in her husband's lips. Mr. Mandal doesn't say much—he's as quiet as Jesse—but I see pain in both their faces. Not disappointment. Just concern that their high-achieving son isn't doing as well as he used to.

"I know it won't be easy being back," Dr. Mandal says. "If you ever want to talk . . ."

She takes a pen and paper from her purse and jots down her cell number. The Mandals were always kind to me. When I became friends with Jesse, his mother approved. *You bring him out of his shell,* she said. I didn't quite know what she meant then. I do now. She saw something in Jesse, a hesitancy, a lack of confidence. She never guessed his brother had a lot to do with that—Jamil was so careful around them. Having someone like me for a friend—brash, bold, maybe a little *too* confident—helped Jesse. Helped both of us.

So I know why she was so kind to me then. Now, though? Now she has every reason to be no more than civil. But she gives me that hug—in front of everyone—and she gives me her number, and I want to cry. I just want—

"There you are." Jesse's voice floats over. "I thought I saw you guys sneak—"

He sees me and stops short.

"I believe you remember Skye?" his mother says, her voice lilting with sarcasm, and even if I can't see her face, I know she's giving him a look.

"I was just inviting Skye to join us for dinner," she says.

"What?" Jesse says.

She speaks slowly, as if he needs it. "We are going out to dinner, and I am inviting Skye to join us."

"I—" Jesse says. "I can't. Homework. I've got homework."

"And you're actually intending to do it? I'd be thrilled to hear that . . . if it wasn't Friday, and your homework can't possibly be due until Monday."

"It's fine," I cut in. "I appreciate the offer, but my aunt's expecting me."

"A cold drink, then," she says. "Afterward, I'll drop you at your aunt's."

"You guys can," Jesse says. "I have to stick around. Team meeting."

"Really? Since when—"

"That's fine," I say. "Really. I do appreciate the offer, but I'm already running late. Mae expected me right after school. Another time?"

Jesse mumbles something, and before I can make it clear that I'm talking to his mother—not him—he turns to go. His dad takes a step that way, as if to speak to him, but Jesse has broken into a lope, already out of reach.

"I am so sorry," Dr. Mandal says. "That was completely unacceptable."

"No, it's fine. This has been hard on him. I get that."

Her lips tighten. "That is no excuse. I'll speak to him, Skye. Clear up this nonsense."

"No," I blurt, in genuine alarm. "Please. Don't. It's tough, and he's having trouble with me being back, and sure, I'd like to talk to him—"

Did I just say that? Not helping, really not helping.

I hurry on, "But there's no rush. I'll be here all year." I try for a smile. "We'll be fine."

Just fine. Just fine. Everything's fine. Really, really, really.

"I should go," I mumble. "I'm sorry if I caused any trouble."

"You haven't done anything, Skye," Mr. Mandal says. "We're the ones who are sorry. If Jasser is . . ."

He trails off and his wife finishes, "If Jasser is being an ass. That's what my husband is too polite to say."

I sputter a laugh at her language, and she gives me another quick hug and says, "Come to tea tomorrow, Skye."

I tense. "I—"

"Tea with me. Only me. Aftab will find some excuse to take Jasser out, and however cranky our son has become, he's still a boy who does as he's told. They'll have a father-son afternoon, and you'll come to tea, and we won't talk about Jasser."

"I—"

"This isn't a trick, Skye. Aftab won't 'accidentally' bring Jasser home early while you're there. I'd just like to talk. To catch up. Can we do that?"

I nod and agree to come by tomorrow at two.

I'm standing outside the Mandal house. It's almost two, and I don't want to be late, but I'm not sure I can do this. I feel the weight of Dr. Mandal's number in my pocket. I can call. Text even. Tell her I can't make it.

The house hasn't changed. Not one bit. It's a beautiful home, an old two-story on a street I know well. We used to live in a place not much different from this, on a similar street, so quiet I can hear leaves rustling in the autumn breeze. One pirouettes down beside me and brings voices from the past.

"Jasser? Can you rake the leaves for your dad? He hasn't had a chance since his promotion and—Oh, Skye. I didn't know you were here. Never mind, then. You two go play."

"Uh, we're thirteen, Mom," Jesse says. "A little old for playing."

"You know what I mean. Why don't I take you two to a movie? My treat."

"We'll do the leaves first," I say.

"And then I'll take you guys to a movie," Dr. Mandal says.

"Sure. I've got my own money, though."

"True, but if you're raking leaves, I'm paying you for it. That payment will be a ticket and popcorn and soda. Or you don't get to rake my leaves."

We went to see an overblown sci-fi flick and snickered at the ridiculousness of it. Jesse's mom took us—"chaperoning"—but she sat a few rows back. Jesse and I whispered all through the movie, sharing our popcorn, and sometimes we reached into the bag at the same time, hands brushing, and my cheeks would heat, and maybe that should seem silly now, but it doesn't.

The more I'm in Riverside—revisiting places that remind me of Jesse, doing things that remind me of us—the more I remember how I felt about him, which wasn't childish or silly at all.

The front door opens. It's Dr. Mandal, and she doesn't call me over, just stands and watches, as if to say she'll understand if I change my mind. I steel myself, and I walk toward her, and she smiles and pushes the door open wide.

I go inside and . . .

Even the smell is enough to make me swallow hard to keep tears from welling. It doesn't just remind me of Jesse. It reminds me of myself. Of who I was. What I had. How my life was before.

Once I get past the front hall, though, the house has changed. Completely changed, as much as it could without gutting and rebuilding.

As Dr. Mandal leads me into the living room, I don't recognize any of the furniture or even the arrangement of it. There are only a few trophies on a bookshelf, far fewer than Jamil earned. There are others, too, bearing Jesse's name.

When I spot an orange cat on the sofa, I smile and say, "Hey, Phurri," and he turns, and I see my mistake and say, "Oh."

"Phurri died a couple of years ago. That's Fluffy." She spells it out as *Phluphi*.

I smile again. "Jasser named him, too, I'm guessing?"

Her own smile falters, and her gaze drops as she takes a chair. "No, I did, following his naming convention."

I sit on the sofa. "I'm sorry. About Jamil. I didn't say that earlier, and I should have. I'm sorry for what happened to him, and I'm sorry Luka . . ." I choke on his name. "I'm sorry my brother . . ." Tears fill my eyes, and I inhale sharply.

Just get this out. It's important. Get it out.

"I'm so sorry Luka . . . Luka . . ."

"You miss him, don't you?"

"What?" I look up sharply.

"Your brother." A wry smile. "Silly question, isn't it? Of course you do. I know how close you two were. You must miss him so much."

I try to say sure, I miss him, kind of, but after what he did, that's all changed, so nope, I don't really . . . don't really . . .

"It's okay to say you miss him, Skye."

I open my mouth to deny it, and I burst into tears.

Jesse

The minute Jesse walks in the door, he knows he's in trouble. Well, worse trouble than he was when he left, which is saying something.

His parents have always been what one might call average disciplinarians, leaning toward permissive. Since Jamil's death, that lean has become a dangerous slant. In a heartbeat, Jesse became their only child. He's struggling, and they want to give him space. He's only sixteen, a junior, bright enough to turn things around in his senior year, or—if that's too much to ask—no one would begrudge him a victory lap.

This weekend, though, he is in trouble. The kind he hasn't been in since before Jamil died. The kind he really can't remember being in at all.

His parents are disappointed. They don't say that, of course. They never say that, even when he does disappoint them. At most, he'll get prods.

Jesse, why don't you call up Mark, see what he's doing this weekend?

Jesse, your teacher says you have a biology project—how about we work on that together?

After last night's track meet, though, they're pissed. Any pride he bought with his win, he more than canceled out by being an ass to Skye.

An ass. His mom actually said that. Well, she told him he was being "a bit of an ass" but only because she couldn't quite bring herself to go all the way.

He had been, though. No doubt about it. A complete ass.

"She came to watch you, Jasser."

"Me? No, she just stopped by—"

"I saw her go to the fence for your race. After you blew her off, she admitted she'd like to talk to you, and then she was embarrassed when she realized she'd said that."

"You misunderstood."

"How can we misunderstand 'I'd like to talk to him'? She made it clear she means when you have time. When you're up to it. She completely understands this must be hard for you and doesn't want to do anything to make it harder. Apparently it's true what they say, about girls maturing faster than boys."

He flinched at that. Flinched not only at his mother's disappointment, but at the knowledge that he *was* being a brat.

Now he comes home after Skye's visit, and he has only to look at his mother's face to know he's sunk even lower.

He tries to avoid the subject of Skye. He shows his mom a couple of shirts he's bought, and even tells a funny anecdote about some little kids in the food court. But his mom has that look on her face, the one that says she has something to say and he can tell her about his trip to the mall later.

So he braces himself and asks, "What did Skye say about me?"

Not a word. That's what his mother tells him. His name never came up.

"She's been through hell, Jasser. Have you even thought about what it was like for her?"

Skye didn't complain to his mother, of course. His mom says she just cried. Cried and cried, and that hurts more than if she *had* complained about how badly he'd behaved.

Jesse has never seen Skye cry. She caught him once, just a stupid thing, Jamil being a jerk on a day when Jesse already felt like shit. Skye found him and sat down and said, "Huh, guess Jamil's been getting the same emails I have," and he said, "What?" confused enough to forget she'd caught him crying. "Emails for penis enlargement pills," she said. "He must be buying them, too, because he's being a bigger dick than ever." That made him laugh so hard he choked. It was only afterward that he realized he'd never even told her Jamil was the cause of his tears. She'd known, without a word.

But *Skye* never cries. He can't even picture it happening.

She did, though. She sat on his couch and broke down with his mother, and he was part of the reason for those tears.

He made her cry.

Guess Jamil's not the one buying those pills these days, huh?

"Do you know how she was treated after she left Riverside?" his mother asks.

Better than she'd have been treated if she stayed.

He doesn't say that—it would sound flip. But as much

as thirteen-year-old I-feel-rejected Jesse resented Skye leaving, sixteen-year-old Jesse understands that Skye was better off elsewhere. Or so he thinks, until his mother directs his attention to the comment sections on old articles.

When he reads those comments, he can barely breathe, outrage and confusion choking him until he says, "But she wouldn't have read those, right?"

"Does it matter? People may not have said this to her face, but this is how she was treated."

He's sick then. Physically sick. And not just for Skye, either. He knows how hard it would have been for his mother to look up those articles, to revisit the shooting. Yet she did it so she would understand what Skye was going through . . . and because Jesse himself couldn't be bothered.

"I'm sorry," he says. "That you . . . had to look . . ."

"I didn't *have* to," she says. "I chose to. Sometimes, showing compassion for others means doing things that are painful for us."

He goes into the kitchen after that. Makes his mother tea and silently drops it off before he retreats to his room. He sits on his bed and thinks. Then he strides into the living room and tells his mom he's going out.

"Can I expect you for dinner?" she asks.

"Probably not."

There's a pause, and he knows she wants to ask where he's going. She won't. That's all part of giving him space. Showing they trust him. She only says, "Do you want to take my car?"

"I'm fine."

A rattle of keys. "Take it. Just be home by dark. You don't have enough experience driving at night."

That's the trick, then. *Please take my car . . . because it guarantees you'll be back by dark.*

Not that he ever stays out late. Jesse isn't exactly a party boy. That's one part of Jamil's life that his brother can keep.

He takes the car. He owes his mom that much, and he doesn't expect he'll be long.

He's going to apologize to Skye. No more following her around, trying to work up the courage to say something. Twice now she's had the guts to make that move. It's his turn.

Skye

I just want to get home. I just want to get home. That's been my mantra for the last twenty minutes, after humiliating myself at the Mandals'.

Except I don't feel humiliated. Not really. I get the sense that I should, but for now I only feel wiped out. It reminds me of the last time I had food poisoning. I'd say I *was* poisoned—I made the mistake of accepting peace-offering brownies from a tormenter—but my guidance counselor told me I was being paranoid. My own stupid fault for accepting them, really, but that was in the early days, when I was still reeling, certain the bullying arose from a horrible misunderstanding and as soon as they got to know me, it'd stop.

Yeah, it's like that speech Chris got in school. Just let them get to know the *real* you, and it'll be fine. It wasn't.

When I finished that bout of food poisoning, I felt like I do now. Empty and drained, but in a weirdly good way, shaking with relief, knowing I've gotten something toxic out of my system.

I take a cab home. Dr. Mandal insisted on getting me one and prepaying it. Arguing would have only increased the likelihood of Jesse showing up.

I text with Gran and Mom on the ride. Then I return to an empty condo with a note on the table, Mae saying something came up at work and she didn't want to disrupt my visit by texting.

I take off my jacket and open the closet door and . . .

My boots are outside the closet.

That gives me pause. I'm wearing sneakers, as I have all week. I wanted to assess the fashion choices at RivCol before reverting to my favorite footwear. So my Docs have been in that closet since I unpacked them.

Now they're outside it.

So? They must have been blocking a pair of shoes Mae wanted, and she forgot to put them back. I pick them up . . . and a clod of dried mud falls off one.

I flip the boots over. The soles are caked with mud, and I know I cleaned them before putting them into my suitcase.

I start a text to Mae: hey, did you wear my Docs today?

That sounds accusatory, which isn't what I mean at all, so I change it to: noticed my Docs are out. Looks like you . . .

Looks like you what? Wanted to see how they'd pair with your business suit? Decided they looked perfect for your morning jog?

There must be a rational explanation. I should just call and ask Mae.

And what do I say when she tells me she hasn't touched my boots?

Okay, thanks. I found them sitting out with mud on them, and I know I haven't worn them since I got here, so I was just checking.

That sounds crazy. But what other explanation is there? That somebody broke into Mae's condo and borrowed my Docs to tramp through the mud?

The door was locked when I arrived. There's a security alarm that came with the place, but Mae hasn't used it since I arrived.

While it's a controlled-entry building, I've only had to use my downstairs key a few times—if someone's coming or going, they hold the door.

Am I really considering the possibility that someone broke in and muddied my boots?

Drop it. Just drop it. Lock the front door. Slide the deadbolt. Figure out later how to use the security system and tell Mae I'd feel more comfortable with that. For now, just lock myself in and read through past online editions of the *RivCol Times,* like I promised Tiffany.

I walk into the kitchen to see my laptop where I left it. On the table, in plain sight.

See, no one broke in. Valuables present and accounted for.

I take my laptop into the living room, and I'm opening it as I head for the couch and—

There's a brown streak on the white fabric. It looks like . . . well, it should be obvious what it looks like. I hurry over and see it's part of a candy bar, mashed in, as if someone sat on it.

When I grab paper towels and scrape it off, I see chocolate with an almond sliver.

I have a Hershey bar with almonds in my bedroom.

I jog there. My food stash is on the dresser, and I can see the brown wrapper. I walk over. The Hershey bar is where I left it, but it's been opened. And it's half gone.

I turn it over in my hands, as if this is some kind of optical illusion. It's not. Half the bar is gone. Smushed into Mae's white sofa.

Even if Mae had a sudden chocolate craving, she'd have left a note promising to replace it. And she would never have dropped it on her sofa—she's already given me side eye for drinking Coke in there.

Someone caked my Docs in mud and left them in the hall.

Someone took half my candy bar and crushed it into the sofa.

That makes no sense. Absolutely no—

Something tinkles behind me. Softly, like wind chimes.

My closet door is ajar. *That* I might have done. Easily.

But the tinkling . . . Mae has wire hangers. They make that sound when they knock against one another.

The closet door is ajar, and something in there jangled the hangers.

I should run. That's what I'd do if I was writing this scene. *And so the heroine—who was not a complete idiot—fled the apartment and called 911 to report an intruder.*

But if I was writing the scene, there *would* be an intruder. As the writer, I'd know it, and my audience would expect someone to be in there. So to have my heroine do anything except run creates a classic too-stupid-to-live protagonist. For the person *in* that scene, though, it's very different. One jangle doesn't prove someone's in my closet.

Um, and also, the boots, the chocolate . . .

I envision fleeing. Calling 911. Then I imagine shame. Shame and embarrassment and a flood of excuses.

I just . . . I panicked. I've had a rough week, and I'm on edge, and I know it sounds crazy, reporting an intruder based on hangers jingling in the closet. But the boots? The candy bar? Okay, sure, it'd be weird for an intruder to do those things . . .

I take out my phone. I hit 9. Then I pick up Gran's heavy silver hairbrush from my dresser. I press 1. Step toward the closet. Brush clutched in one hand. Finger poised over the 1 to hit it again the second I see anything.

I snag the door with my foot, yank . . . and lose my balance, and down I go, hairbrush falling, phone falling, brain screaming that I really am too stupid to live.

Tears fill my eyes. Hot tears of shame. I have this split-second image of my body on the floor, a phone on one side, weapon on the other . . . and I died crying, pitying my stupidity.

I scramble up and snatch the brush, my gaze riveted to that door.

The closet stays silent. The closet stays still.

I manage to scoop up my phone without taking my eyes off that door. Then I consider my options. I can't see inside the closet, even with the door open. The angle is wrong, letting in only shadows.

I need light. Wait—cell phone. I flick on the flashlight. Shine it at the closet. Swing the beam of light at knee level, under the clothing, above the stuff piled on the floor.

I see only the back of the closet.

I move closer, still tensed, and I kick my foot through that knee-height swath, making absolutely sure it's empty.

It is.

There's nobody in my closet. There is, however, one of Mae's dresses snaked on the floor, the empty hanger still on the rack. A dress that slid off, leaving the wire hanger to clink against the others.

Well, there's my rational explanation.

The tears come again, those hot ones that fill my eyes but don't fall. Tears of shame.

Would I think myself smarter if I'd ignored the clinking, gone about my business and ended up dead?

No, what I want is to be the old Skye, who'd have marched to that closet, armed with something better than a hairbrush, and thrown open the door.

If wishes were horses, beggars would fly.

That's what Gran always says, and I have no idea what it means, but I understand what *she* means by it—don't sit around wishing for change; make change happen. Take comfort in knowing I've kinda done the right thing and resolve to do better next time.

Or, you know, hope there won't *be* a next time that I think I hear a deranged Doc-Marten-loving, Hershey-bar-loving killer in my closet.

I reach in to pick up the fallen garment. As soon as my fingers close on the black fabric, I realize it's not a dress. It's a T-shirt. Definitely not what I would have pictured Mae wearing. A throw-back to the days *before* she wore a blazer and pressed jeans for Casual Fridays?

It's a concert tour tee, and I can't help taking a closer look. Maybe she was a Green Day groupie back in her college days. Or even a secret ATF fan. That makes me laugh, and I turn the shirt around . . .

It's not for a band. It's a fake tour T-shirt for the bubonic plague. I bought it at a Comic-Con with Jesse.

"Hey, Luka. Got you something."

He unfolds it and bursts out laughing.

I drop the shirt and run from the apartment.

Skye

I'm at the tiny market a few doors down. I've spent the last ten minutes trying to sternly talk myself into returning to the apartment.

No one planted Luka's T-shirt. Mae rescued it. He wore that tee at least once a month, and I wonder now if that was for me. It was more my sense of humor than his. But he never said so, never stuffed it in the back of his closet. He wore it just as proudly as he'd worn the badly braided bracelets I made him at summer camp when I was nine. Mae must have seen the shirt, taken it as a favorite of his and forgotten to remove it from that closet before I moved in.

It's a logical explanation, but I still can't bring myself to go back. I need to wait for Mae.

I can't stay in the market much longer—the clerk is already eyeing me like she wants to search my pockets for stolen beets and broccoli. I go on my phone to find a nearby cafe. I'll get a caramel latte and hang out on my laptop until Mae comes home.

My Internet search locates two coffeehouses just as the market clerk heads over with a supercilious "May I help you?"

I give her a "No thanks" and head for the doors. The nearest cafe is barely a block away. The second isn't much farther, if the first seems like the kind that treats teens like tech-savvy vagrants, holing up in a corner with a coffee and thinking that entitles them to two hours of free Wi-Fi.

I push open the door and step out of the market, my gaze sweeping the street and—

I stop. I stare. I tell myself I'm seeing wrong. I *want* to be seeing wrong.

There's a figure tucked into a doorway across from Mae's building. He thinks he's hidden, both by the shadows and his pulled-up hood. He's not hidden. Not from me. One glimpse of his profile, and it's like when I first spotted him Monday, a fleeting look that was enough even after three years.

Jesse stands across the road from Mae's building. His gaze is fixed on the doorway. The one that leads to our condo.

I want to pretend it's coincidence. He isn't waiting for me to get back from his place and walk inside the condo and see his handiwork and maybe, if he's lucky, come tearing through the front door, properly spooked. No, that's not it at all. Just coincidence.

He takes his cell phone from his pocket. Hits buttons. Puts it away.

"Is there a problem?"

The clerk's voice makes me jump, and I realize I'm in the market doorway. I back inside quickly and say, "Sorry. I just . . . I'm new here. I thought I saw a coffee place earlier, but now I'm confused. Is the shop left or right?"

The clerk sniffs, says, "I don't drink coffee," and retreats into the store.

I pretend to study the map on my cell while I figure out what to do.

Confront Jesse.

It's daytime. It's a major street. It's safe.

Yes, confront him.

I caught you. I see you. I'm not fooled.

My cell phone screen flashes. An incoming text from a number I don't recognize: You shouldn't eat so much chocolate, Skye. You never know where it'll end up. Hips, zits, all kinds of places.

My heart pounds, and I send back: Who is this?

My message sits, sits, sits . . . Then an exclamation mark appears, telling me it couldn't be delivered.

Then another message comes. It's a video. When I see that first, my gut goes cold. Then I read the message: Leanna wasn't the only kid who died that day. I don't know if you ever met her, but this one should be a familiar face.

I hit Play before I can stop myself. The screen fills with a close-up of a nose. Then it pulls back to show a tongue sticking out, as a voice shouts, "Selfie shots aren't enough for you, huh? You need selfie *videos,*" and the camera keeps drawing back to show a wide grin as a voice says, "Guess who won MVP? *Again.*" The trophy appears and the face pulls back farther, and it's Jamil.

Even as his friends jeer and tease him, he grins into the camera, and it's not the grin I remember—that full-of-himself jerk one. He looks like Jesse, after he beat me in a footrace, an honest grin of pride and—

The clip ends and the screen fills with a pan of an empty school hall. There's blood on the wall—

I jab the Stop button.

I take a moment, my eyes closed. Then I look across the road. Jesse is still there. He's watching the condo building door again, but only a moment ago he was on his phone.

No. He couldn't have. He *wouldn't.*

I just watched him do something on his phone, and then I got the text. Followed by a video of his brother.

It must have been him. So why do I keep making excuses?

Because it's Jesse. The first boy I fell for, and not in that distant-crush way, a guy in class you think is really cute. I got to know Jesse, became friends with him—good friends—and then I fell for him, and it wasn't until I came back to Riverside that I realized how big an impression he made on me.

I've been asked on dates since I left Riverside. And I've refused. Never been out with a boy, never kissed one, and I know those two things don't need to go together but for me, they do. I've told myself I'm just too busy. Too preoccupied. I'm only sixteen. Plenty of time for that later.

The truth is that none of those boys measured up to Jesse.

To think that he could be stalking me? Sending horrific videos of the shooting? Breaking into my home? Trapping me in a *fire?*

That hurts in a way nothing has since the day of the shooting, when I ran to my mother and said, "Tell me it isn't true," and she collapsed, sobbing.

I can't confront Jesse. If I do, I'll be the one collapsing in tears. Everything that's happened will come to a head. I'll break down, and he'll know he's won. I have no idea what the game is, but he will have won.

I watch Jesse, my hands shaking as I clutch my phone. I'm waiting for a chance to dart the other way, to the coffee shop. When he takes out his phone, I freeze.

Don't wait to see what he sends next. Just go. While he's distracted.

I tug up my hood and push the door. Brakes squeal. It's a pickup truck, but it's heading the other way, passing Jesse, who's still busy on his phone. The truck idles in front of the condo until someone drives up behind it and taps the horn. That makes Jesse look, but the truck pulls away, tires spinning.

I duck out in the opposite direction and head for the coffee shop.

Skye

Jesse doesn't send me anything else. I've got my phone in hand, fingers wrapped tightly around it, waiting for the vibration. I'm checking the cell signal when brakes squeak. I look up to see that same pickup in front of me, having turned around and come back. It's idling again. Three guys sit in the front seat. A RivCol football sticker decorates the window.

I'm reasonably sure they didn't spot me earlier. If they stopped for anyone, it seemed to be Jesse. But he only glanced up, no sign that he knew the occupants.

The truck takes off with another chirp of the tires. It turns down a road two intersections away and disappears from sight.

Hello, paranoia.

I still exhale in relief when I spot the coffee shop sign. Then I see the FOR LEASE one. Figures. Oh well, I know there's another cafe around the next corner, which may be why this one went out of business.

My phone buzzes with an incoming text. I jump. When I lift it, my hand is shaking.

It's just Mae.

Her: Home yet?

I type stopped 4 and add a coffee emoji.

The pause tells me she's deciphering. I resend in full verbiage and add: That okay?

Her: np! Can I pick you up in an hour? We'll go out for dinner.

I don't want to go out for dinner, but if I say that, it'll seem like I'm being difficult. I start to reply, asking her to pick me up at the coffee shop. Then I take a deep breath and reply: Just text before you leave & I'll wait at condo.

I pocket my phone. When I look up, I see that truck. It stopped after turning the corner. It's idling. Again.

Because they're looking for a place and pulled over to Google-check their destination. Just chill. Seriously.

Still, I pick up my pace as I make the next right and look for the coffee shop sign, which is . . . farther than I expected.

Again, *chill.* It's not midnight. It's not ten miles away. Stop freaking out.

When I hear a car turn the corner behind me, I don't look back. I will not be paranoid. Will not.

The pickup whips past and veers into a lane I'm just about to cross. The door swings open, and I see the ginger-haired guy who checked me out at the track meet.

Great. I eye-rolled his once-over yesterday, and now he's spotted me and had his buddies drive back so he can let me know exactly how big an opportunity I missed.

I start to give a sarcastic "Can I help you?" before realizing all the ways that can be answered. Instead, I fix Ginger Dude with a cool "Yes?"

"Skye, right? Skye Gilchrist?"

The driver's door opens. It shuts with a slam. A big guy in a football jacket saunters around the front of the truck.

I glance toward the back bumper. That's all I do—glance. But Ginger Dude sidesteps that way, as if I'm making a break for it. The passenger door opens again. A third guy moves into the opening but stays on the seat, sideways, his legs dangling, the door wide.

"RivCol Raiders, huh?" I say, nodding at the big guy's jacket. "What do you play?"

"Wide receiver," he says, and he puffs up, as if waiting for me to . . . I don't know, ask for an autograph?

"How's the team doing this season?" I say, as if I'm some grown-up trying to make polite conversation with the local kids. His eyes narrow, like maybe I'm insinuating something about the team.

"I heard they were city champs last year," I say. "I'll look forward to seeing you guys play this season."

That look stays fixed on his face, waiting for the insult, because this is just too civilized a conversation. Ginger Dude's eyes gleam in anticipation. He's hoping I'll insult his football-playing friend, which will give him an excuse to get up in my face.

"Good luck with next week's game," I say. "And enjoy your Saturday night. You're going to . . ." I follow the lane they've pulled into. "The Lion and Lamb. Hope you've got your ID ready. I hear they can be jerks about it."

I nod a farewell and start around Football Player, who seems the most likely to stand in dumb silence and let me pass. Which he does. But the guy still in the truck, the silent one, springs to life, swinging out the passenger door to cut me off.

He doesn't say anything. Just gives his friends a "Well, dumbasses, say something" look.

Ginger Dude saunters over. "You used to be friends with Mandal, right?"

"Jesse? Sure."

"We spotted him around the corner and wondered what he was doing in this neighborhood. I heard you're staying with your aunt, the dyke who's, like, a CEO or something."

I open my mouth to call him on the slur, but he's still going. "This seems like the kind of neighborhood she'd live in. That explains why Mandal's hanging around. You and him are meeting up, huh?"

"Supposed to be," I say, because I'm becoming increasingly aware of how quiet this street is, most of the shops—including the pub—either closed or not yet open for the evening.

"Well, you missed him over there," Ginger Dude says. "And you might want to keep missing him."

I arch my brows.

"You're new here, Skye. Well, newly returned. And you're having trouble, right? Kids hassling you? Kids can be assholes." He manages to say this with an utter lack of irony. "It might be tempting to fall back on old friends. But Mandal's the wrong kind of friend, if you know what I mean."

"No, actually, I don't."

"He's trouble. Like his brother. You know the truth about the shooting, right?"

I stiffen.

Ginger Dude continues, "It was his fault. Jamil Mandal's. Your brother and his friends were just trying to stop him."

"Stop Jamil from—?" I cut myself short as I realize I really don't want to continue this ridiculous conversation. "I'm going to let you guys go enjoy your Saturday night. Don't drink too much. It seems like you may have already had a few."

I know better than to turn my back on them. So I reverse for a few feet, and then veer to go around them and hoof it to the coffee shop. As soon as I back up, though, Ginger Dude grabs my arm.

I throw him off with a "Hey!"

"What? You can dish it out, but you can't take it?"

I screw up my face. "What the hell are you—?"

Deep breath. I'm not dealing with mental giants here.

I say, "Look, you've had your fun, but—"

"Oh, we haven't started to have our fun, Skye."

Yeah, I walked into that one. Deep breath. Take two.

"I appreciate the advice about Jesse." *Don't laugh. Don't laugh.* "But I'm actually just meeting my aunt at the coffee shop over there."

"Right, the dyke aunt. She teaching you anything? Maybe something we should *unteach* you?"

I have to bite my tongue hard not to WTF them.

"You guys want to take potshots?" I say. "Go ahead. You have two minutes. Insult me, insult my family, my friends. Get it out of your system."

"You've got a smart mouth. How about I show you a better way to use it?"

Don't respond. Don't respond. Don't—

"The way I use it is just fine," I say. "Now get your ass out of my way before I kick it."

Ginger Dude snickers. He grabs for me. I wait until his fingers wrap around my arm, and there is absolutely zero chance he's just testing me. Then I slam my foot into his shin and seize his arm, and as he stumbles, I throw him down.

"There," I say. "Ass kicked. Now, you other guys? I suggest you decide I'm beneath your notice and help your buddy back into the truck. The alternative is that you can try kicking *my* ass, and between the three of you, I'm sure you can, but someone's going to notice, and then you'll be the three jocks who beat up a girl."

The silent guy nods to Football Player, telling him to let it go. Ginger Dude pretends the message isn't meant for him, too.

"Grant." Quiet Guy breaks his vow of silence. "Drop it."

"You think I'm walking away from some smart-mouth bitch—"

"—who put you down?" his friend continues. "Yeah. Come on."

I nod in thanks, and Quiet Guy seems surprised but then gives a curt nod and grabs Grant's arm. "Drop it, bud."

"Screw you, Marco. I'm teaching her a lesson."

Grant lunges at me, breaking from Marco's grip.

I backpedal, and Marco is hauling Grant away when a voice shouts, "Leave her alone!"

Skye

I know that voice. I turn, saying, "I've got this," and Grant hits me from behind. I'm going down on one knee, twisting in recovery, easily ducking Grant, but Jesse charges. I get in his path, hands flying up, and he stops short.

"It's cool," I say.

"Doesn't look that way to me." Jesse sidesteps and bears down on Grant. "You have something to say to her? Say it to me."

"Seriously?" I say. "Did someone spike your OJ with testosterone?" I grab the back of Jesse's jacket. "It's under control. They were just leaving."

Jesse bristles, his gaze fixed on Marco. "We talked about this last week. You're going to leave her alone. Got it?"

Grant grins and bounces on the balls of his feet. "Oh, I don't think I am. Maybe you should do something about that, Mandal. Come on. Take a swing."

Football Player shifts forward, his face lighting in anticipation of a fight. Marco catches my eye and gives a small shake of his head, telling me he's not stupid enough to interfere.

I realize now that they weren't hassling *me*. I was just the bait.

I remember what Tiffany said, the rumor about Jesse being kicked out of Southfield for fighting. He's got a rep, and he's on their turf. They want to put him in his place, preferably while it's three to one and they're guaranteed a win.

"Leave it," I say to Jesse, in a tone not unlike one I'd use on a dog intent on eating something unsanitary.

I keep hold of his jacket, and I can feel the tension strumming through him.

When I say, "Just drop it," and add, "Please," I expect he'll still ignore me. He does stiffen, but there are two long seconds of silence, and then he glances at me, not quite taking his eyes off Grant. A glance and a nod and a "Yeah, okay" that honestly shocks me.

Jesse rolls his shoulders, and I release his jacket. I'm tensed, waiting for him to attack now that I've let go, but he only runs a hand through his hair, his hood falling as he says, "Just leave her alone. Okay?"

"Do we get a 'please,' too, Mandal?" Grant sneers. "That seems to be the magic word."

"Don't be a dick," I say. "I know it's asking a lot, but—"

Jesse give me a sidelong look that takes me careening through a slideshow of memories, all the times I was the one spoiling for a fight—at least the verbal variety—and he'd give me that look to say it wasn't worth it.

I inhale. "Okay, let's leave it there. We're all cool. Let's just back off and say good night."

"Is that an order, bitch?" Grant says.

Jesse rocks forward, saying, "Don't call her that."

"She called me a dick."

"Because you—" Jesse begins.

I can see that last word coming—*because you are*—so I cut in with "Fair enough. We've exchanged insults. We're going to leave it there."

Football Player attacks. I don't see that coming. Neither does Jesse or Marco, all of us fixed on Grant.

One second, Jesse is in front of me. And then he's on the pavement, with a wide receiver atop him.

Grant runs to pile on, and I go after him, but Marco grabs us both, saying, "Nope. One on one. Fair fight. Let them work it out."

"Fair fight?" I say. "He jumped Jesse. That's assault, not a boxing match."

Marco shakes his head. I glower at him. He lets go but keeps one eye on me, waiting for me to charge in. I don't. As long as Marco has Grant under control, I'll stay clear.

Jesse gets out from under Football Player, whose name is Duke. Or that's my guess, judging by Grant's cries of "Get him, Duke" and "Yeah, you go, Duke!"

I snort. "Really? The only Dukes I know have four legs and wear collars. Appropriate, I guess."

Marco's look warns me not to make his self-appointed ref job any tougher.

I turn to the fight. Duke might be big, but he's clueless when it comes to combat. Jesse is fighting defensively, keeping the temperature low, letting Duke wear himself out. Unfortunately, Duke's just bright enough to know he's making a fool of himself when his blows keep landing on thin air. Frustration does nothing to improve his aim, and soon he's snorting like an enraged bull, hitting wildly, more likely to send himself spinning than strike Jesse.

"Duke?" Marco calls. "This isn't my idea of a fun Saturday night. You want a fight, let's go find someone who'll give you that. This guy's just dicking you around."

Duke swings.

Jesse grabs his arm and twists it behind his back. "Why don't you listen to your buddy? This isn't proving anything."

It's a perfectly reasonable thing to say, but Duke's looking for insult, and somehow he finds it, yanking away with a bellow and an uppercut that Jesse blocks.

Jesse grabs Duke by the jacket and throws him down. Putting him down. Saying he's done with him. I know that. But Grant lets out a yelp of outrage, as if Jesse pulled a knife, and he charges before Marco can yank him back.

Grant aims a kick straight at Jesse's head as Jesse bends over Duke. I'm already in flight, and I let out a shout that's more of a shriek.

Jesse sees the kick coming and ducks, but he doesn't quite evade. Grant's boot hits him in the face. Blood flies, and I'm on Grant, knocking him away from Jesse.

I hear a man shout. A door slams. Running footsteps. A hand grabs me back. It's Marco, pulling me off Grant while keeping Grant from retaliating.

Marco's telling us to cool it, everyone cool it, and there's a man demanding to know what the hell is going on. I run to Jesse, who's on his feet, one hand to his face, blood seeping between his fingers. Duke's rising, inching away, his gaze sliding to the approaching man.

The man has his cell phone raised as he says, "You kids want me to call the cops?"

"No, sir," Marco says. "We're fine."

I look at Jesse. "Uh, no, we're *not* fine. These guys assaulted us. They cut me off in their truck, and then attacked. Yes, I would like you to call the police."

The man looks from me and Jesse to the three others and mutters, "Whatever's going on here, take it somewhere else." Then he retreats as I yell, "Thank you for your help, sir! Much appreciated!"

Marco is getting Duke and Grant into the truck. He looks back at us and says, "You're welcome."

"For what? Not being as big a dick as your friends? They're still your friends, and you still came here with them to harass me and antagonize Jesse into a fight. You let them spout their crap and go after Jesse with zero provocation. You want a display of gratitude?" I hold up my middle finger. "Take this."

Jesse taps my arm. "Let's just go."

I turn and start walking. "Assholes."

The truck door shuts and the engine starts, and I can feel Jesse watching me.

"Yeah, yeah, I had to get in the last word," I say. "But I'm not the caveman who came roaring in with 'don't hurt her or you'll be sorry.' Did it look like I was in trouble?"

"No, but—"

"No. End of conversation. I was fine. You made things worse. What the hell was that about anyway, charging in there?"

He shrugs. "I don't know."

I shake my head and keep walking as he trudges along at my side, one hand pinching his bloodied nose.

Skye

We're in the condo. I didn't think before bringing Jesse here. I just walked back, forgetting everything I suspect him of. Jesse is hurt and bleeding. That's all I think about until I see my muddied boots in the hall. And then it's too late for second thoughts. If he did do this, it'd be more dangerous to let him know I suspect him, now that we're alone in the condo.

I bring him into the bathroom and make him sit on the closed toilet seat. Then I clean his face. The bleeding has stopped, and there's no sign that his nose is broken.

Once I finish, I say, "You're fine," and start rinsing blood from the washcloth.

He just sits there. I finish and hang the cloth to dry and walk out, and he follows.

No "thank you." No "I gotta run," either. He just trails along after me.

"You want a cold drink?" I ask.

He shrugs.

"I'm getting one," I say, and I'm heading toward the kitchen when I wave to the living room. "You can wait in there. I'll bring you a Coke."

He nods and goes into the living room. I grab two Cokes and return to see him staring at the brown smear on the sofa.

"That's not what it looks like," I say.

He makes a noise that might be a chuckle, but it's a very low one, and his expression doesn't change.

"It's chocolate," I say. "Don't ask me how—" I inhale as the memory comes back, and I mumble, "I must have sat on it."

He gives me a weird frown, like I said aliens left the stain.

"Yes, I know," I say, trying for levity. "Clearly I should not have gotten within twenty yards of a white couch with chocolate, and I don't remember—" I inhale. "Obviously I sat on some."

He walks over and looks down at the smear. Then he looks at me. Back at the smear.

"Okay, enough already," I say. "I screwed up. It happens. Sit and drink your Coke. Or don't."

"You're shaking," he says as I open my soda. "Is your aunt going to be that mad about the sofa?"

"She won't be happy. Just drop it, okay? I made a mistake."

"Did you change your jeans?"

"What?"

He sits on the clean end of the couch. "If you sat on chocolate, it'd be on your jeans. It's not."

"Thanks, Sherlock."

He keeps eyeing me, and then says, "The obvious alternate explanation is that your aunt sat on chocolate. But you're not even considering that. You're questioning whether you might have. You're getting defensive, and you're shaking. What's going on?"

"Maybe *you* know how that got there."

His face screws up in a confusion he couldn't fake. It takes him a moment before he says, "Are you suggesting I—?"

"Of course not. I'm being a smartass. So, since you seem in no hurry to leave, how about explaining what you were doing across the road from Mae's building? Don't say you just happened to walk by. I watched you standing there."

"I was waiting to talk to you."

"You want to talk? Great."

His gaze goes to the stain. "You think someone broke in and—"

"That'd be crazy."

He stares at the smear. Then he looks at me. "What else was wrong when you got back from my place?"

"Who says I got back? You were *waiting* for me, remember?"

He shifts his weight. "I knew you'd already be here. I was just . . . figuring out what to say. I sat in the car for a while. Then I walked over, but I still wasn't sure how to do this so . . ." He straightens. "Forget about that. When you did get here, there was more than a chocolate stain, right? Something that made you think someone broke in."

"No one broke—"

"You were spooked. Spooked enough to leave. I know you've been having bigger problems than kids being jerks. The fire . . ." He rubs his mouth. "I was there, waiting to talk to you. When I heard the alarm, I took off, but I had no idea it was an actual fire or I would have made sure you were okay."

"That was the second time."

"Second time . . . ?"

"The second time something happened to me after school, and I saw you there. Remember?"

"Wednesday, when I bumped into you. Did something happen then, too?"

"It doesn't matter. I'm just pointing out that I saw you there."

"Then someone broke into the apartment, and you saw me again. Which looks really—" He stops. "You thought I set the fire?" A vehement shake of his head. "No. I didn't break in here, either. I was with my dad all afternoon, and we got back after you left."

"Okay."

"I didn't break in or set that fire, Skye. But someone did, and you need to talk to your aunt. Figure out what's going on. Don't bother with Vaughn. He thinks—"

"Skye?" The front door closes. "You didn't answer my text. Ready to go?"

"Just a sec," I say, rising.

I head to the hall, and Mae starts toward me and then stops short, her gaze fixed over my shoulder.

"Jesse?"

He nods. "Hello, Ms. Benassi."

She looks from me to Jesse. "May I speak to you, please, Skye?"

"I was just leaving," Jesse says. "I came to talk to Skye and got in a bit of a . . ." He makes a face and points at his cheek. "She fixed me up."

"That's very thoughtful of her, *under the circumstances.*" Mae's voice is ice. "But I'm going to ask my niece not to entertain visitors while I'm out."

"I wasn't entertaining," I say. "There was *blood*."

"I apologize," Jesse says. "I should have made sure it was okay for me to be here unchaperoned."

"While you were bleeding?" I say, but he shuts me up with a look and says, "I'll see you at school."

"Have you apologized, Jesse?" Mae says.

I flinch. "Mae, just—"

"No, really." She walks to Jesse and looks up at him. "I heard about your behavior on Skye's first day back. You upset her. Enough that she told me about it, which, if you remember anything about my niece, means she was very upset. Do you think she needed that? From you, of all people?"

I try to intercede, but Jesse shakes his head, gaze dropping as he says, "No, she didn't. I was a jerk."

"Then clearly, if she is bringing you into her home and helping you, you have apologized, *and* you have not done or said anything to upset her since that first time. Seeing her at school caught you off guard, and since that moment, you have been nothing but kind to her. Correct?"

"Mae, please," I say.

"I just want an answer from him, Skye. I know it's yes. To all of the above. Or he wouldn't have the gall to be here."

Jesse is breathing hard enough for me to hear it. His mouth opens. Nothing comes out.

"He's apologized," I lie. "That's why he came here. To say he's sorry. He has. Now he's leaving."

Mae snorts and walks into the living room.

Jesse says, "I—"

"Yes, I know," I whisper. "I didn't hallucinate hearing those words from your lips. I'm still waiting for them."

He nods. "I'm really—"

"I don't want them now."

He looks ashamed of himself, the same look I got shortly after we became friends, when some guys razzed him, and he acted like we *weren't* friends, and I called him on it.

You're right, Skye. I'm sorry. Really, really sorry.

In that look, I see the Jesse I remember, and I don't want to. I've given him ample opportunity to say this, and now I'm in trouble because I helped him—before he even bothered to mumble *sorry*. Now he apologizes, and like the last time, it's only because he's been called on it.

"No, strike that," I say. "I don't want an apology *ever*. Chance missed."

His cheeks darken. "Okay, but please, just let me—"

"Skye? What's this on my sofa?" Mae calls.

Before I can reply, Jesse passes me, striding into the room. "That was me, Ms. Benassi. I bled on your sofa. I apologize. I'll get it cleaned . . ." He trails off. "I mean, no, that's not it. Someone broke—"

I grab his arm and call, "Jesse's leaving. Now."

I haul him to the door as he whispers, "I wasn't thinking. I wanted to help, and that was the wrong way to do it. You need to tell her the truth."

I open the door. "I'll see you Monday."

"And you'll tell Mae, right? She has to know what's happening."

I push him out the door. When I head back into the living room, Mae's examining the spot. "This doesn't look like blood."

"It's chocolate. I'm going to fix it, and I won't eat or drink in this room again."

She turns to me. "We need to talk about Jesse."

"I'm sorry I got snippy. He's right, though, that I didn't think it through, bringing him in when you were gone."

"Because it's Jesse. You know him. Or you know the boy he was." She walks over to me. "What you remember is a child. He's a young man now."

If she's implying that guys go from being sweet kids to monsters, well, we could have a long chat about that. But haven't I been telling *myself* that this isn't the same Jesse, and that I need to bear that in mind? I shouldn't have brought him up here after what I suspected.

So I nod. Just nod.

She continues, "I made the same mistake when I suggested you two could reconnect. I remember the boy he was. Given what he did to you at school, that's clearly not the young man he's become. Maybe it's because of his brother. Maybe it's just puberty, hormones, I don't know. But the boy I remember was sweet and gentle. This one . . ." She inhales. "Jesse was asked to leave Southfield for fighting. *Fist*fighting," she clarifies, as if I might think he got into a dustup on the debating team.

She continues, "When you said he was at Riverside Collegiate, I asked around. Jesse had been in a number of fights, culminating in an attack on a younger boy. He was asked to leave Southfield. Now he got into a fight while coming to apologize to you?" She shakes her head. "He has a problem, Skye."

"He was jumped. Attacked. I was there—"

"Don't make excuses for him."

My jaw clenches. "Lie for him, you mean? I would never—"

"I'm sorry. I didn't mean that. Yes, maybe this was an attack.

Possibly in retaliation for others. My point, Skye, is that I want you to be careful. Accept his apology and move on."

"Are we still going out for dinner?"

She hesitates, as if she wants to pursue this, but the look on my face must warn her not to.

"Where do you want to go?" she asks.

Skye

Monday. School. I catch a glimpse of Jesse in the halls, and I'm not sure if he sees me or not, but he's gone in a blink and I say, "Screw that." I'm not putting myself out again.

I have lunch with Tiffany to discuss the next newspaper. She hasn't mentioned the fire. On Friday, she made sure I was okay, and she seemed mostly confused, as if my story sounded too bizarre to be true. I'm not getting into it with her—she's one of the few people squarely on my side and I'd like to keep her there.

We're talking in the cafeteria when Alberto walks in carrying an envelope. "Fresh leads," he says as he tosses it onto the table and sits.

"Please tell me that's a joke," Tiffany says.

"Nope. Here I was, thinking one good thing came of that fire—the damned leads box burned. Then I'm walking past the main office when the secretary gives me this. Apparently—feeling *terrible* about us temporarily losing our office and our best source of news—they hung this up outside the door."

"I think I heard that on the announcements," I say.

"I would say that makes you the only student who *listens* to the announcements but"—Alberto shakes the manila envelope—"I'd be wrong."

"Let me take those. It's my job, right?" As I reach for the envelope, they both stare at me, and I realize it looks suspicious, me being so eager to take the leads.

"There were ones in the last batch that were . . ." I exhale. "About me. Suggesting the paper investigate me. Wanting me out of RivCol. I'd rather . . . I'd rather be the only person who sees those. I'm used to it."

"You shouldn't be," Tiffany says. "That's harassment, and it needs to go straight to Mr. Vaughn, to be dealt with appropriately."

She takes the envelope and dumps the contents. A half dozen slips of paper fall out. She picks up one and—

"What the hell?" she says.

I read it.

YOU REALLY THINK IT'S A COINCIDENCE SKYE GILCHRIST WAS IN THAT OFFICE WHEN IT GOT TORCHED? NEWSFLASH: SHE DID IT, AND THAT'S JUST STEP ONE IN HER PLAN. SOMEONE HAS TO DO SOMETHING BEFORE INNOCENT KIDS GET HURT.

Alberto reads another. "Whoa." He balls it up and pitches it aside. "Okay, just no. That is not harassment. Someone needs therapy."

Tiffany uncrumples it, and her eyes bug. I lean over to see the sort of comment I won't repeat, about things that should be done to girls like me.

She sees me reading and quickly wads it up.

"I've seen it before," I say. "My therapist said I need to understand that there are some very unhappy and very angry people out there, and not take it personally."

"Not take it—" Tiffany sputters off, unable to finish.

"Yeah, that's messed up," Alberto says. "I vote we accidentally lose that envelope . . . into a shredder."

"No." Tiffany's chair legs squeal against the linoleum as she stands. She scoops up the envelope and discarded notes. "This is going to Mr. Vaughn."

"Please, don't," I say. "It won't help. Just . . . just ignore it."

"Ignore it?" Alberto says. "Someone locked you in a room and lit it on fire, Skye."

"I understand that you're trying to turn the other cheek," Tiffany says. "But this is way beyond bullying. I'm taking it to Mr. Vaughn."

I wait for a call to the office. When it doesn't come by math class, I'm relieved. Then I'm angry, as I realize this means Mr. Vaughn got those notes . . . and is doing absolutely nothing with them.

I arrive in math before Jesse—I make sure of that. If I had to walk past him, I'd feel obligated to say something. I refuse to make the first move again.

So I get to class early, and I wait. I notice him walking in, and when I look up, there's a hitch in his step. Consternation flashes across his face. I wait for him to remember he really needs to be somewhere else right now. He wants to. I can tell. But he only meets my gaze and gives a little nod, and then slides into his seat.

He seems to pay attention during class. Once he takes out his phone, but he holds it below desk level, like he used to in middle school, not wanting to be rude to the teacher. In this class, he's had no such compunctions before. Now he does something with his phone concealed, and then puts it away and goes back to work.

Class ends and as he stands, he palms a note onto my desk, like a magician.

See that empty spot? Abracadabra, a note appears! Did I leave that? No, you must be mistaken. I'm already making a beeline out the door.

I slip into the bathroom before I open it. I'm thirteen again, when Jesse passed me a note for the first time, and I was so sure it was a goodbye. I knew it wasn't easy for him, once others saw us hanging out together.

Jesse and Skye, sitting in a tree, k-i-s-s-i-n-g.

Hey, Mandal, do you like hanging around girls? You do kinda seem the type, nudge-nudge, wink-wink.

When I open this note, I'm taken back to that first one, also read in a bathroom stall, so if it hurt, no one would see me cry.

It's the same note. The same two words.

After school?

Then he goes on to suggest we meet by the gym doors. Between the invitation and the location, something has been crossed out. Heavily crossed out. When I lift it to the light, I can make out numbers.

GPS coordinates.

I remember him on his phone. He was finding those coordinates. Writing them down. Did he smile a bit as he did? Maybe. But then he changed his mind. Crossed them out as hard as he could and wrote the location in text.

I run my thumb over those crossed-off numbers, and my eyes prickle, just a little. Then I pocket the note and leave.

Jesse

Jesse is waiting behind the school when his trainer texts. He ignores it. He knows what it'll say, some variation on the same thing his trainer has been texting all weekend, that they need to talk about Jesse's underperformance at the meet.

Underperformance? He won, didn't he?

That doesn't matter. What matters is that there was a scout in the stands, who declared Jesse a perfectly decent high school athlete. In other words, not destined for anything greater. Which is fine with Jesse. That's all he wants. It's all his parents expect. But his trainer has been pushing for more. And getting more doesn't mean adding ten pounds to his lifting regimen.

Cheat. Fake. Poseur.

It started innocently enough. A new trainer, promising to take Jesse to the next level. Supplements and vitamins to help in the off-season. Some guys need the extra boost to put on muscle. Jesse's one of them. No shame in that. Not until he got his head out of his ass and realized he was getting more than B-12.

Steroids.

When he figured it out, he freaked. Steroids = cheating, it's as simple as that. Not according to his trainer. Lots of athletes use steroids to bulk up in the off-season. Jesse wasn't taking enough to see side effects. He rarely had an acne breakout. He didn't get roid rage. See? No problem.

Or that's what his trainer said. Jesse *does* get acne, which he never had before. Then there's his hair-trigger temper, also new. Zits and fistfights might be normal for some teenage boys. But not Jesse. Not until the steroids.

"Question," a voice cuts into his thoughts, and he jumps. It's Skye, and as he sees her, he feels a flash of panic. He was supposed to be prepping his apology.

She continues, "Are you hiding or is that supposed to look cool?"

He blinks and straightens, and as he does, he pushes his hood back, and she says, "Yes, *that*. The hood-pulled-over-the-eyes thing. Is it hiding? Or trying to look cool? Because it doesn't do either. Just so you know."

Until yesterday, he'd forgotten this side of Skye. The abrasive, in-your-face side. And he'd definitely forgotten what it was like to be on the receiving end.

He's done something. Or failed to do something. And he's trying to figure out *which* thing it is, from a very long list. Judging by the look on her face, though, it isn't anything specific, but rather the culmination of it all. She's had enough of him, and she's here to say so.

He opens his mouth to start his carefully rehearsed apology, but she says, "Forget that question. I've got another. Tell me what happened at Southfield."

"What?"

"Everyone says you got kicked out for fighting. I wouldn't have bought it, but I saw you Saturday. You can fight."

So can you. That's what he wants to say. On Saturday, she threw down one of those guys before he got there, and while Skye has always been more athletic than him, she'd never taken martial arts. But she has now, and while he hopes it's just a newly developed interest, he knows better. He knows things have happened in the past three years that made her decide she needed to learn to defend herself.

The thought makes him sick.

Skye needed to learn self-defense? Nah, of course not. Everything would have been sunshine and roses after her brother was implicated in a school shooting.

"Well?" she says, and she crosses her arms.

He looks at her. No, he stares.

If someone had asked him three years ago to picture Skye at sixteen, this would have been exactly it. Blond ponytail still swinging from marching across the tarmac. Green eyes blazing over some outrage she must set right. Wide lips set in a firm line that makes him want to find exactly the right thing to say, the joke that will make those lips curve in a grin, light up her eyes, bring out her dimples.

The pretty girl he remembers has grown into exactly what he expected—and, maybe, feared, too. A young woman who makes him feel like he's never seen another girl in his life, and all he wants to do is find something to say, anything that will make her stay and talk to him. He sees Skye, and he feels thirteen again, sneaking looks at this amazing girl, and realizing she's actually looking back at him.

"Jesse? Are you listening to me?"

He nods. Just nods.

"Am I going to get an answer?"

He almost asks what the question was. Which would be a very bad idea.

He takes a moment to think first. "Why I left Southfield?"

"Right. Maybe you can answer it instead of acting like there's someplace you'd rather be?"

There's no place I'd rather be.

He clears his throat. "I was asked to leave. After a fight."

"You attacked a younger kid."

"It wasn't—" He inhales and eases back, putting space between them so he can find his balance. "Yes, he was a freshman, but I didn't *attack* him. It was a fight."

"You're saying he started it?"

"He—" Jesse runs a hand through his hair. "No, I went after him, which means I was in the wrong, and I'm just lucky it didn't go on my record. I accept responsibility."

"He provoked it."

"I don't want to make excuses, okay? It's like Saturday. Are you going to say you provoked that fight by being sarcastic? No. Stuff had been going on at Southfield. It escalated, and I blew up. A response disproportionate to the situation. I accepted the blame. Still do. If you're asking whether I deserved to be kicked out? I did. If you're asking if I've turned into a bully? I sure hope not. If you're asking whether you need to worry about your personal safety? No. Absolutely not. I didn't trap you in the newspaper office. I didn't set the fire. I didn't break into your aunt's place. What I *have* done is been an ass to you. And yeah, maybe that *is* bullying. No, not maybe. It *was*. I treated you badly in front of others, which gave them permission to do the same." The words come in a rush, and he has to gasp for breath. "I'm sorry, Skye. I could not *be* more sorry than I am."

Silence. He has his gaze fixed on her forehead, not daring to look her in the eye. When he does, he can't tell what she's thinking. She's just standing there, watching him, and when her mouth opens, he wants to run. He's sure whatever she's about to say he doesn't want to hear.

"I missed you," she says.

He inhales sharply. Those words. The way she says them, her voice quiet, wistful. It's like a power drive to the gut. Everything he's done wrong in the past week—everything he's done wrong in the last three years—comes back, and he has this horrible urge to do something awful. To roll his eyes. To shrug and say, "Whatever." To hurt her and make her walk away—get away as fast as she can. Make her write him off before he can disappoint her. Because he will disappoint her. There is nothing he's done in the past three years that would make her proud of him, make him the guy she remembers, the guy she misses.

But she's standing there, with those words hanging between them, and she's blushing, and while part of him wants to run, the rest just keeps on staring. The rest hears her say *I missed you* and wants to say *I missed you, too.*

Missed you so much, Skye.

She rubs her hands over her reddening cheeks. "Wow. Sorry. That was—I mean—" She waves her arms, a gesture he knows well, a flail, as if physically throwing off sentimentality, her face scrunching, like she's been caught making daisy chains and reciting poetry.

"Okay, so we're good?" she says.

He nods.

Wow, cool. Totally eloquent. Just stand there and bob your head like one of those stupid dolls. Hey, at least that might convince her you're an idiot unworthy of her time and attention.

"Good," she says. "We're done, then. I'll see you around."

She starts to walk away. He jumps forward and says, "Wait!"

She turns. He opens his mouth, and what he wants to say is *Do you still like milkshakes?*

Remember those crazy milkshakes you'd get at the Creamery? With gummy bears and M&M's and so many toppings you had to eat it with a spoon? I'd roll my eyes and act like it was so embarrassing when you ordered that. It was hilarious to watch you try to eat it, but mostly, I liked seeing how much you loved those crazy things. They still have them, you know. It's a bit of a hike, but we can grab a taxi. My treat.

"Hmm?" she says, and he realizes he's standing there, mouth ajar, nothing coming out.

He pulls back. "We should talk. About what's happening to you."

She makes a face. "It's nothing."

"You were trapped in a fire, Skye. On purpose."

"Maybe I wasn't. Maybe I . . ." A gesture, that flail again, out of her comfort zone. "Maybe I imagined it."

"Can you tell me what's happening? I'd like to know, especially since I seem to be a person of interest in the case."

She rolls her eyes. "There's no case."

"Then let's go somewhere and talk. We'll get . . ." *A milkshake. Remember those?* "How about a coffee? Make up for the one you missed Saturday. There's a Starbucks just around the corner."

She hesitates, and he's sure she's going to say no, and he's wildly searching for some other excuse, something they can talk about.

Maybe, you know, the elephant in the room? The shooting?

No, not that. She doesn't need that.

"You should talk to someone," he says. "Work it through. I'd like to hear it."

She finally nods and says, "Okay."

Skye

We don't go to Starbucks. It's packed with kids from school. So we're walking, and Jesse has his cell phone out, having mapped another coffee shop. We've walked at least a mile, and he keeps apologizing. Well, mumbling that sounds apologetic, though I don't catch actual words. He's holding his phone aloft like a compass . . . or an excuse for not communicating.

"Just up here," he says. "On the left."

"Hopefully, it's open," I say, and I tell him about my own coffee-shop quest Saturday, making far too convoluted a story of it. That's *my* way of coping with the awkward silence.

"There," he says, with the relief of a sailor spotting land in a storm. "It's open. Good."

We go inside. Only a few tables are occupied, and I spot the perfect pair of comfy chairs in a corner. He sees it at the same moment and says, "Can you grab those while I get in line? Just tell me what you want."

"I'll buy my own."

"My treat. Really. I told Mom I might be seeing you after school and she gave me—" He pulls a twenty from his pocket. Two more fall to the floor, and he scrambles to pick them up.

"Wow," I say. "We can buy out the pastry counter with that."

He gives a self-conscious laugh. "Yeah, really, huh? 'Cause I need sixty bucks to take you for a coffee." He shakes his head. "They do that a lot. Shoving money at . . ." He trails off with another shake of his head. "Whatever."

Shoving money at problems. As if that will cure what ails us. My dad's the worst for it, depositing weekly money into my account, which I refuse to touch.

Sorry for screwing off when you needed me. Have some cash to make it better.

Even Mom makes sure my wallet is always full.

Do you need anything, Skye? Anything at all?

I want to tell Jesse that I understand. Maybe even explain about my parents. But that's more of the awkward. Oversharing to fill the silence.

So I just say, "Can I get a caramel latte and a brownie?"

A wry smile. "Are you sure you don't want ten?" He waves the cash.

"I'll take the biggest latte they've got."

His smile softens then, a real one for me as he nods and says, "Biggest latte. Biggest brownie. On me. Well, on my mom. Go grab those chairs before someone else does."

Jesse hands me my latte and puts a plate with two brownies on the table, over on my side. I push it to the middle for us to share. He pushes it back again, and he's watching me, waiting for me to smile, to make some sardonic comment. But I can't. I'm struggling here, on this dangerous terrain.

Jesse is showing me glimpses of the guy I knew, reminders of what we had, and I'm too eager to see that. Too ready to jump at it. I'm terrified that if I do, I'll show up in math class tomorrow and he'll sit with his back to me, like this never happened.

I can't handle that. I just can't.

So I murmur a "Thanks," and I know it's not what he wants, but it's all I've got.

I sip my drink, and he does the same, and I'm watching his hand around the cup, the curve of his fingers. I don't recognize that hand. The soft fingers are gone. The chewed nails are gone. The Band-Aids are gone—I swear he always had one from some accident or other. It's just a guy's hand. Could be anybody's.

"My mom says your gran had a stroke," Jesse says. "How is she?"

"Okay."

"We don't hear . . ." He puts his cup down. "Stuff, you know. About you guys. Not much, anyway. I know your parents split. How's your dad?"

"Don't know. Don't care."

Alarm flashes across his face, and I know I've been too forthright. Too old-Skye.

"We don't really communicate," I say. "It's just me, Mom and Gran. Which is fine."

"And your mom . . . ?" he asks carefully. "Did she . . . get better?"

I pick at my brownie. "It's severe clinical depression. They can't seem to find the right meds or maybe she's not taking them or . . . I don't know."

I inhale sharply. "Mom's doing her best. I understand that. We deal. We cope. Or we did until child services decided I wasn't old enough to look after myself." I roll my eyes. "Like you pass some magical age and then, poof, we can trust you not to die of starvation, playing video games 24/7. I did just fine when Gran had her first stroke, but no, that doesn't count."

I'm looking for agreement here. For a nod.

Instead, he's staring at me, and then he says, "I didn't know."

"Know what?"

"About your mom and your gran and your dad. Child services stepping in. I had no idea—"

"They didn't step in, Jesse. They interfered. That's why I'm here, with Mae, who thinks what I really need is to come back to Riverside, chin up. Tough through it. Which is working out *so* well."

He just looks at me. And his expression . . .

I hate his expression. It's horror, and it's pity, and it's everything I don't want to see on anyone, but especially not Jesse.

"Are we actually going to talk about the fire?" I say. "That's what you said."

He straightens. "Tell me what's been going on."

"I already did. The fire and the stuff at Mae's condo. Which is really just the fire. The condo stuff is silly."

"Someone breaking into your home isn't *silly*, Skye."

"Breaking in to put mud on my boots and leave them in the hall? Spook me with Luka's shirt in the closet? Take half my Hershey bar and smush it into the sofa? Who'd do that? It's a waste of perfectly good chocolate."

"Mud on your boots? Luka's shirt in your closet?"

I shake my head. "Mae must have been storing Luka's shirts in the closet, and one fell off the hanger and startled me. I found my boots in the hall, caked in mud, which means I obviously wore them and forgot, because no one is going to break in and muddy my boots. It's crazy."

"It is."

I take a bite of the brownie. Swallow without remembering to chew, and then have to gag it down.

Achievement unlocked. Even Jesse agrees. You are officially losing your mind, Skye Gilchrist.

"I should speak to someone," I say, picking at the brownie. "There's a therapist I can call. She's good. I'm obviously stressed and imagining things, and now I'm lumping that with the fire, which was a stupid prank."

"If you tell me you didn't leave those boots out or eat that candy bar, I believe you."

"You just agreed it was crazy."

He pulls back. "No, I meant it *seems* crazy. It makes no sense. But it has to, right? There's a method to the madness. We just aren't seeing it."

He eases into his chair, settling into a look I know well. Jesse's problem-solving mode.

"Are you sure Mae's just storing the shirt?" he says. "It seems weird that she'd keep Luka's stuff in your closet. Is there more there?"

"I didn't look. Maybe she just kept that shirt. He wore it a lot—the Black Death tour one."

His lips twitch in a smile. "I remember that. Even Jamil said it was cool. I was surprised he got the joke." Jesse's smile flickers, and then he tucks it away and says, "That was probably the most distinctive thing Luka wore. Are you sure it was even his?"

"What do you mean?"

He leans forward, elbows on his knees, gaze distant as his brain works. "I bet it'd be easy to find one online. Whoever broke in could have bought and planted it. Left it half on the hanger, so it would eventually fall and you'd notice it."

He leans back. "The boots. The shirt. The chocolate. All signs that someone else was there. But subtle. Signs no one else would recognize."

He sits up quickly. "*Exactly.* Weird stuff you can't prove. Mae might think you brought that shirt and forgot, like you forgot the boots and chocolate. Or that you're coming up with wild tales to explain tracking mud through the apartment and getting chocolate on the couch. Like the Monty stories. Remember?"

Monty was the name I gave to a poltergeist who was very clearly responsible for every broken toy and missing juice box in our house. Hey, I was four. I had an imagination, and I wasn't afraid to use it.

I pull my knees up. "Maybe I'm doing that again."

"But you knew you were making it up with Monty, right?"

"Yes, but—"

"Stop making excuses, Skye. That's not like you."

He says it with this gesture, a flick of his fingers, dismissive.

That's not like you.

He doesn't mean it to hurt. It does. Because second-guessing myself *is* like me. It didn't used to be, but it is now.

I'll catch glimpses of my old self, when I'm backtalking Mae, or when I was standing up to those thugs Saturday. But they feel like characters in a story I've crafted. Roles I can play, the girl I want to be. But she's the girl I was, too, which makes it worse.

Jesse says, *That's not like you,* and I open my mouth to say "It is now." Then I pause. Say those words, and it's like admitting to my home-life problems. A cry for sympathy. For pity.

I pull my legs up. "I just don't want to jump to crazy conclusions, okay?"

"And subconsciously inventing a poltergeist would be less crazy than thinking someone broke into your aunt's condo? Someone *is* harassing you. Spooking you. Making sure you can't prove the harassment. Is there anything that's happened you *can* prove?"

"The fire."

He reaches for his coffee. "Anything else?"

"What about the fire?" I ask him.

"Hmm?"

"I said I can prove the fire, and you grabbed your coffee."

"I'm thirsty."

I shimmy to the edge of my seat. "You're thinking I need more evidence than just the fire. But I can prove the fire existed. So what you're saying is . . ." I remember the lead in the box, the one that accused me. "Mr. Vaughn thinks I set it?"

"I never said—"

"Then tell me I'm wrong. Tell me you don't have reason to believe he thinks I set the fire myself. Just like he thinks I sent that email."

"What email?"

When I hesitate, he says, "I'm not the only one holding back here. The break-in. The fire. What else?"

I tell him about the petition and the email to Mr. Vaughn. I explain how the VP allegedly knew it came from me, and why it didn't.

"That's easy enough to prove," Jesse says. "There'll be a log showing you've never signed into your account before."

"Unless whoever used it had done so before. That's a start, though, especially if the person signed in from another source—laptop, phone, tablet. I also suggested Mr. Vaughan try to see if anyone noticed me at that terminal. He's not interested in checking."

"Because he isn't punishing you, so he doesn't need to justify his suspicions. Same as the fire. It's like me with the fight—" He stops short and makes a face. "You know what I mean."

"If it doesn't result in disciplinary action, there's nothing to argue. No chance to prove yourself."

"Whoever's doing this knows that. It's all being set up carefully to look like you might be doing this stuff to yourself. Doing it to make people feel bad for you."

"Or to make me seem crazy."

He hesitates and nibbles his lip, as if pursuing a thought.

"Did you hear anything about a petition?" I ask.

He shakes his head. "If Lana had one, she'd have asked me to sign. Last week, she . . ." He makes a face. "Came around. Saying stuff."

"What stuff?"

"That they shouldn't have let you back in. That it's not fair to me. That if I want to talk about it, she's there. Anyway, if there was a petition, she'd have brought it to me. She's been reaching out since I started at RivCol. Weirdly random stuff. She feels sorry for me, I guess."

"Uh, no, I'm pretty sure that's not the reason."

His look is such utter incomprehension that I almost snort a laugh. But I keep my mouth shut. Yes, Lana Brighton has been a bitch to me, but I won't be a bitch back by telling Jesse she's obviously interested in him.

"Well, there *is* a petition," I say. "I heard girls talking about it in the bathroom, and then . . ."

I trail off.

"And then what?"

I won't tell him about the voices. I just won't.

"Lana has been coming at me, too," I say. "In a much less friendly way."

"Which makes her a suspect."

I wrinkle my nose. "Suspect? That sounds like—"

"Like someone is harassing you to the point of criminal activity? What else would you call it, Skye?"

My cell phone buzzes with a text. It's Mae.

"Wow," I say. "First time in a week she's actually home before seven. Nice timing, Mae." I shake my head. "She's making dinner. Which is a little scary, considering what's in her fridge. I need to go. Thanks for hearing me out on this. It was nice to have someone to talk to."

"Here, take the brownies."

He wraps them before I can protest. I put them in my pocket and start to leave. He grabs his backpack and follows me from the shop.

"You know I didn't do this, right?" he says.

"I wouldn't have been discussing it with you otherwise."

"Then you trust me?"

It's an odd question, and I reply with a sound he can take for agreement.

"Enough to give me your school log-in details?" he asks.

I look over at him.

"I want to know what's going on with that," he says.

"You're going to figure out how to hack—"

"I already know," he says. "Not for grades. Just . . . attendance and stuff. I don't skip often, but when I do, I don't want my parents getting a call. Like you said, we're old enough to make our own choices, and sometimes I choose not to go to class. As I remember someone else doing a few times in middle school."

He smiles, and I know he's making light—just normal teen stuff, no big deal—but I have a feeling he's doing more than skipping the occasional class.

"Give me your number," I say, "and I'll text you my account info."

Skye

Apparently, I've unleashed Jesse's inner private eye.

The first text comes before I'm even home.

Jesse: did V say whr msg snt frm?

It takes a few moments to decipher that. I answer no, Mr. Vaughn didn't say where the email had been sent from. That's just the first text in a conversation that lasts into the night. Jesse peppers me with so many questions that I wonder if he's trying to poke holes in my story. Maybe he got home and wondered if I *could* be losing my mind.

Then, just past ten, I get: cn i hv yr e-addy? I'm starting to understand what Mae must feel like, untangling my texts.

I send him my email address. A few minutes later I get a spreadsheet. An honest-to-goodness spreadsheet detailing everything I've told him, arranged into helpful columns. Well, helpful to him, I'm sure. I don't process data this way, and I stare at it, thinking that I'm way too tired to figure this out.

And I'm thinking something else, too.

Why?

Why is he going through all this work to help me? Is he bored? Or does he think I still suspect him, and he's bending over backward to clear his name?

I don't know, but I'm not complaining. I need an ally, and he's the only one applying for the position.

A text follows ten seconds after I open the spreadsheet.

Jesse: is tht e/t?

Me: can I buy a vowel?

Jesse: i gave u 2 :)

Jesse: I asked if that's everything. did I miss anything?

I scan the spreadsheet and send back a thumbs-up emoji.

Jesse: does that mean I have e/t that happened 2 u?

Jesse: or just e/t u told me?

Me: it's good.

Jesse: not an answer to the actual question asked.

Me: can we talk tomorrow?

Jesse: in other words, there's more.

Me: I already feel I'm making too big a deal out of this. mountains from molehills, you know?

Jesse: look at the sheet. that's not a molehill.

Me: can we talk tomorrow?

Jesse: sure. i don't mean to nag.

Me: you're not.

Jesse: tomorrow then. maybe i'll send you GPS coords ;) still got that app?

Me: I'll get it :)

A thumbs-up, and my phone goes silent.

I haven't seen or heard from Jesse this morning. I'm trying not to read too much into that, but it still feels like the early days of our friendship, when we'd spend an hour messaging after school, and then I'd be on pins and needles the next day, waiting for that first moment of eye contact, that first smile, that first word.

If he *is* regretting his offer to help? I won't lie and say that's fine. But I can't force friendship, old or new.

It's lunchtime. I'm at my locker. I open it to see a folded sheet and smile. My mind is on Jesse so that's who I immediately think it's from. Then I see it's a piece of all-purpose printer paper, just like the last note that got shoved into my locker.

This one reads: *There's more to the story. You know there is. Your brother isn't a killer.*

I'm staring at it when a voice says, "Hey," and I shove the note into my pocket. It's Jesse. He has his hood up, and his gaze shifts off to the side before it can meet mine. His hands are stuffed in his pockets, and he pauses a couple of feet away, as if he just happened to be passing and slowed for a drive-by greeting.

I smile. I can't help it. I'm just relieved to see him. When I smile, he shoves his hands deeper into his pockets, shoulders hunching forward, rocking on the balls of his feet.

"Hey," he says. Then the faintest smile. "Again."

"Hey back. What're you up to?"

"Lunch. How about you?"

"Coincidentally, the exact same thing. Must be that time of day."

His lips twitch. "Yeah. Apparently." He knocks back his hood. "So . . . lunch."

"Yep."

"You eating?"

"That's the usual procedure."

"So I've heard. You bring something?"

"Jesse." Chris walks up. "You joining us for lunch?"

"We're going to grab food off-campus," I say. "I think Chris is inviting you. Which I would have, but that's awkward when it's his car."

"Nah," Jesse says, then adds a belated, "Thanks. I've got plans. Just stopped by to see if after school's good with you. For that thing."

"It is. Text me?"

He nods to me, with another nod for Chris as he leaves. I'm reaching into my locker to shove my binder in when the note slips from my pocket. It falls open, and Chris frowns as he picks it up.

"Yeah," I say as he hands it back. "I keep trying to convince myself they're secretly love notes, but somehow, I just don't think so."

"This isn't the first?" he says as we start walking.

I motion that I'll answer once we're out of the school, and I wait until we're in the car. I don't rush to reply even then, but he prompts with, "So, notes?"

"I've had a few," I say. "Variations on a theme. The shooting is a lie. I'm a liar. I had something to do with the shooting. Blah-blah."

His brows shoot up. "You?"

"Apparently."

"Are you sure that's what they mean? That one didn't look like the sender was blaming you personally."

"I've had a couple that were pretty unequivocal on that point."

It takes a moment before he starts the car. "That's weird. How are they saying you're invol—?" He shakes his head. "No, never mind. That's too ridiculous to even waste breath on. Any idea who it is?"

"No, I . . ." I slow as the note triggers something. "Actually, I might. On Saturday, I had a run-in with three seniors who tried to tell me Jamil Mandal was involved in the shooting."

"What?"

I ratchet back the passenger seat. "They said Luka, Isaac and Harley acted to stop Jamil from doing something. Honestly, I was afraid to ask what they meant. I don't know if it was just random crap or if there was some racism happening. Does Jesse get hassled much for that?"

"Not as far as I know, but I'm sure there's some, depending on what's in the news, you know?"

"I do. I think those guys were just spoiling for a fight and lashing out at whatever was convenient. But they're definitely the type who like causing trouble, so they may have decided I make a good target, too, and started dropping off those notes."

"Could be. Have you considered, though, that maybe there's truth there? Not about Jamil, of course. Or about you being involved. But about there being more to the story. I have no doubt Isaac and Harley did it. But Luka was different. He wasn't the type—"

"No."

"So you don't ever wonder—?"

"I mean no, let's not go there. Please."

Silence. He drives a block, and then says in a low voice, "I'm sorry."

"Don't be. I know there are questions, but I don't want to ask them. I'm afraid the answers won't be what I want, and I'm afraid I don't have the right to ask."

"You absolutely have the right—" He stops short. "And that's not what you're saying. You're telling me to drop it, as nicely as possible. So, how do you feel about diners?"

I glance over at him.

"I'm changing the subject very awkwardly," he says. "We went to McDonald's last week. We can go there again, or there's a diner across the road. Your choice."

"Is it one of those places with the greasy burgers that I'll slop all over my shirt?"

"'Fraid so."

"Perfect."

We're still at lunch when I get a text from Jesse canceling our after-school meet. He forgot he had track practice. I pop back a quick no problem and we can reschedule. He doesn't respond, but I won't read anything into that.

Jesse isn't in math class. I won't read anything into that, either. This morning, I started fretting, and he showed up at my locker, proof I'd overreacted.

I'll text him tonight, after dinner, and only to pass on the math homework. Not pushing to reschedule. Not checking that he hasn't changed his mind. Nope, that'd be paranoid and silly. I won't even ask why he missed class. I'll just text to helpfully pass along the homework. And then I'll stare at my phone until he replies.

For the sake of retaining a shred of dignity, I'll pretend I don't leave class mentally composing that text, making sure nothing could be misread into it.

When my phone typewriter-dings with an incoming text, I yank it out, hoping it's Jesse responding to my—

It's from a blocked number. I take a deep breath as I tap the thread. The videos came from a fake number, not a blocked one, so I'm hoping this is just spam or—

> Hey, Skye. Heard you're on the newspaper crew. Also heard some morons have been saying you set that fire. I think I can help you find the real culprit. I remember Jesse saying once that you guys would communicate in GPS coordinates, so let's do that ;) Meet me at these ones at 4 PM today.

I try sending back a response. Of course it doesn't go through. I consider. I check my watch. Then I take off.

Jesse

Jesse is running laps again. He told his parents he was seeing Skye after school, and his dad is working from home today, meaning Jesse can't show up at four o'clock. Also, he did tell Skye he had training. So he hasn't lied.

No, he totally lied. And now he's running as fast as he can, pain shooting down his calves as he pushes harder, waiting for that moment when he's so exhausted he can't think anymore.

That moment isn't coming nearly fast enough.

"Hey! Jesse!"

He looks over to see Chris Landry by the stands.

Jesse turns his attention forward and hunkers down, pushing to his limit. When he comes around the curve, his gaze is focused straight ahead.

Sorry, Chris, don't see you there. Otherwise, I'd stop.

Chris moves onto the track . . . where Jesse cannot possibly miss him. Then he puts his fingers in his mouth and whistles.

When Jesse looks, though, Chris only motions that he'll be waiting in the stands until Jesse is done.

Jesse curses under his breath.

He knows what Chris is here to talk about, and Jesse does not want to have this conversation. He likes Chris. One of Jesse's earliest memories of Skye is in fourth grade. A few older kids picked Chris as their target of the year. Jesse noticed but—and this makes him a little sick to his stomach—he didn't pay much attention. In fact, if pressed, he might admit he was just glad the kids hadn't targeted him. He never had problems with that, but he was always braced for it, feeling as if it was only a matter of time before others picked up on whatever made Jamil hate him so much.

They were all in the cafeteria when one of the guys knocked Chris's tray, sending his lunch to the floor. Skye picked up Chris's milk carton . . . then reached over and took the burger from the bully's tray, gave it to Chris and said, "Accidents happen." Everyone laughed, and the bullies might have glared at her, but they didn't say a word.

Jesse was ashamed. He knew what Chris must feel like, yet it had never occurred to him to step in. After that, while he never could stand up to the bullies the way Skye would have, he did what he could, subtly, sitting with Chris on trips or making sure he wasn't the last one picked for groups and teams.

Jesse didn't see Chris much after they went to different high schools. It wasn't until Jesse came to RivCol that he realized how much had changed for Chris. He was on the student council. Yearbook committee. Volleyball team. While he didn't hang out with the most popular clique, he had his crowd, kids like him, heavily involved in school activities. Well-liked kids, popular in the truest sense of the word. And he had girls. Chris Landry had no problem with girls.

Jesse was happy for him. A little envious? Sure. But that was Jesse's problem, not Chris's. It was good to see Chris doing well. He deserved it.

And then . . .

Well, then came that moment, standing at Skye's locker when Chris came by to pick her up for lunch.

Which had nothing to do with Jesse canceling out on her.

Very little to do with him canceling out.

Jesse pulls over on the next lap. He walks to the bench, takes his water bottle and drinks deeply.

"I think I'm going to stay upwind," Chris says as he strolls over. "That is a serious workout. I saw you from class—I guess you got a spare last period, huh?"

Jesse shrugs.

Chris peers around and checks his watch. "When's your trainer coming by?"

"Hmm?"

"Skye said you had a session with your trainer after school, but maybe she misinterpreted, and you just meant you had to practice."

He says it casually enough that Jesse must be imagining the soft jab in his tone. A guilty conscience hearing what's not actually there.

"Skye told you?" Jesse says.

"I was there when you texted. I could tell she wasn't exactly thrilled with the message. I asked if everything was okay, and she said you had to cancel your plans."

Here it comes. The reason Chris is here. To tell Jesse he's stepping on Chris's turf. To politely let him know what's what.

Jesse chugs more water.

"It's good to see you guys hanging out," Chris says. "I know there was some tension when Skye first came back. I'm glad you've moved past it."

But . . .

Chris sits on the bench. "I remember when you guys got together in middle school. Well, not 'got together,' but you know what I mean."

Jesse grunts. Strips his shirt and towels off the rivulets of sweat.

"I had a crush on Skye," Chris says. "I think a lot of us did. She was that kind of girl. Not the most popular. Not the prettiest. But the most . . . interesting, you know? Like we couldn't take our eyes off her."

Jesse keeps toweling dry, says nothing.

"But when you and her started hanging out, I wasn't jealous. I was happy. In that weird way, like when you watch a movie and you want two characters to get together. Seems silly now, but it was middle school. I wanted you guys to get together."

Jesse reapplies his deodorant and pulls on a fresh shirt.

"You were good for Skye," Chris continues.

Jesse notes the past tense in that sentence.

"You were a good guy. She deserved someone like you."

Also past tense. All of it.

"So I'm sure I'm wrong about this, but I need to say it. Just in case."

Jesse tenses. Here it comes.

"When you bailed on her today, I really hope the timing was coincidental."

Jesse looks at him. "What?"

"You saw me and Skye at her locker, and we were going for lunch, and then you canceled your plans with her. It could look like you got pissed, seeing her hanging with me. Which I'm sure is not the case. But you should know how it could look. To her."

"It wasn't like that."

Nope, not at all.

"Good," Chris says. "But in case there's any question, it really was just lunch, and I'm not trying to make it more. Skye doesn't need more. She made that clear from the start."

Jesse raises his brows.

Chris chuckles. "It's Skye. She's not going to beat around the bush. She heard I have a rep with girls. She wanted to be totally clear that lunch is lunch, and that's all. It is. She's having a tough time, and I wouldn't take advantage of that. I want to help. Like she helped me."

Chris makes a face. "Which makes it sound like charity work. I enjoy hanging out with her—as a friend. Anything else would be wrong, under the circumstances. She doesn't need that. Well, not from me. You and Skye are different. You have history."

Chris lifts his hands. "Which is not me pushing you guys together. I'm just saying she could use old friends. Me, you, whomever. While I'm sure you didn't bail on her because of me, I figured I should take a page from Skye's book and be blunt about it, so there are no misunderstandings."

Jesse can see why Chris is so good on the student council. He knows exactly why Jesse canceled, and he's giving him an easy out. Which only makes Jesse feel like an even bigger jerk.

"I was going to reschedule," Jesse says. Which is the truth.

"I figured you would. But if you're done practicing, you might still be able to catch up with her."

Skye

I'm walking when I get a text.

> **Jesse:** u still around?
> **Me:** following a lead 4 paper

We fire texts back and forth as he tries to figure out where I am. He apparently hoped to un-cancel our meet-up if I was still near school. I tell him I'm pursuing a lead about the fire, a mysterious source who texted wanting to talk off school property. Two seconds later my phone rings.

"Tell me that's a joke," Jesse says. "Tell me you are not actually heading to meet someone who anonymously texted. Because you know that would be a trap, right?"

"I know it could be. I also know the text sounds legit. Yes, it's from a blocked number, but that makes sense if it's anonymous. The others came from fake numbers."

"What others?"

I hurry on. "I've mapped out the meeting place. It's a coffee shop, which would make a lousy setting for a trap. Am I supposed to show up and find no one waiting? Waste an hour sitting in a comfy chair, enjoying a caramel latte and free Wi-Fi? Oh, snap, that'll teach me."

He's quiet for a moment, and I know he's struggling to come up with a better motive. Finally, he says, "This person could be planning to publicly humiliate you. Call you out. Accuse you of setting the fire."

"In a coffee shop nearly three miles from RivCol?"

"I'll come with you."

"If it really is a lead, and I don't show up alone—"

"I'll stay outside. If you need me, I'll be a text away. If you're stood up, I'll come in, get a drink and you'll tell me what you meant by 'other texts.'"

I'd already walked a mile when Jesse called. I'm afraid if I wait for him to catch up, I'll be late for the four o'clock meet time. Silly thought. He runs. When I see him coming, another text arrives, this one from my mystery source.

> Hey, Skye. I'm early. Place is packed. New coords coming!

Jesse jogs up in time to see me reading the text. I pass my phone to him. He takes out his and plugs in the new coordinates and . . .

"No," he says as the map appears. "Oh, hell, no."

Skye

We have reached the location described by those final coordinates. Reached them over a tirade of protests from Jesse, and perhaps the closest thing we've ever had to an argument. Now we stand on the sidewalk, looking at a massive brown brick building, with every window boarded up. Even the name has been taken down, but it's a pointless effort. For almost a hundred years those letters hung on the brick, and once they were removed, the impressions remain in dark brick, unbleached by a century of sunlight.

North Hampton High.

"I thought they were going to tear it down," I say.

"Every year, the city council promises it, and every year, there are excuses. They closed it, and they seem to think that's enough."

It's not enough. It's like taking those letters off the front. We still see the ghosts.

These are the secondary coordinates my "source" provided, proving I'm not here for a tip on the fire. The coffee shop was a decoy to get me close enough that I wouldn't be able to resist. Get me close. Get me curious. Lower my defenses and yes, perhaps then I would stand on this spot, see the setting of my nightmares and consider going in.

No, not *consider*. I am going in.

And Jesse is furious.

He says I'm punishing myself. A dare has been offered that I cannot refuse. He's right. It's like those video clips. Even when I knew what they were, I had to watch. To refuse seemed to deny my brother's crime, deny the victims their due.

I haven't told Jesse about the video clips. That really wouldn't help.

He's furious. Yet he's here, beside me, as he seethes. Our argument ended with me asking him to watch my back, and admitting that if he refuses, I will not do this. But I want to. I need to see where this is leading.

It's more than guilt and self-punishment. It's even more than standing up to a bully. I have been lured here, and either the destination is the message—in which case, it's been delivered—or my tormenter is inside, waiting for me. This may be my only chance to confront that person, which is why Jesse has stayed.

He isn't happy about it, but he knows I'm making the choice I need to make, and he won't stop me, even if all that would take is to walk away and say "I won't help."

Jesse is not the boy I remember. Too much has happened for that. But there is good in the changes, too. He stands firmer, more resolute. My old Jesse might have let me do this, but only because he'd be afraid to refuse, unsure of his own opinions. This Jesse tells me I'm making a mistake, and then stands by my side while I make it.

Going in might be pointless. This front entrance could be

both the destination and the message. *Remember what happened here. Remember those who died. Remember what your brother did.*

Yet the exact coordinates lie within. And the front door is open.

Jesse leaves me here. He can watch my back better if he isn't right beside me. He's found another way into the school, and he'll use that.

I step up to the front door. The street is empty, and while I know people live in the surrounding houses, the neighborhood feels as abandoned as the school.

I've already checked the front door, and I know it's open, the lock forced. I could read that as an obvious trap, but it's an empty building—I suspect kids have been sneaking in here for years.

I pull open the heavy door and—

I look down the cavernous, dimly lit hall. "God, this place is old."

Luka smiles. "You say that like it's a bad thing."

"It is. It stinks."

"It's called character, Skye."

"No, it's called mold."

He shakes his head. "Go find a seat. Auditorium's right down the hall. I need to get to costuming." Before I go, he says, "If you're lucky this place will be shut down before you go here."

Tears prickle my eyes. *You were right, Luka. But I'm not lucky. Not one little bit.*

The smell brings every memory rushing back, from that first time I came to watch Luka in a play to the last time, on a school trip, seeing him down the hall as he hurries to class, and he waves at me, and I pretend not to notice, like I'm way too cool for that, and he jogs over to give me a hug, properly humiliating me for ignoring him, and Jesse laughs and—

I can't do this. Barely two steps past the doorway, and I'm ready to flee. Then I look up and see . . .

I see what seems like trash blocking the hall. There's only a bit of light coming in through boarded-up windows, and so all I can tell is that stuff has been piled in the corridor. As I walk closer, I see a stuffed animal. A worn bear. I slow. If someone is squatting here with a child, I shouldn't go farther. Shouldn't intrude.

Then I notice the flowers. Daisies. Real ones, with a vase and water. There are other flowers, too, some starting to wilt, but none dead. More flowers. More stuffed animals. A baseball helmet beside a picture frame. A football jersey off to the far side, hung up as if on display. A North Hampton High jersey, with the number 63, and a name I can't quite read until I move closer and—

Mandal.

I stagger back as if slapped. I stare at the jersey, still streaked with dirt, as if Jamil had just come off the field and thrown it aside and . . .

This is a memorial. Like the ones people put at the roadside where a child has died, but this one . . . This one is massive. It's been divided into quarters. Jamil's jersey marks his place, and it's surrounded by things left for him, objects that reminded people of him. There are other jerseys, folded neatly, from other players, as if his teammates left theirs in memory. There are photos in cheap frames. Jamil and his teammates, Jamil and his friends, Jamil and a girl, and as I bend in front of that last photo, I remember her.

"She's nice," I say to Jesse as Jamil leaves with her.

Jesse chuckles. "You seem shocked."

"Uh, yes . . ."

"Yeah, me too. Weird thing is, he really seems to like her."

"Pretty sure you should like the girls you date."

"You know what I mean. He usually picks the ones who hang all over him, make him feel good, put up with his crap. Peyton doesn't. Last week, I heard her call him out on something, tell him he'd been a jerk, and he actually agreed. Even apologized."

There's a note below the photo. A note from Peyton. Five words.

I miss you so much.

I stand quickly and turn my attention to the other memorials.

There are photos of Nella Landry with her little brother and sister. With friends. With family. There are awards, too, for her community service, her advocacy work. Copies of letters from politicians and activists, names I recognize, praising her accomplishments and offering condolences on the "violent end" to such a "bright future."

Leanna Tsosie grins at me from photos shot on a trip to Paris, with classmates and friends. An even bigger grin as she holds up a scholarship offer, and yet those smiles are nothing compared to those of her parents, standing beside her. Two old science fair projects have been left, first-place ribbons still attached. And books. Her favorite ones, dog-eared and piled. I've read those books. All of them, and I look at Leanna's memorial, and I wish I'd known her as I realize how much we had in common. Then I think of her under that desk, texting her mother.

I'm fine, Mom. Don't worry.

For Brandon, there is art—sketches and portraits of his family. One is framed—including a drawing of his sleeping infant son. There are photos, too, of him with friends and family, and with his girlfriend and baby. People have added newer ones of his son, from baby to toddler to preschooler. In the last photo, his son celebrates his fourth birthday, blowing out candles, his mother beside him, her hand stroking his hair, a sad smile on her face, a distant look in her eyes.

I kneel by the flowers and touch a petal. Someone brings these. Every week someone must bring these. Three years have passed and still they come and lay fresh flowers. And notes, so many notes, some rolled or sealed, as if meant for the dead. Words left unsaid. No matter how many people have been through here—looking for a place to sleep or smoke up or make out—no one has opened those notes. They have respected the dead and the living, and left them alone.

I want to leave my own note. Tear out a sheet of paper and write four times, "I am so sorry." Roll them up. Lay one in each quarter. But that feels self-indulgent and wrongheaded. These were left by the grieving, and my pain has no place here.

I straighten and look around. My phone vibrates.

Jesse: ok?

I force my finger to the emojis and poise it over the thumbs-up. But I can't do it. Just can't. I reply with OK. Then I take a deep breath and continue down the hall.

As the hall gets darker, I use my flashlight app. When I spot something written on the wall, I nod. There will be more memorials. I need to be prepared for that.

I continue down the hall, and I want to ignore that writing, but that feels like ignoring this summons.

This is what the shooters did, damn it, and you will stop and look. You will respect the dead.

So I glance at the wall and see the words: *Rot in hell, you sick son of a bitch.*

Below that, written in marker, there is an arrow. An arrow pointing to the floor with *RIH. Luka Gilchrist.*

I look down . . .

Blood. There is blood on the floor.

I stumble back so fast I fall, and then I'm on the floor, staring at a wash of dark red, as if someone made a haphazard attempt to clean up . . .

To clean up . . .

I squeeze my eyes shut. *Fake. This must be fake.*

Then I lift my gaze . . . and see the boys' bathroom.

Skye

No. No, no, no.

This is not the place. It cannot be the place. It . . . It . . .

I know now why I'm here. To face this. To picture it. Luka walks out of that bathroom—

"Geez, Luka, I thought you were going to take up residence in there."

He laughs. "Sorry. Just trying to get the rest of this makeup off. I swear, if I have to do another hundred-year-old musical . . ." He makes gagging noises. "You need to write me a part, Skye. One that I can . . ." A theatrical wave. "Truly inhabit."

"Annoying geeky older brother?"

"No, annoying geeky older brother superhero." He slings his arm over my shoulders as we head for the exit. "Like Spider-Man, except without the costume. Just a regular-guy superhero."

"Uh-huh, you need a tragic backstory for that."

"I have one. Forced to live with an annoying geeky little sister." He grins. "You asked for that."

I sigh.

He squeezes my shoulder. "Write me a story, Skye. Make me a hero."

I see us walking out, his arm still draped over my shoulder as the lights extinguish behind us.

Make me a hero, Skye.

I can't, Luka. I want to. I want to so badly and I . . . I can't.

My gaze falls to the red wash on the floor, and I see him again. I see him lying in a pool of blood. His eyelids flutter open, and he sees me, and he winks, like it's a scene in one of his plays.

That's all, Skye.

Just a play.

It's not real.

He reaches up, and I drop to my knees.

And then he's gone.

Luka is gone.

My brother is gone, and he is never coming back, and I failed him. Somehow I failed him.

My fingers touch the faint streaks of blood, and I see the truth. I see him lying in a pool of blood, and there's a gun by his side.

I touch the blood, and I hear him coming out of the bathroom again, like a tape on replay.

". . . just trying to get the rest of this makeup off . . ."

A sob doubles me over. I want to grab that memory, grab it as hard as I can and forget this, forget the blood on the floor and the truth—the truth that my brother was as far from a hero as anyone can get, and this is *his* memorial: these words on the wall.

Rot in hell.

Sobs rip through me, and I cry harder than I have ever cried for my brother. Harder than I have ever been able to cry for him.

When I hear running footsteps, I look up sharply, and I almost expect to see Luka race around the corner.

What's wrong, Skye?

It's okay, Skye. Mom's getting better. I know she is. Dad'll be home soon, and she's always better when he's here. Everything will be fine. We just need to hold on a bit longer.

It isn't Luka, of course. These are actual footsteps. From a flesh-and-blood person who has heard me crying and come running to see what's wrong.

I text a quick I'm okay, and the steps halt.

Jesse: i think we should leave.

Me: Soon.

A pause; then, from Jesse:

i heard something.

Me: I scared myself. Yelped. Ugh.

Jesse: no one's here. I'm coming to you.

Me: Let me get to the exact coordinates. I'm close.

Jesse: five minutes.

I pull up the GPS. I'm not sure if those coordinates will lead anywhere at all—I'm starting to think they really were just rough ones intended to get me to the school. Like Jesse says, there's no sign of anyone here. Nothing I've seen so far has been planted or staged, and the message seems simple.

Face what your brother did.

Face how your brother died.

I suspect whoever brought me here isn't even the same person who's done the rest. That's why the number was blocked instead of faked. This is just a student who knew about the fire, knew suspicions had fallen on me and knew about my GPS game with Jesse, which hadn't been a secret back in middle school.

I follow the coordinates to an open door on the first floor. It's a classroom. Nothing odd about the door being open—half of them are. I step through and brace myself for a more personal message, maybe written on the blackboard. I also keep my foot in the doorway. After what happened in the newspaper office, I am taking no chance that this door will mysteriously shut, locking me inside.

Maybe that's the point here. Trap me inside North Hampton High and force me to call for help and explain what I was doing here.

I see nothing on the blackboard. Hear no footsteps creeping down the hall, which is dark and empty and still.

I move into the classroom, my foot blocking the door. When I hear a soft sob, I jump. It's cut short. Stifled. I strain to listen. A whimper. Then a sharp "Shh!"

The sound comes from inside the room. The *empty* room. I peer around, shining my cell phone flashlight over posters on the walls. I pause on one for a theater production of *A Midsummer Night's Dream*, and I remember that Luka was the understudy for Puck in a local production—

And I must stop that. Focus and banish my brother. It's not the same poster, anyway. This one is from Broadway. Beside it, another poster lists fifty of the most commonly misspelled words. Then one for Banned Books Week. Below that are shelves of books.

An English classroom.

Turn in your badge, Detective—that took way too long.

English.

That sparks a connection. Something about Luka.

Yeah, it was his best subject. His favorite class. Move on.

No, there's something—

That whimper comes again, and I tense. Other voices follow.

"Shh!"

"I can't—"

"Shh!"

Silence.

"Where's Luka?"

I spin. The last voice comes from across the room, a harsh whisper.

"Has anyone seen Luka?"

Now the connection hits. English class. This is where Luka was when the school went on lockdown, and then he snuck out and the next thing anyone knew, he was walking out of the boys' bathroom with a gun.

I forget that I'm supposed to stay in the entranceway, making sure the door doesn't close. I hear that whispering voice, and I'm bearing down on it.

The voice has stopped, but I know where it came from—an empty corner next to the blackboard. There's nothing that anyone could hide behind. Meaning the "speaker" is exactly that: a speaker of the technological variety. I'll find it and—

A light flashes. I wheel as the opposite wall lights up like a screen.

At a gunshot, I start to drop to the floor, but the sound reverberates from all corners of the room, and I realize it's a recording.

The light flickers and brightens, and figures appear on the wall. A moment frozen in time. Frozen in this very classroom. The photo was taken seconds after that first gunshot. I see that in their faces. A couple of kids sit at their desks, their heads up, like startled deer. Someone else is diving for the floor, and beside him, a girl laughs and points. *Look at the idiot, diving for cover when a car backfires.*

Two more shots sound in quick succession. Then a siren. The school siren. A teacher shouts "Everyone down!"

The first wall goes dark and a second wall lights up with another photograph. It's the teacher, her arms raised, her face taut with fear. Kids in the first row are scrambling to their feet. A desk is falling over. One girl stands with her eyes wide, and I recognize her. Even with the blurred shot and imperfect projection screen, I know her.

It's Tiffany.

She's standing at her desk, and she looks utterly terrified.

She was in Luka's class.

I remember that—she and Luka were doing homework together once, and he said she'd skipped sophomore English and gone straight to junior.

She's looking at something beside her. That wide-eyed look of terror fixed on an empty desk.

Where's Luka?

Has anyone seen Luka?

The speakers come alive again. Blasting from all corners. A girl sobbing. A boy telling her to shut up, just shut the hell up. Then a scream. A high-pitched scream of pain from another part of the school, and a boy shouts, "What the hell is that?" and more screams. Gunfire and endless screams.

Skye

I tear out of the room, and I swear the screams and shots follow me. I race along the hall, and when I hear footfalls, I spin, my hands going up, ready to defend myself.

Jesse runs over. "I heard shots. Like a recording. What the hell is going on?"

I stop and struggle to catch my breath. "Performance art."

"What?"

"It's . . ." Breathe. "It's performance art. An installation with an audience of one. It was set up in the English room. Luka's last . . . His last class."

Jesse's expression says he still doesn't know what I mean. He takes my elbow, as if to steady me, and I breathe deeply.

"I'm okay," I say.

"Yeah, no. You're not. And this was a lousy idea. But you've seen what you needed to see, so we can go now."

I nod. He keeps hold of my elbow, and we start down the hall. The audio is still going. Sounds of the shooting. Every time a gun fires. I flinch. We both do. Jesse walks closer to me, his hand tightening on my arm.

"It's not real," he says.

I nod.

"It's not even from the shooting," he continues. "Someone's made a loop tape of random shots and screams. Probably from a movie."

Performance art.

We turn a corner. The gym is ahead, and Jesse hesitates.

The gym. It reminds him of Jamil.

"We can go this—" I say.

"No, this way is faster." His fingers lock in mine. "Ignore it. Just ignore it. It's all fake. Some sick asshole—"

The sound of a door slapping open. Right beside us.

The gym doors.

We both wheel, but the doors are shut. *Chained* shut.

The sound comes again, the distinctive squeal of a metal door. The smack of it hitting the wall.

Light flashes. The wall across from the chained gym doors lights up with a still image of two boys.

I see their faces, and my hand clasps Jesse's.

"Isaac and Harley," Jesse says, and I nod, as if it was a question, but I know it's not. I can't remember if Jesse was ever at our place at the same time as Luka's friends, but it doesn't matter. These are the boys who murdered his brother. Jesse will no more be able to forget their faces than I can.

Isaac and Harley.

Isaac is in the lead. He was always in the lead. He has a gun. A handgun, and I see the news articles again. *Isaac Wickham sup-*

plied two handguns, owned by his father. Harley Stewart brought his uncle's hunting rifle.

Isaac holds the pistol like an action-movie villain. Harley has the rifle in both hands, carrying it more than wielding it. Harley looks . . . bewildered. Like he stepped onto a stage, and someone handed him this gun, and he has no idea what role he's supposed to play.

And Isaac?

Isaac is grinning.

"It's a distance shot," Jesse says, and the sound of his voice startles me.

"Distance shot?" I say. "You mean the rifle?"

"No. The image." He walks to the wall, and I follow, our hands still entwined. "See how crappy the resolution is? It was taken from a distance." He turns and points. "Down there, I bet. Someone was filming—kids did, during the shooting. Isaac and Harley burst out of the gym, and a kid must have caught that on film. Probably wet himself when he realized it."

Jesse looks at Isaac. He's standing eye-to-eye with his brother's killer. I'm about to speak when he turns sharply and he says, "There was stuff online. Photos. Videos. Kids were supposed to hand them in for evidence, but some emailed themselves copies and others just didn't submit theirs. After the shooting, my parents were part of a group of victims' families, and one thing they did was try to get this stuff off the Internet. It didn't work. So that's where this comes from. So that's where we can start looking."

He turns back to Isaac and he nods, as if in satisfaction.

I have reduced you to a clue. A useful clue. Nothing more.

He peers around the dark hallway. "And there," he says. "That's the source." He points to what looks like a dot on the opposite wall, near the top. "The video feed. If I boost you up, can you get a better look?"

This is how Jesse will handle the ghoulish performance. Turn the fear and grief into something we can use against whoever is doing this.

I'm struggling to follow his lead. I can't tear my gaze away from Isaac. I can't stop seeing his expression. His joy. I can't stop hearing the screams and shots echoing around us.

I want to run. Just get out.

Which is exactly what my tormenter hopes I'll do. Run home sobbing and pull up my sheets and tumble into a world of endless nightmare, faced with the reality of what my brother did. The stark reality that I've been spared until now.

I will not give anyone that power.

I will take what has been given here, and I will use it.

I block the sounds of the shooting and turn my back on Isaac and his grin and his gun, and I let Jesse boost me. There in the wall . . .

It's a bullet hole.

"Skye?"

"It's . . ." I swallow. Then my light glints off something inside the depression. "Hold on." I take a pen from my back pocket and poke inside. Bits of plaster crumble, and I see a lens.

I tell Jesse, and then say, "The projector must be on the other side of the wall."

He nods. "It'll be in a room off the next hall. We'll get to that in a second. First, let's see if we can find one of those speakers, too."

"Just follow the screams?"

A wry smile. "Exactly."

We pass the gym. Jesse has homed in on a source up ahead. We seem to be leaving one speaker behind, the sound growing softer as another increases in volume, and Jesse has his chin up, his gaze on the right wall, flashlight app lifted. He's gotten two steps ahead of me in his eagerness, and when the wall to our left lights up, he's already moved past it.

I'm going to do the same. Just keep walking. Jesse doesn't see the projection, and so I'm not going to look . . .

I look.

And I see a picture of Jesse.

That's what I think as I'm turning, my gaze in motion, catching a flash of a figure on the wall. I realize my mistake in a heartbeat. This boy has the same hair as Jesse. Similar features. Wider shoulders.

Jamil.

The camera caught Jamil turning, his body in motion, as if hearing something over his shoulder. Jamil has heard or seen something, and he's—

That's when I realize Jesse has stopped. He looks to his left, noticing I'm no longer at his side.

"Skye?"

I lunge, saying, "Right here," and I prod him forward. *Keep going. Just keep—*

He sees his brother's photo on the wall.

"Let's go," I say, grabbing his hand. "Forget the speaker and—"

He pulls free and walks to the wall, one slow step at a time. Then he stops in front of Jamil.

Seconds tick past. I want to grab his hand again and drag him out. But I know I can't, no more than he could have pulled me from that restroom door.

"Mom used to say—" Jesse's voice cracks, and he clears his throat. "Sometimes, he'd pick on me in front of them—just little things, like elbowing me aside. Kids' stuff. Mom would tell him to be careful, because someday I might be bigger than him. He'd laugh and say that would never happen."

Jesse stands in front of Jamil's photo, and has to look down to meet his brother's eyes. It's not much, maybe an inch. But he is looking down.

"He seems so . . . young." Jesse rubs his mouth and gives a shaky laugh. "That makes me sound old. I just mean . . . when I remember him, at the end, he was practically grown-up. And now . . ."

And now Jesse realizes Jamil was our age when he died.

"He's scared." Jesse pushes his hands into his pockets. "He looks so . . ."

He swallows hard.

I put my arm around Jesse's waist and lean against his shoulder, and I look at Jamil, and I remember the boy I hated. Hated as I have never hated anyone in my life.

No matter what happened to me in the years after that shooting, I never hated my tormentors the way I hated Jamil Mandal. In my memory, he looms huge, this brawny, sneering, preening bully who tormented his little brother, simply because he existed and as long as he existed, Jamil could never be the center of attention at home, the way he was at school. He always had to share. Share a house, share his parents, share the limelight, with his little brother.

Jesse had refused to play sports because he didn't want to compete with Jamil. He stepped aside for his brother and shone in his own corner of the universe. He would be the academic to Jamil's athlete.

But that didn't help, did it? It divided the limelight between them, and Jamil's ego—the ego of the older brother, the first in line—could not accept that. So he shoved Jesse down every chance he got.

I hated Jamil. Hated him so much. I used to dream of the day when Jesse would be an engineer or a doctor, a guy with a string of letters after his name and an amazing career ahead of him . . . and Jamil would be that loser in a crappy job, looking back on his glory days of high school football.

But now I look at Jamil on that wall, and I don't see the ogre from my memory. I just see a boy. Smaller and younger than I remember. And scared. So incredibly scared.

What you did to Jesse was unforgivable, but I wish you'd had a chance to ask for that forgiveness. I wish you had a chance to grow older and grow wiser and realize what you did and ask him to forgive you. Jesse would have. I know he would have. I wish that for you, and I wish it for him.

"I'm sorry he was so frightened," Jesse says, his voice barely audible. "I'm sorry . . ." His voice hitches. "I'm just . . ."

I step in front of Jamil's image, and I put my arms around Jesse and hug him as tight as I can.

"I'm sorry, too," I whisper.

Skye

Jesse and I are in what remains of the bleachers behind NHH. It looks as if some haphazard effort was made to tear them down, but there's still a section remaining. On the scoreboard, someone has spray-painted *#63 Jamil Mandal. Never forget!*

Jesse shouldn't be here. I want him anywhere but here. This, however, is where he wants to be. Sitting on those bleachers. Staring at those words.

"When he first made the team, I came to see him play," Jesse says. "I thought that might make things better. If I . . ." He shrugs. "Supported him, I guess. It made Mom and Dad happy. But then Jamil said I was doing it for them, sucking up, and I thought that meant he didn't want me there, so I stopped going. Things got worse after that. He was on me all the time, and I didn't know why. I'd stopped going to the games, like he wanted."

Jesse pulls one knee up, hugs it. "I wonder now if he was challenging me, you know? Seeing if I'd just been doing it for Mom and Dad, and when I stopped, that seemed to prove . . ."

He brushes back his hair and sighs. "I don't know."

And he never will. That's what hurts the most.

"Whatever Jamil did," I say, "is on him. If he wanted you at those games, he needed to act like it. Otherwise, he was setting up a game with rules you didn't understand, and then punishing you for not following them."

He nods.

"Can we go now?" I ask.

When he hesitates, I say, "I'll stay if you want to, but I'd like to talk about what this adds to the case."

He straightens, expression relaxing. It's like flipping a switch on a track, reminding Jesse of the direction he needs to go. The path out of the dark place he's in right now.

We start walking.

Jesse wants to begin by discussing suspects.

Lana Brighton is one. She's gone quiet since the petition thing, and she's been avoiding me at school, but as Jesse says, "That doesn't clear her. She might have realized it makes her the number one suspect and so she backed off."

We talk about the three seniors, too—Marco, Duke and Grant. I tell Jesse what they said about the shooting and Jamil. I hate doing that, but apparently they'd already made it clear that they weren't Jamil fans, so Jesse isn't surprised. As for them as suspects, Jesse seems to be the one they're trying to antagonize. None of what they said to me was any variation on "*you* shouldn't be here." Still, Jesse wonders if he was their focus only as a way to keep us apart—ensuring that I don't find an ally in Jesse. We'll have to see if any of them have a connection to the shooting.

Jesse also tells me what he found last night.

"Your school account was hacked," he says. "The password was reset. That's how they did it. They claimed to have forgotten your password, which was only a system-generated one. You hadn't linked an outside email to the account, so it asks you a security question. Except, since you never accessed it to set a security *answer,* it bypassed that step and used a captcha."

"Those things that make sure you're not a spambot."

"Right. Awesomely lame security. Get past that, and you're in. The password you gave me—the default one—didn't work, so I had to hack it. Took me exactly four minutes."

"Which means it didn't require killer tech skills."

"My *dida* could do it, and she needs my help with Facebook. The account was accessed on one of the school library computers, which only tells us that the email was sent by a student, staff or volunteer. No one is going to sneak into the school and access our computers."

"Once, maybe. Not twice. And not leaving me notes, trapping me in the office, setting the fire . . ."

"Don't forget the texts." He glances over as we cross a street. "You are going to tell me about the texts, right?"

I do.

"Let's see them," he says, putting out his hand.

When I don't give him my phone, he looks at me. "Skye?"

"It's not just texts. There are . . . video clips."

I tell him about Leanna's clip. Then I show him the text that accompanied it.

"I'm going to ask for a copy of the video," he says. "I know you don't want me watching it, but that's the only way to narrow this down. I said earlier that those images at the school were taken from video clips . . . and someone's been sending you video clips."

"So it's probably the same person."

"Yes, which means those clips are a huge clue. I'm going to need them."

We cross another street in silence. Then I say, "Can I just send you that one?"

"How many are there?"

"Two."

More silent walking.

"It's about Jamil, isn't it?" he says quietly. "The other clip."

I nod. "Please don't ask me to send it, Jesse. You didn't want me going into NHH, and you were right. There was . . ." I inhale. "Outside the bathroom. Where Luka . . . There was . . . On the floor, there were still traces of his . . ."

He reaches to take my hand, and I push it into my pocket, as if I didn't notice him reaching for me. I'm shaking, and I don't want him to see that.

He stops walking. "Skye . . ."

I keep going. "Don't ask me to send Jamil's video, okay? Just don't. Please."

"All right." He catches up and swings in front of me. "Can you stop walking for a second and talk to me?"

I shake my head and turn away as my eyes fill. "I'm fine."

"No, you're not."

I walk past him. "I'll forward you all the texts. I can tell you content from the second video—the parts that have nothing to do with the shooting, in case it helps you track down a source."

"That's fine, Skye, but can you—"

"There's something else, something that makes a lot more sense after today." I tell him about the voices in the hall. "It'd be the same person, I'd guess. Using similar tech. If it happens again, I'll find the speaker."

"If it happens again, I hope you'll text me immediately," he says as he falls in beside me. "Since we're apparently not talking about what you found at NHH, I'll move on to the audiovisual part. It isn't my area of expertise, but Chris might be able to help."

"Right. He's mentioned setting up systems for people. We can talk to him. But that doesn't explain what I heard. I was in the bathroom stall, and two girls were talking about the petition—the petition that doesn't exist. Then I heard the *same* conversation in the hall. How is that possible?"

"Do you know who the girls were?"

I shake my head.

"Was there anyone else in the bathroom at the time?"

"No, and that's the problem. If no one else was there, who recorded it?"

He walks a little farther, and then says, "Other than that conversation, did you hear the girls in the bathroom say or do anything?"

"No . . ." I think it through. "Which could mean even those voices were recorded. Someone came in, played it, and then left."

"Exactly."

Mae texts shortly after that, and I jump at the excuse to leave, before Jesse tries to circle back to what I saw in the school. If I talk about that, I'll break down. Jesse remembers a tougher girl, and I'm going to be that person for him.

I hold it together for Mae, too, retreating after dinner for homework. It's only after sleep comes that my defenses drop, and I descend into nightmare.

The next morning, I manage to make it to school with plenty of coffee and concealer under my eyes.

It's a quiet day. No notes. No voices. No calls to the office. No talks with Mr. Vaughn.

Tiffany needs me to do newspaper work at lunch, and then, after school, Jesse has his trainer over. He invites me to drop by in the evening, but I'm . . . I'm feeling off. Part of it is still finding my balance after yesterday. Part of it is the rough night. And part is, yes, that I'm worried I'm going to disappoint him.

I don't cold-shoulder Jesse. I wouldn't do that. He was there for me yesterday—really there for me—and this is my issue to work through. In math, I smile and chat. When I pass him in the halls, I give him another smile and a nod. When I tell him I can't come by after his track session, I smile and make up some excuse about Mae wanting me home.

But I'm smiling. Always smiling. You're fine. I'm fine. We're fine. Everything's fine.

He buys it, and that's all that counts.

Jesse

Rejected. That's how Jesse felt all day Wednesday, and it's how he feels on the way to school Thursday morning. Like a guy who asks a girl out and everything seems fine, and then the next day, all he gets are fake smiles and excuses.

Not that he's ever been in that situation. He's had exactly two dates in his life . . . if you could call them dates. The girls in question probably wouldn't. They were situations where a girl asked him to lunch, and he didn't want to say no, because it took a lot of guts to ask. The girls were nice enough, so maybe if he got to know them better there'd be a click, and it'd turn into something more. Only it hadn't.

Worse, it felt like the girls thought he only went out with them to be nice. Which he kinda had. *He* wouldn't want a girl doing that to him. On the other hand, would he want her not giving him a shot, either?

Was it worse to have Skye refuse to give him a second chance after he was a jerk to her? Or to get that second chance . . . and blow it?

It doesn't help that he can't figure out *how* he blew it. Also, it doesn't help that his whole analogy is crap. This isn't getting rejected after asking a girl on a date. This feels bigger. So much bigger.

He did all the right things Tuesday at NHH. He's sure of it. They'd argued over going into the school, but he'd stepped aside and let her, and she agreed he'd been right. They'd been fine until she admitted what she'd seen in there—with Luka—and he'd wanted to talk about it.

Was that the wrong thing to do? It *seemed* right.

All he knows for sure is that Skye is avoiding him, and he feels rejected, and he doesn't know what he's done.

Jesse takes a deep breath and texts her.

Him: lunch?

He holds his breath. Waits. Waits. Stares at the screen. Waits. It takes exactly three minutes for her to reply with:

Can't. Need to proof & send paper.

I could join you.

I could bring you lunch.

I could just sit there and watch you edit.

Mmm, no, thanks for offering, Jesse, but maybe not. Also? That's kinda creepy.

He's staring at the screen, trying not to read too much into her answer, trying not to feel like she's ducking him . . . when another text dings.

Skye: After school?

He exhales and sends back a thumbs-up, says he'll see her in math, and puts his phone away.

Skye

It only takes ten minutes to proofread the school paper. I consider texting Jesse a quick: *Hey, you still free for lunch?* It's what I want to do.

Instead, I text Tiffany to say the *RivCol Times* is officially published.

> **Her:** Awesome! Haven't even gone 2 lunch yet. Will come by & grab u.

I meet up with Tiffany and give her back the newspaper office key.

As we're walking to the cafeteria, I catch a glimpse of a dark-haired boy, and my heart double-thuds as I realize how bad it'd look if Jesse saw me going to lunch with Tiffany. The boy isn't Jesse, but I should let him know I was done early. When Tiffany stops to talk to someone, I quick-type the message.

> **Me:** achievement unlocked! I have published my 1st newspaper!

My fingers hover over the Send button.

Hit it. Just hit it.

Still hovering.

Seriously? What is your problem? You think he's going to find out you've changed and walk away . . . so you'll push him away instead? Make him feel like he's done something wrong?

That's not fair.

I move my finger over the button again and—

"Okay, let's . . ." Tiffany walks up beside me and looks at my screen. "Is that Jesse?"

I nod as I press Send and push the phone into my pocket.

She pulls back. "Sorry, I didn't mean to pry. By the time I realized what I was reading"—she taps her temple—"it was already there."

"I know you warned me about him."

"Warned you about Chris, too. Which means I should probably *not* warn you about the guys who are *real* trouble."

I tense. "If you're implying I 'went after' the very guys you warned me against, Chris and Jesse were friends of mine from before."

"I know. Sorry. Lame joke." She hugs her books to her chest. "I'm not very good at them. Jokes, I mean. Not lame ones. I'm really good at lame ones. You're right. I just . . . I know what it can be like, trying to rekindle friendships from before the—"

"Hey, Tiff, did you get my ad in the paper this week?"

It's one of the seniors. When Tiffany stops to talk to him, Jesse comes around the corner. He has his hood up, earbuds in, as he weaves through the busy hall. Then he sees me.

He stops short. His gaze rises to the hall clock.

I take out my phone. My text is still there. Unsent.

I look up. Jesse's walking the other way. I quickly interject with Tiffany and the senior—*forgot something, gotta run, see you later.*

I jog up beside Jesse and say, "The problem with text messages? People don't respond if you fail to send them."

He stops. "What?"

I hold up my phone. "I've been waiting for you to answer this. Which isn't going to happen if I don't hit the Send button."

His gaze flicks to the screen, and he grunts something unintelligible.

I continue, "I saw you walking away, and I just wanted you to know I wasn't blowing you off earlier."

"What?" He shoves his hands in his hoodie pockets. "No, I didn't see you. I turned around because I remembered I forgot . . . something."

"Oh. Well, then, I look kinda stupid, don't I? Let's back up." I press Send. "Message sent." His phone dings. "And delivered. Now I'll withdraw from this awkward moment, and see you in math."

I get about three steps before my phone pings with a text.

Jesse: i lied

Another ping.

Jesse: totally thought u were blowing me off. totally saw u in hall. totally ran other way.

Another ping.

Jesse: totally an idiot.

I turn, and he's right where I left him. He mouths, "Sorry," and I smile and start toward him. There's a group of kids huddled against the lockers, whispering and watching. I've almost reached

Jesse when someone says, "What the hell?" and the voice is loud enough to catch my attention. It's just a guy reading his cell phone. I start past. Then he sees me and barrels forward, saying, "What is wrong with you?"

"Nothing," Jesse says. "She's just trying to get an education, like everyone else here. Now step off—"

"I'll 'step off' when she explains what the hell she was doing."

"Doing with what?" I ask, but Jesse starts going around him, his hand on my elbow.

The guy blocks. Jesse sidesteps again. Guy blocks.

"If you want to dance, you really should ask," I say. "Consent is important."

That gets snickers from the growing crowd.

We start walking again. Then Jesse staggers, and I wheel to see the guy pulling back after shoving him.

I say, "If you need to shove someone, shove the person you're actually pissed off at."

The guy crosses his arms.

"No, really," I say as I step up to him. "You're mad at me. Don't push Jesse because you can't hit a girl. That's sexist. Come on. Take a swing."

"Skye . . ." Jesse tries to stop me, but I get past him and move closer to the guy, getting in his face.

"There," I say. "Go ahead and—"

His hand slams into my shoulder, and I fly into the lockers. Jesse grabs the guy by the back of the shirt and yanks him away. My attacker spins, both hands smacking Jesse's chest.

"You want to get into it, Mandal? Come on, then. Let's get into it."

I grab the guy's arm. As he yanks away, my nails rake down his forearm. He yowls. I retreat fast, hands raised.

"I didn't mean that," I say. "I was just trying to stop you."

He advances on me. "You really do want to get into it, don't you?"

Jesse takes him by the shirt again. The guy spins, swinging. Jesse grabs his arm and wrenches it up. Someone yells, "He's playing with you, Caleb. Hit him." Others join, the crowd closing in.

Caleb swings with his free hand. Jesse dances away, but another guy pushes him forward, saying, "Get back in there, Mandal. You want to defend your crazy girlfriend? Do it right."

Before I can intercede, a girl steps into my path, a girl I vaguely remember from a year below me in middle school.

"Forget them," she says to me. "Just answer his question. What is *wrong* with you?"

I turn away, trying to see what's going on with Jesse, but the girl yanks me back.

"I'm talking to you," she says. "Do you know who I am?"

When I don't reply, she says, "Meg Johnson. My cousin is—*was*—Brandon Locklear, who died because of your brother."

She's scowling and gripping my arm tight enough to hurt, but her eyes glisten with tears. "I've heard your mother is mentally ill, and I'm hoping that's your excuse. Really, really hoping it is. When I heard you were back here, I wanted to talk to you. I wanted to tell you that I understood what happened wasn't your fault, and I hoped you were doing okay. But I couldn't work up the nerve. And then you do this."

"Do what?"

She thrusts her phone at me, but it's so fast I don't see anything. "If you are mentally ill, Skye, then you need help. And if you're not, then you need even more help, because you are one sick bitch."

"May I please see what you were trying to show me?" I ask, as calmly as I can.

Someone else shoves a phone into my face. On the screen is today's *RivCol Times*. The edition I just published.

"Is something wrong with the newspaper?" I ask carefully.

"Hey, Mandal," someone says. "She's asking if something's wrong with the paper? Do *you* see anything wrong with it?"

I look to see that the guys have stopped fighting, and Jesse is staring down at his phone.

I scroll down the page. The first article should be a headline crowing about the track meet victory. Instead, it's a massive two-line header: REMEMBERING THE NHH VICTIMS. With my name as the byline.

"No," I whisper. "I just published the paper. That wasn't—I didn't write . . ."

I scroll faster. Jesse's at my side now, and he's reaching for the phone, saying, "Someone tampered with the newspaper."

I backpedal before he can take the phone from me. I'm skim-reading the article. In it, I apologize for my brother's participation in the shooting, while making it clear that he never actually hurt anyone, and as I read that, I cringe.

The article goes on to say I want to offer my condolences to the family members at Riverside Collegiate . . . and then it lists every one of those relatives.

Below that is an embedded video.

My trembling finger hovers over the Play button, and I realize the crowd has gone silent. I look up to see them watching, expressions ranging from confusion and curiosity to barely contained outrage.

Jesse touches my arm, saying, "You don't have to—"

I meet his gaze. "I do."

I hit the button. The video starts with the clip from Leanna's second birthday. Then the ones of Jamil and his friends. Next is Nella dressed up as a lion for Halloween, chasing her little brother, dressed as a mouse. Then Brandon at the hospital, meeting his son for the first time. My eyes well up. Then the screen clears and—

A blood-splattered hall. The camera pans to a body—Brandon's—sprawled across a pool of blood, cell phone in his hand. Words flash on the screen.

He started texting a message to his girlfriend and baby son. He never got a chance to finish it.

I want to drop the phone. Drop it and run. Instead, I clutch it and force myself to watch the clip of Leanna under the desk, telling her mother she's all right. The video ends with another slow pan of a blood-streaked hall. And then the final words:

Remembering the victims of NHH.

"I didn't—" My chest heaves and I can't get the words out. "I would never—"

Jesse gently takes the phone from my hand. "I know you didn't." He raises his voice. "Do you really think she'd post that for me to see? *Me?*"

"Skye?" Shoes click down the hall, and I turn, still numb, and see Tiffany walking toward us.

"We need to talk," she says.

"I didn't—"

She takes my arm and steers me away, calling back to the others. "We are very sorry for this mistake. It will be corrected immediately."

Jesse catches up. "Skye didn't—"

"I understand you want to set the record straight about Luka," she says, her voice low as we walk fast toward the newspaper office. "I know you must have thought a public apology would help."

"And posting a video of their dead bodies?" I say.

"*What?*"

Jesse holds out his phone. She snatches it and plays the video as we walk. Her face pales.

"I . . . I didn't see that," she says. "I just read the article."

"Skye didn't post this," Jesse says. "Not the article or the video. Someone set her up. We need to get the newspaper down."

Tiffany unlocks the newspaper room door.

"Can the files be accessed remotely?" Jesse asks.

"Hmm?" She looks at him, clearly shaken.

"The door was locked, meaning no one snuck in and published that version. Can it be done remotely?"

"No."

"Is there anyone else with access?" Jesse asks.

She turns on him, key raised. "Are you suggesting I—?"

"No, I mean someone else on the staff."

"I'm the only one with a key, Jesse. And if you want an alibi, I can provide it, considering I was with Skye right after she published the newspaper."

"Okay, so we're looking at a hack. I wasn't accusing you, Tiffany. I'm sorry if it sounded like I was."

She doesn't seem to hear him, just ushers us inside.

"I don't know what happened," I say. "I published the right version. I have the test copy in my inbox. I also checked the link when it went live."

"Let's just get it down."

She logs onto the computer. Jesse stands behind her, saying, "Do you use your school log-in? Or is it a different one for the newspaper?"

She doesn't answer.

"It's different," I say.

"And do you each have unique log-ins? Or is it universal?"

"It's one to get on this computer and another for the publishing service. Both are used by everyone."

"Okay, so it's a two-step process with separate universal log-ins. And the paper can only be published from here, but—"

Tiffany cuts in. "This is the newspaper office, Skye. We've just had a serious security breach. I don't need someone hanging over my shoulder asking questions."

"He's figuring out how someone hacked in and published that version of the newspaper," I say. "He knows this stuff. I don't."

She glances over at him. "You know how to hack, Jesse? Huh. That's interesting . . . considering we just had a hack. One that is going to make life a whole lot worse for Skye. I've heard you have a problem with her being at RivCol."

"Then you've heard wrong," he says evenly. "I was caught off guard when she enrolled, and I've apologized for that. I'm sorry if I was distracting you. Getting that video taken down is the important thing right now. I'll ask questions later."

"It's down," she says after a few more keystrokes. "I've pulled the newspaper and deleted the video clip."

I check the link on my phone. Jesse does the same on his and nods.

"I'll get the real paper up," Tiffany says. "If I can do it fast, that proves we had another version."

She's flipping through the directory, saying, "The only version I see here is the one that was published."

"Then someone erased the original," Jesse says.

Tiffany says nothing. She's typing when Mr. Vaughn walks in.

"Skye?" He seems surprised to see me there. "I heard there was an . . . incident. With the paper."

"It's fixed," Tiffany says. "Someone replaced the lead story with a fake one."

"Allegedly written by me," I say. "A very disturbing article that is going to have serious consequences for me at RivCol. Which is why I'm going to ask for a full investigation."

He looks from me to Tiffany to Jesse and then back, and I know what's coming. He's going to say as long as it's been fixed, we can just ignore it. No harm. No foul.

I'm preparing my argument when he opens his mouth and says, "I agree. I'd like you to wait in my office, Miss Gilchrist, while I speak to Miss Gold."

Skye

While we wait in Mr. Vaughn's office, Jesse asks me questions and takes notes about the newspaper publication system. I don't know how much of that is simply busywork. I don't care. I need to be busy.

A full hour passes before the door opens. Mr. Vaughn steps inside and sees Jesse. "I don't believe I asked you to join us, Mr. Mandal."

"Oh?" Jesse says. "My mistake."

Mr. Vaughn stands in the open doorway, waiting for Jesse to leave. Jesse just pushes his notes forward and says, "I've been working out possible explanations for what happened. The newspaper might be a closed system, but it publishes via the Web, which means someone could hack in. You need an expert to assess incoming transmissions."

"There were no incoming transmissions. Mr. Dennis has confirmed that."

"Dennis? There's a reason I stopped taking comp-sci when I transferred here. Dennis hasn't coded since Windows 1.0."

"*Mr.* Dennis is an accredited computer expert—"

"The only thing he's an expert in is the power-off power-on method of troubleshooting."

"I'm not a fan of this newfound sarcasm, Mr. Mandal. Perhaps you ought to rethink your current circle of associates."

"I wish I was being sarcastic. Do you know what Dennis uses as his password? 'Password.' Kids log into his account when they want to surf porn sites. If you don't believe me, check his account history. Dennis babysits the lab and teaches courses he's not qualified to *take*. Which means you can't trust any assessment he gives."

"I suppose you're offering to do that assessment for me, Mr. Mandal."

"No, I'm telling you to get an expert. An outside opinion. I'm neither. Also, my name is either Jesse or Jasser. Mr. Mandal is my dad, and calling me that isn't respectful—it's patronizing."

I cut in with, "I don't know what you think I'd hope to accomplish, sir, by setting the fire or writing that article."

He unlocks a drawer on his desk and takes out a folder. Inside, he's printed my record. For easy access, it seems. He opens it and says, "Page one. Kindergarten. A pair of boy's underwear was found hanging from the classroom flagpole. You accepted blame." He looks at me. "*Readily* accepted blame."

"Josh kept pulling up girls' skirts to see their underwear. So I showed off his. I tried putting it on the *school* flagpole, but I wasn't tall enough to reach the winch."

"How'd you *get* his underwear?" Jesse asks.

"I promised I'd never tell. Having his Superman Underoos run up the flagpole was embarrassment enough."

"I'm glad you're amused, *Jesse*, but you both fail to recognize the point, which is that Miss—*Skye*—has a history of attention-seeking behavior."

"No," Jesse says. "She has a history of harmless revenge pranks. Avenging *other* people."

"There may be a few actual pranks in my record," I say. "And sure, pranks by their very nature are designed to get attention, but you're talking about the kind where someone falls down the steps and says she was pushed. I don't do that."

"No?" Mr. Vaughn flips through the pages. "I see several incidents three years ago where you've claimed persecution related to the shooting."

My cheeks heat. "I didn't *claim* to be persecuted. I was."

"There's no evidence of that."

Jesse cuts in. "Because bullies know enough not to leave evidence. No one sees it. Even their parents—"

He stops and pulls back sharply.

"You'll notice I stopped complaining after the first year," I say. "That's because I stopped telling anyone. We're supposed to report bullying, but those who are bullied know that never goes well. That's why I haven't reported anything at RivCol."

"Instead, you've staged serious incidents, knowing that reports of simple verbal bullying aren't taken as seriously—"

"*Simple* verbal bullying?" Jesse says. "Wow. Are you going to recite the sticks-and-stones line, too?"

"*Mr.* Mandal."

I lift my hands. "We aren't getting anywhere here."

"I would agree," Mr. Vaughn says. "You both seem to be under the impression this is a court of law. It's a school. We have our own investigative practices—"

"*What* investigative practices?" Jesse says.

I stop him with a look, and then say to Mr. Vaughn, "Okay, I get it. You think I set a fire. When you refused to accuse me of it, you believe I tampered with the newspaper. So open an investigation. I'll cooperate in every way."

"I have opened one. And closed it. In light of your previous activity—"

"You mean previously *unproven* activity? Previously *uninvestigated* activity?" I shake my head. "Fine. I'll do my own investigating."

"An excellent idea. It will keep you occupied during your suspension."

"Suspension?"

"For a week."

"You can't suspend her on a suspicion," Jesse says. "If you're accusing her, then do it. That's why I'm here—to verify everything that happens in this room. And in case you try to claim we both lied?" He holds up his phone. "I've been recording this."

Mr. Vaughn's jaw works. Then he turns to me. "Whatever else you have done, Miss Gilchrist, this is your gravest offense. Turning a good student into a fellow troublemaker."

"Good student?" Jesse chokes on a laugh. "You aren't talking about me, right?"

"You have been a model student, Mr. Mandal."

"I have a C average, and I don't know why it's not a D. I barely show up for class."

"You're a star athlete. Your grades may suffer for that, but it's only a matter of finding balance. Your IQ tests prove you're very bright. It's a rare combination—intelligence and athleticism."

"Athleticism . . ." A weird note in Jesse's voice makes me look over.

"Yes," Mr. Vaughn continues, oblivious. "You're the best runner this school has seen in years. You inspire the entire team."

"Inspire?" Jesse's laugh sends dread prickling down my spine, that first sense of an approaching storm.

"Steroids," he says.

"I beg your pardon?" Mr. Vaughn says.

"The secret to my success, if you must know. Anabolic steroids. To build my muscles, because I don't have my brother's physique. I need 'help.' That's what my trainer says—the trainer who was recommended by Coach Albright when I was trying to decide which high school to attend. I chose Southside, but my parents took *your* coach's recommendation. They hired that private trainer to take me 'to the next level.' That's how Coach Albright put it."

His voice is so eerily calm that I'm sure he's kidding, and Mr. Vaughn echoes that, saying, "I believe you should leave the jokes to Miss Gilchrist. That particular one could smear the reputation of your entire team."

"Forget what I said about Albright. Maybe she had no idea *how* her recommended trainer turned average runners into champion sprinters. This isn't about dragging your team through the mud. It's about me. How I got to be the best sprinter in Riverside. Hint? It's not hard work and dedication."

I'm staring at Jesse, and he has his gaze fixed on Mr. Vaughn. His voice stays eerily calm, but a bead of sweat trickles down his cheek.

"That's enough, Mr. Mandal. I'm going to ask you to leave—"

"The team? Sure. I'll take a suspension, too, and whatever else you're offering."

"Your sense of humor—"

"Not joking. Really, really not joking. I don't know how you want to handle this, but I'm ready to take my punishment. Return my trophies. Get expelled from RivCol. Whatever you want."

"I *want* you to leave my office. Go to your last class, and I'll pretend this conversation never happened."

Both Jesse and I stare at him. Silence falls, so thick I swear I feel it.

"What?" Jesse says.

"You heard me, Mr. Mandal. Return to class."

"I just confessed to using *steroids*."

"In an effort to divert attention from Miss Gilchrist's antics. I would applaud your chivalry, if it were not so misguided. I will do you the favor of pretending this conversation never happened. If you continue in this vein, Mr. Mandal, I would suggest that suspension would be the least of your worries."

"Are you threaten—?"

I wrap my fingers around Jesse's arm and whisper, "Let's go."

When he hesitates, I add, "Please," and he takes my hand, fingers interlocking with mine, and marches from the office.

Skye

Mr. Vaughn comes after us, warning Jesse that he'd better get to class and I'd better get back in his office so he can formalize my suspension. We ignore him until he threatens to call security. Then Jesse says, "Call my parents, too, please. I'd like to tell them that I confessed—"

Mr. Vaughn cuts him off with a cough and says, "I expect you both to go to the library and wait for me there." Then he retreats to the office.

Jesse mutters under his breath, "If we actually went to the library, how long would it take him to show up?"

"Monday," I say.

Jesse shakes his head, and we continue out of the school.

Jesse walks to the bus stop. He doesn't seem to realize he's still holding my hand, but he's clutching it hard. I don't say a word. I hold on just as tightly.

We've just reached the bus stop when he spots a taxi and hails that instead.

It's a silent ride. Jesse stares out the window. He hasn't even put on his seat belt, and he jumps when I place the metal end on his leg. Then he nods and clicks it into place.

The car stops at Fletcher Park: the playground where we used to hang out and pretend we were still children.

Except we *were* children. In so many ways.

Jesse leads me through the gate. Then he stops. The swings are gone. The spiral slide is gone. So is the teeter-totter. Instead, there's a bright red plastic climbing contraption with short slides and walking rails barely a foot over the ground, so even a toddler couldn't get hurt falling into the bed of shredded rubber below.

Jesse squares his shoulders, as if he's going to make the best of it. He turns toward the wall . . .

They've put plastic shielding along the base, so no one can climb it.

Jesse's shoulders slump. "I didn't know they redid it. I haven't been here since . . ."

"Neither have I," I say, and I smile, but he just keeps looking around for something—anything—familiar.

"It changed," he says.

Everything's changed.

Everything's changed, and we can't go back.

I squeeze away the prickle of tears. He doesn't need that. Neither of us does. I tug his hand, and he follows as I lead him to the picnic shelter. He sits on a tabletop, but I say, "Uh-uh. Too easy."

I climb onto the table, grab the shelter roofline and hoist myself up. He follows. We crawl to the opposite edge and sit looking out at the ball diamond, a new housing development under construction behind it.

"It's true," he says after a few minutes of silence. "About the steroids."

"I figured it must be."

"I cheated. All those awards . . ." He swallows. "My parents keep them in the living room. With Jamil's. I won't go in there. I didn't earn any of them. I cheated. Every last race, I cheated."

"Your trainer gave you steroids for weight training in the off-season. You didn't take them at race time."

"Don't."

"I'm just—"

"Please." He looks over at me. "I know what you're trying to say, but I cheated, and I don't want excuses."

"Okay."

"I just . . ." He pulls his legs up, sitting cross-legged, like we used to do on his garage roof. "With Jamil gone, my parents missed going to his games. Being in the stands. Cheering him on. You can't do that at a spelling bee."

"They did."

"It wasn't the same. They acted like it was, for my sake, but I knew they missed sitting in the bleachers. I'd always been a good runner, so I tried out for track and made the team. When I started high school, my parents got me that trainer. He suggested—" He takes a deep breath. "I'm not blaming anyone. I figured I'd use the steroids for one season to jump-start my training. But then I started winning, and it was the one thing . . ." His breath catches. "The one thing . . ."

He can't finish. I take his hand and squeeze it. He just stares out at the ball diamond.

"That's why I was a jerk to you the first couple of days," he says. "I didn't want you to see—" He inhales. "I'm not the kid you knew, and I was ashamed of that."

I open my mouth, but he's still talking. "Everything you liked about me, everything we shared, it's gone. The shows we used to watch, I haven't seen in years. The music we listened to, I don't even have on my phone."

"That's—"

"That's little stuff. I know. Tastes change. But I didn't replace the shows or the music. I just . . . I just did nothing. I'll watch whatever's on TV. Listen to whatever's streaming. I cut class, and I'm not even skipping to do something fun. My grades have tanked, and it isn't because I don't have time to study. I just don't do anything. Except run. I run, and I run, and I run and . . ."

His hand trembles in mine. "Jamil used to call me a loser, and as much as that hurt, I knew he was wrong. I was smart, and I had hobbies, and I had friends. But now? I'm exactly what he said . . ."

His voice cracks, and his eyes fill, and then they widen in horror as the first tear falls. He releases my hand to wipe it away quickly. "Damn it. Sorry. I—" More frantic wiping as he turns his head, mumbling apologies.

"Jamil was an asshole," I say.

His shoulders tense.

"I know I shouldn't speak ill of the dead," I say. "And he was your brother, so if you want me to shut up, just say so."

Silence.

"You were smart, and I think he knew, in the long run, that would count more than being good at football. Now he's gone, and I'm pretty sure I'm the only person who knows how he treated you. You never told your parents, did you?"

"I can't. Not now. It's too late."

"So you're stuck with it. Stuck pretending you miss this guy that everyone thought was so great. Except he wasn't great to you. He made your life hell, and you're trapped with that secret. I can't imagine how hard that was, and I'm sorry I wasn't there for you."

He smiles, a sad twist of a smile. "You haven't changed at all, have you? No matter what's happening to you, you're thinking of others. You were a lot closer to Luka than I was to Jamil, and the circumstances . . ."

He inhales. "It was worse for you. Much worse. Your brother was dead, and I went to your house because I was hurting, and when you couldn't be there for me, I turned my back on you. I felt rejected so I abandoned you when you really needed a friend. I was a selfish brat."

"When did you go to my house?"

"I threw pebbles at your window, remember? You looked out, but . . . It was lousy timing. You weren't ready to see me. And I never tried again. I told myself . . ." He throws up his hands. "I don't even know what I told myself. I felt rejected. I sulked and waited for you to come to me, and the next thing I knew, you'd moved away."

"I . . ." I stare at him. "I thought you were angry."

"Angry?"

"That night. At my window. You looked angry. Really angry, and I didn't blame you. My brother was part of the shooting that killed your brother."

"But that had nothing to do with you."

My mouth opens. I can't find words. I think of all the time I've spent agonizing over that moment. All the pain it caused me. All the outrage that my best friend had let me down. Even if I told myself I understood, I didn't really.

All it would have taken was a few words. A text. An email. A phone call.

Are you okay?

Three words would have solved everything.

Three words. Three years lost because we hadn't said them. Now *my* eyes are filling, and Jesse's look of confusion changes to horror, and he's patting his pockets and pulling out a half-shredded paper napkin and shoving it at me.

"I'm sorry," he says. "I'm so, so sorry. I was upset, and when you didn't come to the window, I *did* get mad, and if you saw that, of course you'd think I was angry. I should have—"

"I should have—" I say at the exact moment he does, and we sit there, unfinished regret hanging between us.

I should have . . .

Should have. Could have. Didn't.

Finally, I break the silence with, "You say I haven't changed. But I have. That's why I brushed you off yesterday. I didn't want *you* to be disappointed."

"I could never be disappointed, Skye. Not with you."

My cheeks heat, and he says, "You might *think* you've changed, but I don't see it."

"I have. My goals . . . What I wanted to do with my life . . . It's all gone."

"So you don't want to be an astronaut anymore?" he says.

His lips curve in a gentle smile, but I burst into tears, which he scrambles to fix with the napkin while tripping over himself to apologize for making me cry. And I apologize for crying. And then he has to say no, it's okay.

A vicious cycle of apologies and embarrassment, ending with me drying my tears and pulling back and saying, "See? Not the girl you remember."

I smile when I say it, but he gives me a hard look and says, "Just because I never saw you cry doesn't mean you never did."

"Not as much as I do now."

"And I curse more than I used to. People change."

I choke on a laugh at that, and the tears threaten again as I say, "I'm so far from becoming an astronaut it isn't even funny, Jesse. I'm not even sure I'll go to college, because I have no idea what I'd do. I quit everything I loved, and I didn't find anything to replace it. I just . . . am. I exist. I get through my days, and I thought that was enough, and then I came back here and remembered what I used to be, the dreams I had and . . ."

He hugs me. Puts his arms around me and hugs me tight. When he lets go, he says, "We kinda both lost our way, huh?"

"Kinda."

He puts his fingers on my chin and tilts my face up, and his lips are parting to say something . . . or I think he's going to say something, but there's this little bit of me that hopes—

My phone vibrates. It's been vibrating for a while, and I've been ignoring it, but he hears it now and says, "Your phone?"

I want to tell him to forget that. What was he going to say? What was he going to do? But there's no returning to that moment, not while he's waiting expectantly.

I check the string of texts and wince. "It's Mae. She's heard about the suspension, and she's freaking." I hold my phone over the edge of the pavilion. "Think I can accidentally drop it?"

"Drop it, yes. Accidentally, no. And having already read her messages . . ."

I sigh. "Sure, be all mature about it."

"One of us has to be."

I start a retort, but I move too fast and teeter. He grabs me and hauls me back onto the roof, saying, "Careful."

"I was being careful. Which means if my phone fell, it would totally have been an accident. Which you ruined. Spoilsport."

"Next time I should let you break your neck?"

"Yep, teach me a lesson."

"Never has before."

"Um, pretty sure I've never broken my neck before."

"Just your wrist. And your arm. And sprained *both* ankles."

"Not all at the same time. I need to try harder."

I look over the edge.

He laughs and grabs me. "Don't even think about it."

"Can't stop someone from thinking."

"Can sure try."

I pretend to settle on the roof. Then I spring and leap over the edge as Jesse lets out a curse behind me. I hit the grass in a crouch and turn, grinning.

"See? Nothing broken. It's not nearly high enough. Next time? Top of the school."

He gives a deep sigh. "Believe me, Skye, you have not changed nearly as much as you think you have."

I make a face and wave for him to jump. He crab-crawls sideways along the edge, tensing for a leap, and then changing his mind and trying a new spot.

"And apparently, neither have you," I say. "Get your ass down here."

He moves to the edge over the grass and jumps. He hits the ground and hisses in pain, dropping to a crouch, hands going to his ankle.

I hurry over and drop beside him. "Are you—?"

He tackles me, too fast for me to see it coming, and the next thing I know, I'm flat on my back, and he's beside me, laughing.

"Too slow," he says. "Still way too slow."

I rise to sit. "I saw it coming."

"Liar."

"I was humoring you."

"*Such* a liar."

A phone sounds. It's not mine. Jesse takes his out and curses.

"Let me guess," I say. "Mae isn't the only one who got a call."

"Yeah." He scrolls through texts. "Vaughn phoned my mom to report an 'incident.' He didn't tell her what it was, only that I'd 'gotten upset' and cut my last class."

"And she's freaking?"

"Nah. Mom doesn't freak. She's just concerned. She wants to talk." He sighs. "Vaughn won't tell her about the steroids. But I have to. Get it over with."

"Best thing."

"I know."

"She'll understand."

Another sigh. "That's the problem. They've been so careful since . . . Jamil. Giving me space. Letting me work it through. Which seems great, but sometimes, what I really need is less handholding."

"As someone with parents who *aren't* there for me—can't be or won't be—I can tell you, it's not any better. Whether it's unwavering support or a kick in the ass, I think the only people who can give it to us are ourselves."

"Or each other."

I give him a quick hug. "Definitely each other. So let's put out these fires and reconvene in cyberspace."

Skye

When I open the condo door, Mae's there with "Where have you been? I've been calling for hours."

I bite my tongue against saying it's been forty-five minutes since her first call and twenty since I texted her back.

"Is *he* with you?" she says.

I reply calmly, "If you mean Jesse, he's gone home to explain to his parents."

"I said I don't want you hanging out with him, Skye. He's the one who got you into this, isn't he?"

I want to say that Jesse's the one keeping me sane, but that'll just start a fight. We've already been texting, both of us unable to hold to that "talk tonight" promise, our stream of chatter keeping my mood exactly where it was when we parted.

It reminds me of the time I tried pot—new school, trying to impress. I expected a state of blissful euphoria, like what other kids described. Instead, I threw up. But how I imagined it would be? That's exactly how I feel right now.

Jesse and I have cleared away the misunderstandings, banished the anxieties of reconnecting and truly reconnected. I feel free. Free and light and giddy, like I'm back behind our old school again, and he's just asked me to the All-Time Five concert.

I'm not that girl again—I never will be—but I've recaptured something, and I want to just calm Mae down, go to my room, lie on the bed and grin like I'm thirteen again, waiting for his text.

"Skye? Are you listening to me?"

I nod and slip past her into the hall, saying, "Let's go in the living room. I need to talk to you."

"I should hope so. Suspended? Do you have any idea how serious that is, Skye?"

Again, I resist a retort. Stay mature. Like Jesse said earlier, one of us has to be. I smile at the thought.

"Do you think this is funny, Skye?"

"No, of course not." I sit on the sofa. "I don't know what Mr. Vaughn told you, but someone at school has targeted me. Trying to scare me off, I guess. Jesse and I are trying to find the culprit. Right now, we're—"

"Mr. Vaughn says there was a fire."

"Yes. Last week. I should have mentioned that, but I was fine. Shaken up mostly. Anyway, after the fire—"

"He thinks you set it."

"That's the problem. There weren't any witnesses. Not surprisingly, given that it happened after school—"

"Mr. Vaughn also says you wrote an article in the school paper, linking to a . . . to a terribly tasteless video clip."

By this point, I really want to tell Mae to let me get through my explanation. Or complete a sentence. But I'm still calm, focused, not losing my temper. Staying the course.

"I didn't write that article or make that clip. The problem is that I'm the one who published the latest edition of the newspaper. Jesse's looking for evidence of a hack—"

"Mr. Vaughn says there was no hack."

My temple throbs. One tiny spot, like a needle driving in every time she cuts me off.

"Mr. Vaughn says a lot of things," I say. "He is convinced I'm staging my own persecution. As for why—"

"He says you're looking for attention."

The needle drives in, and my words come out sharper than I intend as I say, "Which I don't do. You know that."

"I know you're very dramatic, Skye. You always have been. Your mother used to joke that the principal had her work number on speed dial."

The needle explodes to a full-scale spike, and I squeeze my eyes shut, forcing my temper back. "Yes, and the fact she *joked* about it means it wasn't serious. I goofed around. I pulled pranks. Sure, some of that was to get laughs, but *this* is—"

"I know how hard the last few years have been on you, Skye. With your father gone and your mother's illness and your gran's stroke, you feel overlooked. Neglected, even."

"Uh, no, I do not feel—"

She lowers herself beside me on the sofa. "It would be understandable if you did. You've been there for everyone, and no one's been there for you. You're the child. We're the adults, and even here, you haven't had my undivided attention."

"I don't need attention, Mae. Undivided or otherwise. I'm perfectly capable of looking after myself."

"But you shouldn't have to. You need more, and I would understand if—"

"If I lit a *room* on fire? Posted a video of the *shooting*?" My voice rises, and I push to my feet. "I didn't do this, Mae, but I can see that having a mature conversation about it is out of the question."

Her voice hardens. "I *am* having a mature conversation."

"No, you're treating me like a kid in need of serious therapy."

"Well, that's a starting point."

I stare at her. Then I head for my room. I won't escalate this. I won't.

Mae leaps to her feet and grabs my arm. "Don't you walk out on me, Skye."

I spin on her. "You say you've neglected me? Newsflash? I'm okay with that. I don't want to eat whatever organic, free-range crap you call dinner. I don't want to watch rom-coms. Remember what happened to the Barbies you gave me for Christmas? I turned them into ninja princesses. Not that you paid any attention—ever. You certainly didn't when we were falling apart, Mom hardly ever getting out of bed and Dad off on business trips screwing his business partner. We lived five miles away, Mae. *Five* miles. I can't even remember the last time you checked in on us."

"I—"

"You were busy. I get it. Now you say you want to help, but do you know what helping would have been? Taking a couple of weeks off and coming to look after Gran when she had her *second* stroke. Visiting just long enough to assure child services that everything was fine. If you couldn't find time for that, then maybe you could have listened when I begged—*begged*—not to come back here. But no, this is what I needed. To return to a town and a school where my brother was part of a school shooting. Where every day I see people who knew the victims, and others who think having me in Riverside is an *outrage* to the victims. People shove it in my face, and then tell me I'm masterminding my own fake persecution. You wanted me to toughen up, Mae? Well, I'm sorry to break it to you, but I'm not that tough. I'm just not."

I stride to my room and close the door behind me.

Jesse

Jesse tells his parents about the steroids. He sits in the living room to do it. He hasn't done more than pass through there since his parents proudly displayed his first track trophy. Now, though, he needs to let them look at those trophies and realize he hasn't earned a single one of them.

He talks. They listen. And he must witness every emotion that passes over their faces.

Trepidation at first. They don't know what happened at school, only that there was some "incident" involving Skye, and Jesse left with her because of it. When he got home, the first thing his father said was "We aren't angry."

Get that out of the way quickly, as they always do, because they are never angry. No matter what he does. No matter how far he falls.

Mom says they knew he must have walked out in solidarity with Skye, and while she isn't sure that's the proper response, they understand. They always understand.

When he repeats that he needs to talk to them, he gets the looks of trepidation. Then, as he begins to explain, trepidation turns to bafflement.

Track? What could an incident with Skye possibly have to do with track?

He says the word.

Steroids.

Their confusion grows. Is he telling them that other kids are juicing? Is he feeling pressured? That must be it, because their son would never—

Did he just say . . . ?

They look at each other, searching for clarity, proof that they have misunderstood, because Jesse would not—

Astonishment. No, he is clearly saying what they thought he was saying.

Their son used steroids.

Disappointment. Dismay. They cover those quickly—his father rubbing his beard, his mother glancing out the window—before recovering. Disappointed? No, no. Surprised. That's all. They're just surprised.

He finishes. Then he waits. They have spoken volumes with their eyes and their faces and their gestures but haven't said a word since he began.

His father opens his mouth. It takes another moment for the words to come, and when they do, they're slow, the thought still forming.

"I don't understand. How . . . ?" He trails off. Jesse knows what would have come next.

How could you?

His father would never say that aloud. He's quieter than Jesse's mother. Dad leaves the big conversations to her and sits in the background as support. Yet it is always support. His father would no sooner accuse Jesse than his mother would, and so he lets that "How . . . ?" hang there, the rest booming inside in Jesse's head.

How could you?

Jesse wants to explain. Wants desperately to explain.

You guys missed Jamil. You missed going to his games. I couldn't give you back Jamil, but I could give you back your place in the stands to cheer on your son, to be proud of your son.

He says none of that. They'll feel it as blame, even if that isn't what he means. Starting track was a gift to them, not fulfilling an obligation.

So he says nothing. But his gaze slips, only for a second, to the wall of trophies, and that's enough. His mother gives a sharp intake of breath and his father exhales at the same time.

"Was this about—?" she begins.

"No," Jesse says. "This was about me. *All me*. My mistake."

"But—"

"I screwed up," he says, rising. "And I'm sorry. I am so sorry."

His mother rises to hug him, but he sidesteps, his gaze averted so he can pretend he didn't see her reach out.

"I'll be in my room," he says.

He has to pass the trophies. He stops and looks at them, beside his brother's.

"Could you take these down?" he says. "Just . . . get rid of them. Please."

Skye

It doesn't take long for Mae to come to my bedroom door. She wants to talk. I don't. I've heard enough.

We might not be close, but it never occurred to me that she'd actually think I did this. That hurts more than I could have imagined.

"I'd like to be left alone," I say.

"I just want to talk."

"I don't. I'm going to ask you to respect that, Mae."

Silence. Long silence.

"I just want to talk," she says again.

I sigh softly. "If you insist, then I'm going to walk out that door and continue straight through the front one. I don't want to storm off. That's what a child does. I am not a child. I don't want to argue anymore, so I'm trying to do the mature thing and just stay in my room. Okay?"

A few minutes pass before her footsteps recede.

I want to call Gran. I want to talk to someone who will believe me. But I can't bring my grandmother into this. While I've been doing my daily calls—to her and Mom—I haven't mentioned any of what's been happening. They don't need my problems on top of their own.

I check my phone. Jesse asked me to text when I was done, presuming my talk would take longer than his, but . . .

I look at the clock on my phone. Nope, mine didn't take long at all.

I do have a message, though. From Tiffany.

Tiffany: Can we talk?

I hesitate, but I don't want to be too quick to text Jesse, in case I interrupt his conversation with his parents, so I send Tiffany a quick: What's up?

My phone rings twenty seconds later. I sigh. While I really didn't want to tie myself into a phone conversation, I can't pretend I'm away from my phone mere moments after texting her.

I answer, and she says, "I'm sorry."

"About what?"

There's a pause, and I get the feeling she's been anxiously awaiting my reply so she can apologize, and now she's confused. But she's not the only one, and I'm racking my brain to figure out why she'd be apologizing.

"I'm sorry that I didn't speak up with Mr. Vaughn," she says. "Jesse had your back, and I didn't."

"That's fine—"

"It's not. I know you didn't post that video. Instead of saying so, I got on Jesse's case, and he didn't deserve that. I'm sorry."

"Okay."

"It's not okay, Skye. I've been a bitch to him, and I've been weird about you guys getting back together. I kept telling myself that I must sense an ulterior motive. I finally realized that's not it at all. How does the cliché go? It's not him, it's me."

Before I can speak, she continues, "Jesse stood by you. That's what a friend does. Stands with you. Doesn't hide in the newspaper room while you get chewed out by a VP for something you didn't do."

"It's—"

"I don't like Jesse because he's a reminder of the shooting," she blurts. "Of the fact that my boyfriend killed his brother, and I should have seen it coming. There must have been signs with Isaac, and I missed them and Jamil died, and if Jesse's messed up, that's why. Because of something I failed to do."

"You didn't—"

"But I *feel* that way. Right or wrong. Isaac was my boyfriend. I knew he had issues, and I—"

She takes a deep breath. "I was glad when Jesse went to Southfield. One fewer person in the halls to remind me. I already had to see Chris and Owen and others. That was hard enough. Maybe that's why I don't care for Chris. In his case, I do get the feeling there's more to it—he's too nice, too smooth, and it rubs me the wrong way. And Owen?"

Another deep breath. "Owen was my softball coach the year of the shooting. He had a crush on me, and I thought he was cute, and after the shooting that was just . . . awkward. But this isn't about Owen. Or Chris. It's about Jesse, who has never been anything but nice to me. I feel like he's another victim, like Isaac and Harley took a good, brilliant kid and wrecked him."

"Jesse isn't wrecked. He's having problems, but he'll be okay."

"I didn't mean—Anyway, that's my apology. And it's not just empty words. I'm going to fix this. With the newspaper and with Mr. Vaughn. I'm going to prove you and Jesse didn't do anything."

"You don't need to—"

"I know the newspaper system better than anyone, and I have a few ideas. I'm going to work through them and let you know what I find."

Jesse

Jesse lies on his bed and stares at the empty walls. His shelves are almost as bare—he prefers to keep his belongings in drawers.

He remembers the first time he walked into Skye's old bedroom. It looked like the set of a teen movie. Every wall was papered with posters and dog-eared comic-book sketches. Every shelf crammed with books. Even the perimeter space on those shelves was lined with figurines and toys and shells and rocks and whatever else had caught her eye.

That's what it seemed like to him—that she'd just dumped all this stuff and forgotten it. Which wasn't the case at all. The comic-book sketches were Luka's, rescued from the trash when he wasn't looking. The toys had been childhood favorites. The shells and rocks came from vacations. The figurines were from her favorite TV shows and movies. Even the posters had significance, not just "an ATF poster" but one from a performance in Australia that she and friends had stayed up all night to watch live.

Skye's room said, "This is me." And he loved poking around

and asking about stuff. She had stories for everything, right down to a shell the size of her pinky nail.

While he envied her crazy room, he didn't try to emulate it. He liked to store his things away, neatly. But he declared he might hang a poster or two. Yes, he might do that.

He didn't, of course. Then came December, and Skye asked if they celebrated any holidays, and he said that, besides Eid, his parents recognized the secular side of Christmas, with Santa and gifts and a family meal. So on Christmas Eve, she gave him a present. Two posters. One from the first ATF album they'd listened to together and one from their favorite *Doctor Who* episode. He put them up that night.

Three days later, Jamil barged into his room to take his deodorant, saying, "Not like you need it yet anyway."

As Jamil was walking out, he spotted the posters. "What the hell are those?"

"All-Time Five and *Doctor Who*. Skye gave them to me."

"A boy band and a geek show? Tell me you just put them up to score points with her."

Jesse could have said yes. Ended the conversation there. But that wasn't true, so he said, "I put them up because I like them."

His brother's face screwed up in disgust. "You don't even try, do you? Just keep this door closed when I have friends over."

Jesse walks to his closet, opens it, reaches into the back corner and pulls out the posters.

They made him happy. He liked seeing them neatly displayed on his wall. He took time with that, measuring the distance from the room corners and using a level to get them just right. Then he lay in bed and admired his work and thought about Skye, and remembered listening to the album and watching the TV show, and her giving him the posters, and how she lit up when he was pleased.

He tugs off one rubber band, and he's just about to unroll the poster when his phone beeps. A polite beep. Quiet and unobtrusive, but he's been listening for it.

It's a text. Just one word: talk?

Jesse: here.

Silence. Silence. He checks his signal, but of course it's fine.

Skye: that sounds ominous.

Jesse rereads his text and realizes she misinterpreted the single word as terse. He forgot that about Skye. Her own communication is so expressive—her face, her gestures—that she flounders when she doesn't get that from others.

He remembers that as kids, even after they'd been hanging out for weeks, Skye was still wary, as if she expected him to stop talking to her at any moment. Finally, she gave in to her blunt side and said, "If you're not okay hanging out with me, just say so. You don't have to do it to be nice."

He asked what made her think that, and she said, "I can't tell with you, Jesse. You seem to like talking to me, but . . . I just can't tell." Which made him laugh, because he'd been worrying he was giving too much away, making a fool of himself.

Skye: Jesse?

He snaps out of his thoughts and sends: here. Then he curses under his breath, and quickly types: everything's fine. well, not fine, but ok. i think they're disappointed in me and—

Skye: if it's a bad time, just say so.

That's the problem with not using text-speak. It takes so long to type a message that the other person thinks you aren't answering.

He switches to video chat. It pings Skye, and when she picks up, at first all he sees is . . . well, boobs. She's holding the phone at chest height, and his screen fills with her T-shirt, stretched tight across—

"Whoops," she says, and then starts raising the camera. "Better?"

"Uh . . ." He starts to laugh, except it's more of a snicker, a completely embarrassing thirteen-year-old-boy snicker.

"Okay, bad choice of words," she says, laughing. "It'd be kinda weird if you said, 'Yes, the view of your neck is much better, Skye.'" The camera continues shifting until he has her face. "There. Perhaps not better, but more appropriate."

The camera moves again as she flips onto her back, holding the phone over her face. She's lying atop bedcovers, hair out of her ponytail, fanning around her face, and he's close enough to see her freckled nose and the birthmark just over her lips, those wide lips parted in the ghost of a smile, green eyes still dancing with her laugh.

He swallows and sits up, cross-legged on the bed. "So, as I was trying to text—very slowly, in full words, because *someone* is eighty and can't read text-talk—I spoke to my parents. It went . . . pretty much as one would expect. Confusion. Disbelief. Quickly disguised disappointment. More confusion."

"It'll be okay."

He has braced for her to offer some meaningless platitudes, tell him his parents *weren't* disappointed. Lie to him. Which only proves that he's still adjusting to having her back.

"Feel better now?" she says softly as she tucks stray hair behind her ear.

He smiles. "Yep. Ripped off the Band-Aid. Hurts like hell. Wish I'd done it long ago."

"And . . . exhale."

He chuckles. "Exactly." Which is true. That's how he felt. Like he could finally breathe again. "So how about you? Glad to get it all in the open with Mae?"

Dismay and regret flash, and then she blinks. "Oh, you mean telling her what's happening."

"Uh-huh. But that's not all you got in the open, apparently."

"Yeah. I . . . I tried not to. I went into it totally calm. But what I expected was hurt and confusion, like with your parents."

"What happened?"

"She didn't believe me."

"Huh?" He stretches on his stomach, phone in front of him. "Which part?"

"All of it."

"*What?*"

"She thinks I set the fire and made that video. I'm clearly in need of attention, having been neglected by my entire family, including her."

"Her?"

"She's had to work late. I've been traumatized."

He snorts. "More like relieved."

"Kind of what I said. Which was, yes, rude. Now I feel bad,

but if I go out there to explain, it'll start all over again. I'm calm now. I'd like to stay calm."

"Have you had dinner?"

"Not exactly my priority at the moment."

"Your growling stomach begs to differ."

She rolls out of sight. When she returns, she's opening a Hershey bar.

"That's not dinner," he says.

She smiles. "You sound like . . ." The smile falters, and she trails off, and Jesse remembers Luka giving her crap for not eating right.

"I'll bring you pizza," he says quickly.

"Is that any better than this?" She waves the bar.

"Sure. Meat, veggies, cheese, bread. All the food groups. I'll sneak it to you through the window."

"Did you forget I'm on the twelfth floor?"

"My parents got me a drone for my birthday. I could fly it up."

"I don't think it'll carry a whole pizza."

"Slice by slice."

He has her laughing now, and he closes his eyes, just to listen to the sound. When he opens them again, she's smiling at him, her expression softer, wistful.

"Missed you," she says.

"Missed you, too."

Her eyes glisten, as if she's going to cry, and he quickly says, "Can you sneak out?"

"What?"

"Sneak out and grab dinner with me. Put on music or something so Mae thinks you're in bed."

"Wow. That's downright devious."

"I've changed, remember? Just leave her a note, in case she figures it out, so she doesn't worry."

She smiles. "You haven't changed *that* much. Yes, of course, I'll leave a note. Can you get away?"

He nods. "I didn't storm off. I just retreated."

"Naturally."

"I'll see if I can get the car and text you in a few."

Jesse walks into the kitchen, where his mother is baking bread. That's what she does when she's stressed. For months after Jamil died, Jesse's dad would make daily food bank runs to donate fresh loaves. Now, when Jesse walks in, his dad is at the table, silently watching as she kneads.

He spots Jesse, nods and goes to leave the kitchen. Jesse motions for him to stay, but he shakes his head and squeezes Jesse's shoulder as he passes. It's only then, as his dad leaves, that his mom notices Jesse's there.

"Oh," she says.

"Hey, I—"

"I want to talk to you," she says, and wipes flour from her hands. "About the steroids."

He stiffens, and then he reminds himself that he's the one who wanted to come clean. That means he's going to have to talk about it.

"You said you took them for training," Mom says. "During the off-season."

"Yes, but if you're going to argue that that makes it okay—"

"Did you know what kind you were on?"

He tells her, and she wants to know the dose, and when he finishes explaining, she says, "That's a common one, and at that dose, it's hardly going to—"

"Mom . . ."

More towel wiping, though he doesn't see a speck of flour on her brown hands. "Steroids serve medical purposes, too, so I'm familiar with them. The one you were on is widespread among recreational weight lifters, and to them, it's not much different than protein shakes and egg whites."

"If it wasn't a problem, my trainer would have asked you to get them for me."

"Yes, but on a scale—"

"I don't want to judge this on a scale."

"Using them for training is very different from using them on the field. Even a drug test wouldn't have shown any trace. They'd be out of your system."

"Great. So if I announce that I used steroids for training, no one will care? The coach won't get in trouble? No one will demand I return my awards?"

She stops the hand wiping. "I'm not sure you'd want to go that far."

"Exactly. What I did was wrong. I knew it was wrong. I kept doing it." Jesse leans against the counter. "I made a mistake, and I'm going to ask you to let me own that mistake. I'm not going to publicly announce that I juiced—but only because it would cause problems for the team. I'm just going to quit, okay? But between you and me, we know what happened and that those trophies belong in the trash. Keep the ones I earned. My academic ones. I want to get back to earning more of them."

She throws her arms around him. "I'm so proud of you."

He sighs. "I know. Just . . . don't be afraid to let me stumble, okay, Mom? I appreciate the support, but these days I really need a kick in the butt more than a pat on the head. Anyway, I was coming in to say that I'm going to visit Skye. She's dealing with some stuff—"

"That's right. What happened at school?"

"Stuff."

"More specifically?"

He checks the microwave clock.

"You can spare two minutes to tell me what's going on, Jasser."

"She's being hassled, and she's being blamed for it."

"Blamed for *being* hassled?" His mother straightens to her full five foot two. "That is unacceptable. Even to suggest that someone is responsible for being bullied—"

"They don't think she *is* being bullied. They think she's making stuff up for attention."

"It's that VP, isn't it? Mr. Vaughn. I don't know what's happening in his personal life, but lately he seems to view his job as an inconvenience. I tried to talk to him about your attendance record, and he made excuses for you."

"Okay, but—"

"Accusing Skye of orchestrating a campaign of bullying against *herself* is preposterous. It's an excuse for the school not to dig deeper. I presume Mae is handling it."

"She's siding with Vaughn."

"*What?*"

"I don't know what's going on there. Maybe she's just confused. Skye's upset, though, and I want to get her out of the house for a while."

His mother nods. "Good idea. If you'd like me to talk to her aunt—"

"Mom? No."

"I just want—"

"You want to help. I know. If things reach that point, then sure. But for now, just let us handle it, okay? We'll ask for help if we need it."

When he checks the clock again, she says, "Go. Take my car. Just be home by eleven, please."

Skye

I hate sneaking off on Mae. It feels childish. It was different when I *was* a child and I snuck out as a lark. That was innocent stuff, only going as far as the corner store to get a candy bar. Those bars tasted of bravery. Today's escape tastes of cowardice.

Except it isn't cowardice as much as exhaustion. I'm too tired to fight with Mae. I'm hungry, and I want to flee this bitterly cold condo and hang out with a friend.

I start a playlist on my laptop, keeping it low enough that Mae won't think I'm trying to piss her off. Then I bunch up my comforter so if she glances inside, it'll seem like I've gone to sleep. Finally, I leave a note. *Gone for dinner with Jesse. Back by eleven.*

Escaping the condo isn't a problem. Mae's in her office with the door shut. When I'm in Jesse's car, I say, "Pizza?"

He turns a corner. "I was thinking since you found that option less than nutritionally sound, we should just abandon all pretense and eat . . ."

He points to a sign ahead, and I laugh.

"Yes?" he says.

"Please."

We're waiting in line at the Creamery.

"You're getting frozen yogurt, aren't you?" I say. "With fresh strawberries."

"Hell, no. I've changed, I eat *far* worse now."

"Uh-huh. So, strawberry *sauce* instead?"

"Ha-ha. Nope, I am getting a milkshake. With"—his hand sweeps the candy jars—"all of that."

"Uh-huh."

We get up to the counter. I place my order. It takes a moment for the clerk to stop gaping as Jesse snickers behind me. Then she says, "I, uh, don't think we can put gummy bears in a shake."

"The blender chops them up. It's fine. But I'll need a spoon." I turn to Jesse. "And he'll have . . ."

"A milkshake with . . ." He's looking up and down those candy jars, with an expression of mild panic, as if realizing his folly.

"May I?" I ask.

He exhales softly. "Sure."

I turn to the clerk. "He'll have a shake with frozen vanilla yogurt and peanuts. Oh, also chocolate-covered peanuts. And peanut butter."

When we head for a seat, he says, "Apparently, I really like peanuts."

"It's for protein."

"And I need protein because?"

"Because I saw you run."

He stiffens, just a little, and stops unwrapping his straw.

I continue. "I saw your face. You love running. It's the crap that came with it that you hate. I don't want to see you throw out the baby with the bathwater."

"I've never understood what that means."

"It's a stupid idiom but a fine sentiment. If you're cleaning up your life, get rid of the crap, not the good stuff. Quit the track team. Keep running. Maybe train for a half marathon. I could do it too, and then you'd be guaranteed to beat at least one person."

He laughs. Then he bumps his milkshake against mine, like a toast.

"Missed you," he says.

"I know."

He laughs again and leans over the table. "But if I keep running, you have to do something too."

"Cheer you on?"

"That goes without saying. But you also need to write me a story." He puts his straw in. "That's the deal. You can make it about me running."

"From a bear?"

"Only if I escape."

"You won't need to, I'll rescue you."

"Awesome."

"So, deal?"

"Deal."

We drink our shakes and talk. We don't discuss what's going on. We just talk. We've been there about an hour when I get a text.

Tiffany: I have something.

Tiffany: It's important.

Me: What is it?

Tiffany: Can't say. Need to show you.

Me: Out with Jesse. Swing by your place after?

Tiffany: Dad won't like that. He doesn't want me associating with . . . people connected to the shooting.

Me: Tomorrow?

Tiffany: It's urgent.

I check the number again. It's definitely Tiffany, but this sounds suspicious.

Me: Meet now?

Tiffany: Please.

Me: Fletcher Park?

Tiffany: Perfect!

I tell her we'll be there in twenty. Then I sign off. I show Jesse the thread. He reads it, and then looks at me.

"No," he says.

"I didn't say a word."

"You want to go to Fletcher Park. At dusk. Because if it is her, she has information we can use . . . and if it's not her, you can turn the tables on whoever *does* show up."

"Yep."

Jesse looks at me. One long, hard look. Then he waves for me to finish my shake so we can leave.

Skye

Despite the cosmetic changes at Fletcher Park, the layout remains the same. Playground next to the road and parking lot. Picnic pavilion behind it. Baseball diamond behind that. Beyond the bleachers is what used to be open field. Now it's under development, with a few partial homes. Machinery and turned-up soil mark land where we once played tag and hide-and-seek in the long grass.

I even had a fort out there once. The first time I brought Jesse, I showed him what remained of it, and he was very impressed by my construction skills. Typical Jesse—not "Wow, that's a cool fort," but "Wow, you built it properly." And I was so much more pleased with that.

My fort is long gone, and this afternoon, when we sat on the pavilion roof, I gazed into the field and felt what I suppose is nostalgia. Seems weird at my age, but that was what I felt, seeing the playground revamped and the field torn up.

As we get out of the car, I text Tiffany.

Me: We're here.

Tiffany: On my way!

"I'm sure you are," Jesse mutters as he peers around the playground. Dusk has settled hard, and the park grounds are more shadow than light. He looks at my phone and opens his mouth. Then he shuts it.

He isn't happy about this. On the drive, I phoned Tiffany to check whether she sent those texts. She didn't answer.

We climb onto the playground equipment, giving us a good place to see from and *be* seen from. Then we wait.

Jesse spots the figure first. He nudges me and discreetly gestures toward the pavilion. Someone's standing half hidden in shadows. Someone who is too tall to be Tiffany.

The figure pulls back around the building.

I text Tiffany.

Me: You here?

Her: Not yet! Give me 5!

Uh-huh.

Jesse reads the texts. Then he says, "Can you scroll up?"

"That's all she sent tonight. Well, except for this." I move to our brief conversation earlier in the evening. He reads it and frowns.

"Problem?" I say.

"She uses full words. Like you."

I shrug. "A writer thing, I guess."

"Yes, but—"

A phone sounds. Just the first notes of a ring tone, cut short. We both look up fast. The figure beside the pavilion has his head down, hands in front, as if silencing that ring.

The figure looks up . . . and sees us looking straight at him. He takes a slow step back. I slide down the climber, my feet hitting the recycled rubber with a squeak.

"Skye!" Jesse whispers.

The figure takes off. I go after him.

I hear that rubber squeak again as Jesse jumps down, and then the pound of his footsteps as he calls, "Skye! Get back here!"

I know I'm doing something reckless, but I need to see this person. It might be the only chance to clear my name. Just one glimpse of a face, and I'll know who's behind this.

As I run, I see every dirty look I've gotten in the past three years. I hear every whisper behind my back. I reread every online comment. Everyone who thinks I did *something.* That I knew something. That I failed to stop my brother. That I'm cursed with the same taint, and what's happening now is just proof I have a few screws loose, like Luka and my mother, and that my father was right to abandon us, to get as far as he could from his messed-up family.

As I pass the pavilion, I fumble to get my phone out. I can see the figure ahead as he tears toward the housing development. I just need to get close enough to startle him. Make him turn, and when he does, I'll have my phone ready for a photo.

I glance back. Jesse got a late start, and I'm running full out, but it's not enough. Jesse's gaining.

Just a few more seconds. I'm gaining on my target too, close enough now to be positive it's a guy. He's dressed in black, which makes it increasingly hard to follow him as the streetlights fade behind us.

I can't shake Jesse. His specialties are sprints and hurdles, and he's in his element here, running fast and leaping over debris.

I race around a stack of building lumber. Behind me, I hear a grunt of pain, as if Jesse jumped and landed wrong. I resist the urge to slow.

The guy swings behind a half-constructed house. I'm about ten paces behind. I turn to follow and—

My target is gone.

"Skye!"

Jesse's voice trails off in a hiss of pain. I don't hear his footsteps. I haven't heard them since that grunt when he misjudged the pile.

"Skye!" The thump of a step then. A slow thump, followed by a drag. He's hurt.

I look around. My target has vanished. I've lost him.

"Skye, please!"

I turn toward Jesse. A hand grabs my jacket. I try to clasp his wrist, but he's behind me, out of reach.

"Skye?" Jesse shouts.

A hand claps over my mouth. Jesse's footfalls are moving faster now, but he's heading the other way. He's heard or seen something that sends him in the wrong direction.

I try to bite the hand over my mouth, but I can't get a grip. My captor adjusts and locks his arm over my throat instead. His forearm pushes against my windpipe. I can't breathe, and I fight harder, trying to kick, punch, no longer caring about getting a proper hold.

I smell something chemical. Metallic.

The guy reaches around me, holding a cloth soaked with that chemical stink.

I grab him by the wrist. He's wearing a jacket and gloves, but I clamp down as tight as I can, and then try swinging him into a hold. It's not perfect, and that sleeve is nylon, slipping under my fingers. He drops the cloth, though. Drops his arm off my throat, too. That gives me room to move, yanking his arm—

There's something in his other hand. The reason he let go of my throat. To take a knife from his belt. A blade slices toward my arm.

I don't let go. I can't let go. If I do, I'm lost.

I see that blade coming, and I grit my teeth and keep twisting his arm, keep trying to throw him. The blade slashes through my jacket. Slashes through skin and into flesh.

I barely feel it. Everything is focused on what I'm doing.

This attack is no prank. No game. If I let go, he'll put that stinking cloth over my mouth and nose, and I have no idea what will happen then.

I'm still holding his arm, but there's blood, and then there's pain, and my muscles will not do what I need them to do. I can't throw him. I can't get the leverage, and there's blood on his nylon jacket, and my hands slide.

He backhands me across the face. I reel. He shoves me. I see him coming. I see his face for the first time.

And there's no face to see. He's wearing a balaclava: a tight black hood over his head, with only holes for eyes and mouth. He's moving so fast I can't even see the color of his eyes. All this, and I get nothing.

He shoves me, and I come back swinging, but I'm already falling.

I keep falling, and when I finally hit the ground, the crash is hard enough to knock the air from my lungs. I lie there, struggling to breathe.

Then I look up. Way up. To see the guy standing at least eight feet overhead, on the edge of a hole.

"Skye!"

It's Jesse. He's heard the thud of me falling, and he's running this way. My attacker hesitates for a split second. Then he takes off.

Skye

Jesse's still calling. He's heard me fall but can't pinpoint the noise, and he's frantically shouting, his voice moving deeper into the subdivision.

I stay silent, as terrible as I feel about it. If I yell, Jesse might run right into my armed attacker. So I wait until I'm sure my attacker is far enough away. Then I rise and say, "Jesse?"

He comes running. As he does, I realize I've fallen into the basement of a partly constructed home. I'm trying to find a way out—with one hand gripping my bleeding arm—when Jesse appears.

He scrambles down before I can stop him. He jogs to me, limping slightly.

"I screwed up," I say. "I—I just wanted to see him, to end this, to get proof—"

My voice cracks, and Jesse's there, and I collapse against him, still apologizing, as the shock passes and I realize exactly how much danger I've been in—how much danger I ran *straight into.*

When tears well, I pull away, apologizing harder, but he hugs me and says, "It's okay," and rubs my back.

I get it under control, and I'm about to straighten when he tenses and says, "Do I smell blood?"

His gaze shoots to my arm. "You're—Oh, hell. Sit. Just sit." He doesn't give me a chance to obey as he propels me to the dirt floor and strips off my jacket.

"You're cut, Skye. You're really badly cut."

"He had a knife. I—I—I was stupid. I never thought—I didn't expect—"

I swallow. "He had a cloth, too, that smelled like chemicals. He tried to put it over my face. I—I don't know what he planned to do. I don't want to know."

"Neither do I," he says grimly as he clamps a hand over my bleeding arm. "But you're not the only one who didn't expect anything like that. I'd never have brought us here if I did."

He wraps my jacket sleeves around my arm, and then tugs off his belt and fastens it over the top. It's a bulky, awkward tourniquet, and he gives a grunt of dissatisfaction but only says, "Let's get out of here before he comes back."

Getting me out of that basement isn't easy when I have only one working arm. There's no helpful set of stairs leading up. Construction hasn't proceeded that far. After several failed attempts, I'm finally able to get onto Jesse's shoulders and climb out. Then I use my good arm to help him scrabble up the dirt side.

Jesse's limping less now, and I ask about his foot, but he says he just twisted it. Enough to slow him down, nothing serious.

We go quiet after that, lost in thought as we walk through the housing construction site.

When we reach the pavilion, he says, "I'm taking you to my mom. For your arm and to talk. I told her I wanted to try handling this on our own, but we've gone way past that."

"Agreed." I check the time on my phone and notice I have texts. I was vaguely aware of my phone vibrating earlier, but I was a little occupied at the time.

When I see that I've missed six texts, I cringe. "Mae must have found—" I stop as I open my messages. They aren't from Mae. The string starts twenty minutes ago, around the time I was battling my attacker.

Tiffany: Okay, I'm here. Sorry I'm late.

Two minutes passed.

Tiffany: Skye? You still around? I don't see you.

Another two minutes.

Tiffany: There's a BMW in the lot. Is that yours?

Tiffany: I see a parking pass for the hospital staff lot. Jesse's mom's car?

Tiffany: I'd make an awesome detective, huh?

Tiffany: Speaking of detective work, is that you guys in the field? I think I hear Jesse calling for you. Heading that way.

I'm scrolling and reading faster, whispering, "No, no, no."

"Call her," Jesse says.

I punch in the numbers. The line connects . . . and we hear a phone start to ring not far from us.

We both run toward the sound, Jesse hobbling but keeping pace. The phone stops, and voice mail comes on. I hang up fast. Dial again. The other phone rings as we walk, the sound getting louder and louder until . . .

The ringing is coming from the ground at my feet.

I bend to find Tiffany's phone in the grass.

We're in the car, and Jesse's driving faster than I suspect he's ever driven in his life. We haven't called the police. That was, of course, my first impulse. Jesse stopped me. We need to be sure Tiffany's gone. Otherwise, I could report her kidnapping . . . and discover that she's at home, and someone stole her phone and sent those texts.

I get Tiffany's home number from directory assistance. I don't know her family—only that she lives with her dad and stepmom and a couple of half siblings. I call their landline. No one answers. I leave a message saying I'm a classmate, and we were supposed to meet for a project, but she hasn't shown up, so I'm worried.

I email her next. As I do, Jesse's fingers drum the steering wheel. When I finish, he says, "We'll be at my place in two minutes. I think we should have my parents call 911. The police will listen to them."

"Agreed."

"I can't imagine why he'd take her hostage, but I also can't imagine why he'd stab you."

"I don't think we're dealing with a rational person here. Do you think he actually abducted her?"

He says nothing.

"The texts," I say. "That's what you meant earlier. I was so sure they didn't come from Tiffany, but they *sounded* like they did. That's what you were thinking, before I ran after him."

I look at him. "So if it really was Tiffany texting, how did he end up at our meeting place?"

"Either he's been following you or he has access to your texts somehow."

Jesse slows for a stop sign and a right turn. I glance toward his house.

"I don't think anyone needs to call the police," I say.

"Hmm?"

He looks over to see two cruisers parked in front of his house.

Skye

As Jesse pulls into the drive, I spot officers through the front windows, talking to his mother.

Are there police at Mae's condo, too? I check my phone, but I don't have any messages from her.

I should quickly call 911. Report Tiffany's disappearance before we walk into the house. But it's too late.

Now we know why my attacker took Tiffany: so he can frame us for her disappearance.

We have to face this. Prove that we've been framed. And, more importantly right now, convince the police that Tiffany really is in danger.

We take a few seconds to clean up in the car. On the way, I rebound my arm, using the first-aid kit. If I walk in there covered in blood, we're liable to be hauled off to jail before we get a chance to explain. So I leave my bloodied jacket, and Jesse lends me his hoodie.

We're walking up the front steps when the door opens. It's

Dr. Mandal, saying, "It's okay. We're sorting this out. Just come in and sit down."

"Skye's been—" Jesse begins, but one of the officers shoulders past his mom and says, "Jasser Mandal? We have a few questions for you."

"Sure," Jesse says. "We have to talk to you, too. First, I just need my mom to—"

"Your mother is right here, son. We aren't questioning you without her present."

"Okay, but I need her to—"

"I have to search you. Please turn around and put your hands against the wall."

Jesse glances at his mother.

"Go ahead," she says, her voice brittle. "They have a warrant. And since I'm quite certain the grounds for it are baseless"—she shoots a glare at the officer—"it's best to just comply and get it over with."

"Mom, Skye's—"

"Son . . ." The officer puts a hand on Jesse's shoulder, and Jesse tenses, as if to throw it off, but I give him a look and shake my head. My arm is fine for now.

The officer searches Jesse. He takes his phone, pats him down and finds nothing. Then he tells Jesse to go upstairs with another officer and remove his clothing, which will be taken for further examination.

When his mother protests, Jesse says, "It's fine, Mom. I haven't done anything."

"I know. I just—" Another glare for the officer. Then to Jesse, "Go on. Skye and I will be right down here."

They're heading to the stairs, and I'm about to tell Dr. Mandal about my arm when an officer from the upper level says he's found something. The officer prods Jesse up the stairs, and Dr. Mandal follows. I go after her. On the stairs, I whisper, "Whatever it is, someone planted it."

"That's what I'm worried about," she says grimly.

When we get upstairs, I see Jesse's dad arguing with the officers searching Jesse's room.

"It's a penknife," Mr. Mandal is saying. "He's a sixteen-year-old boy, and he had it in his dresser drawer."

"Take it," Jesse says. "It's too small to hurt anyone, but go ahead and analyze it."

"We aren't looking for evidence that you've hurt someone," the officer who brought him upstairs says. "We're looking for evidence that you plan to. And with something much more lethal than that knife." He turns to another officer. "Bag it and have it analyzed for chemicals."

"Chemicals?" Jesse turns to his parents. "What's this about?"

"They received a so-called credible tip that you have bomb-making material in your room."

Jesse gives a choked laugh. "Bomb-making material?"

"I bet it's those idiots," I say. "The seniors who attacked you Saturday. This is their revenge." I look at the officers. "We can provide names. They were giving Jesse—Jasser—a hard time, talking crap about the North Hampton shooting."

"North Hampton . . ." One of the younger officers straightens from where he's been searching under Jesse's bed. He looks at Jesse's parents. "Mandal. You're . . ."

"Yes," one of the older officers says. "And while we offer our deepest condolences for that, it has no bearing on what we're investigating here."

"It might not be those guys," Jesse says. "There's something else. The reason we thought you were here. Skye and I—"

"Son? I really need you to take off your clothing. Now."

"But we have to report—"

"Clothing, off. Miss? I think it's time for you to go home. You'll need to provide your name, in case we have cause to question you."

"It's Gilchrist," I say. "Skye Gilchrist. I'm Luka Gilchrist's sister."

That gets their attention, as I hoped it would. But it doesn't mean they're going to let me explain about Tiffany. They just want me to go downstairs and stay there.

Before we leave, Jesse taps his upper arm. I mouth "I will," and follow Dr. Mandal down the stairs.

We're in the kitchen, and I say, "Jasser and I ran into a problem tonight. When we saw the police were here, we thought that's what it was for."

"Skye . . . ?" she interrupts, and I follow her gaze to my arm, where blood has seeped through Jesse's hoodie.

"Yes," I say. "That's part of the problem, but the more important part—"

"Get that sweater off. Now. I'll decide which part is more important."

I try telling her about Tiffany as I pull off the hoodie. I get as far as explaining who Tiffany is and that she'd been trying to help and she'd contacted us and . . .

And that's when Dr. Mandal unwraps the bandages, and once she sees my arm . . . Well, she's not listening to anything I have to say after that.

I've been trying to pretend it's just a little cut on my arm. It's not. It's a deep slice through muscle, and it needs attention—immediately. She wants to take me to the hospital, but by then, Jesse's downstairs, and he brings a bigger first-aid kit, which contains suture tape.

We convince Dr. Mandal to fix me up here. The longer we wait to explain about Tiffany, the worse this is going to get. We try telling her again, but it's pointless. His mother is focused on my arm and keeps telling us to wait, just wait. The police are upstairs, and it's clear they aren't interested in listening either.

Finally, Dr. Mandal starts working on my arm, and we resume explaining. She's halfway done when we reach the part about Tiffany's phone. That stops her.

"You found her *phone?*" she says. "Where was *she?*"

"That's what we've been trying to explain," Jesse says. "Tiffany *was* there. Or we think she was—we tried checking with her family to make sure the phone wasn't planted. Then we saw the police cars here, and we thought we were being set up for kidnapping Tiffany."

His mother mouths an oath. Then she looks down at my arm. "Get your father," she says to Jesse. "Quickly."

Skye

It does not go well after that. We tell Mr. Mandal, who tells the police, and it seems to take forever to get their attention, to the point where Mr. Mandal is threatening to just call 911 and report Tiffany's disappearance, because apparently he can't report it to the four officers currently in his house.

When the officers do listen, they seem to decide this is some lame story Jesse and I concocted to distract them from their search. Eventually, they realize we're serious. And it's all downhill from there.

The officer in charge accuses Jesse and me of failing to report a serious crime. Jesse's mom accuses the officers of failing to listen when we tried to report it. By that point, one of the officers has called it in, and soon there's a car at Tiffany's place, and her dad confirms that she went out earlier. Went out and didn't return.

The officers then decide that our failure to report it is extremely suspicious. As for the fact that we *did* report it, well, that's only because we panicked when we found police in Jesse's house. We obviously decided the best way to divert attention from ourselves was to be the ones to report the crime.

We're taken to the station. There's no getting around that. Jesse's parents come, and Mae gets called, and that only makes things worse because she never realized I wasn't home.

Jesse and I are questioned separately, with our guardians. We explain everything. Mr. Vaughn is called, and Mae and I sit in that room for what seems like an hour before the detective returns. He's had a long conversation with the VP and now believes this is yet another escalation in my fake persecution.

I don't know what the police think we've done with Tiffany. They seem to be leaving their options open. Their questioning suggests we may have kidnapped her and are holding her hostage somewhere. Or worse—that she summoned us to confront me with proof of my complicity, and in the ensuing argument, something terrible happened. There is a third possibility, though, and that's the one they seem to like the best. That Tiffany is part of this. That the three of us faked the whole thing, and she's hiding somewhere while we report her disappearance.

Mae has been restrained so far. Listening. Saying little. Not looking my way. The weight of her silence feels like abandonment, as if she's already put child services on speed dial.

When the detective raises the possibility that Tiffany is involved, Mae says, "And the logic of that?"

"Pardon me?"

"Why would Skye and Jesse collude with Tiffany to fake her disappearance?"

The detective looks at Mae as if she's been asleep for the last hour. "For the same reason the school believes your niece is responsible for all this. To get attention."

"To what end?" she says, still carefully, like she's not challenging him but simply reasoning it through for herself.

"Attention is an end in itself."

"Maybe with the smaller things Skye has been accused of. Claiming there's a petition to have her expelled. Claiming someone has been leaving notes in her locker. Even claiming she was trapped in the VP's office after detention. Skye didn't want to come back to Riverside. I failed to understand—"

She swallows and straightens, her hands folded on the table. "I failed to understand how difficult it would be for her. Is it possible someone in her position would exaggerate persecution to get out of such a distressing situation? Yes. But to do that, she would have needed to *tell* me what's happening to her. She didn't. And simple attention-seeking makes no sense on this scale. We're talking *kidnapping.*"

"We aren't yet convinced there's been a kidnapping."

"There has," I cut in. "And the longer you ignore it, the more danger—"

"I'm sure that's what you'd like us to believe," the detective says.

Before I can respond, Mae says, "Back to my original question, even if you believe my niece did this for attention, that doesn't explain why Jesse and Tiffany would get involved."

"I'm told Jasser Mandal was friends with your niece before the North Hampton incident. Skye is an attractive young woman, and I'm sure it would be possible for her to renew that *friendship.*"

I gape at him. "You're saying I—?"

"As for Tiffany Gold, she would be involved in it for the same reason as your niece." He reaches into a folder by his elbow and takes out a sheaf of pages. They're the ones someone put in my locker. The ones about the shooting.

I keep my mouth shut, in case he's come by them some other way, but he sets them in front of Mae and says, "These were found in your niece's locker."

"Your warrant didn't cover that," Mae says.

"Lockers are school property and may be searched at any time. Mr. Vaughn did so earlier today, after suspending your niece. When we contacted him on this matter, he brought these over."

"What are they?" Mae asks.

I start to answer, but the detective begins going through the stack, explaining. I see articles and typed notes and—

"Hey, is that the police report?" I say.

He slaps the folder shut and looks at Mae. "Your niece has been investigating the incident at North Hampton. Trying to clear her brother's name."

"What?" she says.

"No," I say. "Those pages were put into my locker. They're part of this whole thing."

"This conspiracy," the detective says. "Against you."

I look him in the eye. "I have never used that word. It's not a conspiracy. It's an escalation of bullying."

"So you're telling me that the person who is blaming you for these incidents is the same one who's trying to say your brother *didn't* collude with Harley Stewart and Isaac Wickham?"

"Maybe my persecutor wanted me to start claiming Luka was innocent. Turn people against me that way. But I knew better than to even read that stuff."

"You're telling me you haven't read any of this?" He taps the folder.

"I didn't dare," I say. "Claiming that my brother wasn't guilty only raises hopes I can't afford to have. Of course I don't want him to be guilty, but I know he was."

"He was," the detective says, and his voice softens, just a little. "I do understand how hard that is to hear. But Luka had a gun. Multiple witnesses saw him holding it. He was *fully* involved. We had a very credible source who verified that."

"Harley," I say.

"The terms of Harley Stewart's plea bargain do not allow me to discuss his statement, but Luka was not an idle bystander who happened to find a gun."

"I know that," I say, my voice low. "The shooters were his friends. Luka had a gun. Therefore, Luka was involved." I point at the folder. "I don't know what's in there, but my only guess is that someone wanted me proclaiming Luka's innocence to discredit me. To turn others against me. But you can analyze that for fingerprints. I unfolded the pages, saw what they were, shoved them into my locker and left them there. The only reason I didn't throw them out was because I was afraid if someone found me with them, I'd get blamed, just like I am now."

I look at him. "I didn't do any of this. But if you think I did, then I'm okay with that, because it means you'll investigate, which is more than Mr. Vaughn cared to do. Whatever you decide, though, please look for Tiffany. She's in danger." I put my hand over the bandage on my arm. "She's definitely in danger."

Skye

We find Jesse's parents in the hall. Dr. Mandal hugs me and says Jesse is just in the restroom, and he'll want to see me before we leave. Then she turns to Mae.

"I trust this has convinced you that your niece isn't orchestrating her own persecution?" she says.

Mae's gaze shoots my way, giving me a guilty look.

Dr. Mandal says, "No, Skye would never complain to me about you. She talked to Jasser, who relayed it to me when I made the mistake of presuming you were supporting your niece."

"I was confused. I spoke without thinking—"

"There's nothing to *think*. It's about trusting your niece enough to hear her out and then make a decision." Before Mae can respond, Dr. Mandal turns to me. "I'd like you to come by the hospital tomorrow morning so I can check your arm. Jasser will bring you. I won't expect him to go to school under the circumstances."

"I can bring her," Mae says.

"Jasser will."

"No, really, I—"

Dr. Mandal cuts her off with a slow, appraising look. "Do you have a problem with my son?"

Mae flushes. "No, of course not."

"Good. Then he'll bring Skye. I'll leave my car with the pass for him. Jasser?" she says as he approaches. "You'll bring Skye to the hospital in the morning."

"Sure."

"You two can make arrangements. We'll head on outside. Ms. Benassi? I'd like to speak to you."

I can tell Mae really doesn't want to hear anything more from Dr. Mandal, but she nods and follows them as I say goodbye to Jesse.

We're almost to the condo before Mae speaks.

"I'm taking some time off work," she says. "You're right—I've been neglecting you."

"I never said—"

"If I'm going to be your guardian, I have to act like it. You need me right now. So I'm staying home."

"I'd rather you didn't." I chose my words with care, but she still flinches.

I try again. "I don't need you to stay with me." *The time for that was back when Gran had her stroke.* "We can do something this weekend, if you'd like, but I'd really rather not interfere with your schedule."

"You aren't—"

"Just go to work, okay? Please."

○○○

I spend my night fixated on that folder from the police station. I see the flash of the report on the shooting. Then I see the detective quickly closing the folder. I remember his expression when I said I hadn't read the pages. It looked like relief.

What's in those pages? I had them for days and never even realized it, and that's good because my fingerprints aren't all over it, but I wish I'd looked. I desperately wished I'd looked.

I've always trusted the official investigation in the shooting. The police had no reason to cover up anything. If nobody questioned the findings, then their conclusions must be correct.

But someone *did* question. Someone sent me those pages.

Yes . . . someone hoping I'd wave it around as proof of my brother's innocence, further damning myself in the process.

My persecutor didn't send me those pages to be helpful.

They are lies. Falsified reports. That's why the detective slapped the folder shut. The last thing the police need is a dead boy's sister claiming she saw a police report proving his innocence . . . leaving the department scrambling to prove it was doctored.

I still wish I'd looked.

Really? Do I want to see doctored police files? Plant false doubt in my head?

Too late. It's already planted.

Even when I finally fall asleep, my brain stays fixed on the file. On everything that could be in it.

In my dreams, I read that there was no gun in Luka's hand. He lifted his hands while holding his cell phone to call and tell me he was okay, and the police mistook it for a gun and shot him.

I wake from that dream, and I know it's not true. Luka had a gun. No one has ever disputed that.

Then I fall asleep again and dream that he *did* have a gun. That he shot kids. That he killed Jamil. That he was the worst of the shooters, and afterward, there was confusion, an error in the lab mistakenly showing that the bullets came from Isaac's gun.

I wake, and I know that's not true either. Again, there were witnesses who saw Isaac shoot Jamil and others.

When morning comes, I know there's only one way to put my mind at ease. Learn *all* the details of the shooting. Understand exactly what happened, as best it can ever be understood.

Jesse drives me to the hospital the next morning. His mom cleans and redresses my arm. It's fine so far, and while I can feel it, the pain isn't enough for medication or a sling. Soon we're on our way again.

There's been no news about Tiffany. I searched online for that as soon as I woke up. Dr. Mandal has called the police to check, and they insist they're investigating. A missing person bulletin will go out after she's been gone for twenty-four hours. Until then, they have no proof of abduction, and she turned eighteen last month.

"I'm debating whether to hack into Tiffany's email account," Jesse says as he pulls out of the hospital parking lot. "It might show what she wanted to tell us."

"But if that can be traced back to you, it won't look good."

"I know. I've hit a dead end otherwise on the hacking stuff. I zeroed in on the birthday part of Leanna's video, thinking it suggested your stalker is connected to her and has access to family footage. But no—that clip is online as part of a memorial video. I watched the bits side by side. It's an exact copy."

"So someone downloaded the memorial video and took that part."

He nods. "But on that note, one thing we haven't had a chance to follow up on is the AV tech. We should speak to Chris today."

"Text and see if he can meet you for lunch. I'll be at the main library. There's something I want to research."

"I'd rather we didn't split up, Skye. That seems to be asking for trouble."

When I hesitate, he says, "What are you researching?"

I hesitate again.

He glances over as he idles at a stoplight. "Is it about the shooting?"

"They found part of the police report in my locker. Someone put it in there, saying I needed to look closer at the case. I didn't read them. I'd gotten notes that seemed to suggest I knew more about the shooting, so I thought it was more of that. I still think it's just a variation on it—my persecutor hoping I'll start claiming Luka was innocent."

"And you don't want me helping because of Tuesday night at NHH. How I reacted to that projection of Jamil."

I shake my head. "No, I didn't want to tell you I was researching it because it looks like I'm hoping to clear Luka."

"I know you better than that, Skye," he says. "And thank you for *not* leaving me out to spare my feelings about Jamil. I . . ." He turns his gaze to the road. "I get a lot of that. It makes me feel like an imposter. Almost as much as the steroids did."

"I know."

"There were so many times I wished he was—" He inhales. "Not dead. I used to dream he'd get a sports scholarship to a boarding school. But not dead. Never dead." His fingers clutch the wheel. "I have nightmares of that, though, of him coming back and saying I wanted him—" He stops short.

"I have nightmares of Luka. That he's home, and everything's okay. Which aren't nightmares until I wake up and remember the truth."

He reaches and finds my hand, giving it a squeeze before taking the wheel again.

"I do mourn Jamil," he says. "In my way. I feel bad that he never got to grow up. I remember Dad saying he hated his brothers when he was a kid. They were always picking on him. Once they grew up, that changed, and they're really close now. I think that's what I miss most—that I never got the chance to find out if it would be like that with Jamil."

"What he did was more than just picking on you, Jesse."

"I know. And I think, if he lived, once we were both grown up, I'd have told him what a jerk he'd been to me. How he'd made me feel. But I won't get that chance now. It just . . . ended. He's gone, and there's nothing more. There can't ever be anything more."

Skye

Jesse and I have an early lunch, and then spend all afternoon working in a quiet corner of the central library. We supplement what we already know with what we learn at the library, both from digitized newspapers and computer searches.

No one knew how the shooting was *supposed* to start. In the aftermath, Harley could say only that Isaac made the plan, and they were to follow his lead. As for motive? "Make people pay," according to Isaac. That's all Harley needed.

Whatever the plan, it went awry from the beginning. The police received an anonymous call reporting a kid with a gun at North Hampton. The call came from a cell phone that had been taken from a girl's backpack and dumped into the school trash, no fingerprints left.

Harley said he'd been the one who called it in. That he had second thoughts about Isaac's plan and reported it, but then he'd been forced to join Isaac in the shooting or Isaac would shoot *him*.

When the call came, the police had a car nearby and got there within minutes. The school went into lockdown, but Riverside had never experienced such a thing. It was chaos—kids running to classrooms, kids running *from* classrooms. Then police saw Luka coming out of the bathroom with a gun. One shouted for Luka to drop it. Instead, he raised it. That's when the officer shot him.

The officers moved in to disarm my brother as he lay on the floor, dying.

That's not what my mother told me. She said he died instantly. That he never knew what happened. The police saw him with a gun and fired, and he was dead before he hit the floor.

He wasn't.

I don't need to know this. I really do not need that image in my head. Now it's there, and it always will be. This is the price I pay for choosing to dig deeper.

Could Luka have been saved if the ambulance had arrived faster? That's another question that will haunt me, because nothing in these reports answers it. What happened next meant there was no way for the paramedics to get into the school quickly, no chance for the officers to administer first aid.

What happened next.

When Luka fell, the officers must have presumed they had their perpetrator. The report said there was a gun. Here was a boy holding a gun. Situation averted.

But there were kids in the hall when it happened. Kids running for their classrooms. One heard the shot, saw Luka on the ground and freaked out, shouting that someone had shot Luka Gilchrist. The mayhem of the lockdown became panic. Teachers lost control of the situation.

That's when Isaac acted. He took advantage of the tumult, and

Isaac and Harley pulled the guns from their backpacks and began shooting.

Four dead.

Ten injured.

Then Harley got shot in the shoulder and went down. Isaac ran, escaping in the chaos of kids fleeing the scene.

Two days later, a dog walker found Isaac's body. He'd shot himself in the temple shortly after the shooting. No suicide note. No explanation. There could never be an explanation.

Any answers had been lost with Luka's death and Isaac's suicide. Harley pled guilty and went to prison. He may have tried to avert the crisis with that phone call, but it didn't excuse the fact that he'd killed one person and injured three others.

After we finish our research, I curl up on an armchair, legs under me, staring into space, lost in thought.

When Jesse says, "I've never really thought this through before, but why was Luka in the bathroom with a gun?" I pull from my thoughts, a little annoyed with the interruption and maybe snapping a bit when I say, "What?"

"The school is on lockdown. Luka walks out of the bathroom holding a gun. Why?"

"How should I know?" Now I'm definitely snapping, but I can't help it, annoyance and frustration sparking.

"I don't know why he did any of it," I say. "I'm not even sure I knew *him*."

"You did. We both did. And it makes no sense for Luka—"

"Just don't, okay?"

After a few minutes, Jesse says, "What the papers said about Jamil. That's not true."

Jesse's quiet tone is enough to make me soften mine as I say, "Hmm?"

"The papers say he saved a kid. Shoved her out of the bullet's path. It's not true." Jesse sits back, one knee drawn up. "There was this guy who saw it. He didn't like Jamil much. Hated seeing him portrayed as some kind of hero and felt the need to tell me otherwise."

"Asshole."

Jesse shrugs. "Yeah, I thought the same thing. Why bother, right? But he had to set the record straight. He said Jamil and the girl were both running for a doorway. Jamil shouldered his way through first. That's when Isaac shot him in the back. I could have told myself this kid was just trying to cause trouble because he didn't like Jamil. But I had to know. So I asked the girl. She said it didn't matter how it happened—Jamil still saved her. Which I guess answered my question. I thought that proved what a selfish jerk he was. Then I saw his face, in that projection. He was so scared. I don't think he meant to shoulder her aside. He just wanted to get out of the hall. I'm not sure I wouldn't have done the same."

I stand and motion for him to shift over in the armchair. It's wide, but not wide enough for two. I still squeeze in beside him, partly on his lap.

"I'm sorry," I say.

Jesse puts his arm around my shoulders. I lean against him.

"I still have the tickets," he says. "For All-Time Five."

"Jesse Mandal, are you asking me to go to the concert with you?"

He finds a weak smile. "I don't think they'd take those tickets. And, confession? I'm a little over ATF."

"Ditto." I lie against him for a minute, listening to his breathing, and then say, "I still have the bear you won for me at the fair."

He pauses. "Bear? I thought it was a dog."

"I went with bear. It didn't complain."

"Either way, it was ugly. I think I spent twenty bucks winning it, when I could have bought it at the dollar store."

"Nah. They have better ones at the dollar store."

He laughs. "You actually kept it?"

"I felt obligated. You worked so hard to win it."

"Thanks."

"I'm kidding. You know why I kept it? 'Cause I really kinda liked the boy who won it for me."

He goes silent, and my heart's pounding, waiting for him to say something, anything. Finally, his voice low, he says, "And if that boy doesn't exist anymore?"

"He does. All the parts that matter, anyway."

I twist to look at him, and I move forward, just a fraction, testing whether he'll pull away, turn aside, flash a subtle stop sign.

Jesse shifts forward, but no more than I did, just closing the gap a little.

He grins and says, "I dare you," and I can't resist that, obviously, so I press my lips to his and—

"Oh!" a voice says behind us, and we jump apart, me scrambling off his lap like we'd been caught doing a whole lot more than kissing.

"Sorry," I say. "We were just—"

"I could see what you were doing." It's not a librarian, but one of the elderly volunteers. She's smiling and shaking her head.

"Sorry," Jesse says. "We really have been working."

"I see that, too." She nods at the terminal, the last article still displayed. Her gaze moves to my pages of notes, and she takes a closer look at the terminal. "Is one of the high schools doing a project on the shooting?"

"Project?" I say.

"You're the second student digging through those recently. I suppose a teacher has decided it's been long enough to assign it as a research project, but I'm not sure I'd agree. There are still children at school who were affected by it."

I nod, expressionless. "I know. It did seem weird that it was on the list of topics. I'm surprised anyone else dug this deep. We thought we'd ace the assignment if we came here. Seems we have competition."

I glance at Jesse. "I bet it was Brittany."

"No, sorry," the volunteer says. "I haven't been volunteering here long, and I don't know as many students as I'd like, but this particular boy goes to my church. I was surprised to see him printing out those files last week. I should have known it was for a project. He's not likely to go looking otherwise. His family was one of the ones affected. His cousin was killed."

My heart starts thumping. I say, "It wasn't Tim Locklear, was it?"

I'm hoping she'll say yes, that's exactly who it was, but I know better. I just do.

"No," she says. "It was Chris Landry."

Jesse

Skye looks like she's going to be sick. She's had that same look on her face for the past ten minutes. After the volunteer left, Skye took the chair beside him, pulled up her knees and disappeared into her thoughts.

"He told me I should investigate," she says finally.

When Jesse turns to look at her, she says, "Chris was there when I got the pages. The ones the police found in my locker. He asked me about them, and I told him, and he said maybe there was something to it and I should investigate. He practically *told* me he was the one who left them, and I still never suspected him."

Jesse could point out that Chris's suggesting she follow up hardly proved he'd left the pages. She doesn't want to hear that, though. Doesn't want to hear anything right now. She's just thinking out loud.

As he watches her, he remembers the kiss. He shouldn't, not at a time like this. But it would be weird, too, if he finally kissed

Skye and then promptly forgot it. That door has been opened and all he really wants to do is walk through it. And . . . yeah, *so* not happening right now.

Chris Landry.

When the library volunteer first said that Chris had been looking into the shooting, Jesse's honest reaction was "Huh, that's odd." It was only when he saw Skye's face fall that he made the connection. Then there was a little spark of . . .

Relief. Admit it. One spark of relief at seeing a potential competitor thrown off the field. Of course, that lasted only a split second, before the full weight of it hit him.

"We were going to talk to him about the tech." She shakes her head. "He was the *first* person we thought of to ask, and I never even considered the possibility he could have *done* it. I know his cousin died. I know he has the skills for the videos and the speakers. I still never suspected him."

"Neither of us did."

She turns to face him. "The guy we saw last night. The one who attacked me. He was Chris's build. Chris's height."

Damning evidence, but not concrete proof. Jesse doesn't say that. Skye doesn't want to hear it right now.

Skye continues. "I thought Chris was just being nice to me. I'd been kind to him, so he was repaying it."

"That's what he told me," Jesse says. "Exactly that. If I suspected anything, it was just that maybe he wanted to be more than friends, eventually. But that he was setting you up? It never crossed my mind."

"He stabbed me," she says, her voice barely above a whisper. "He had a knife and he—he—" She looks over. "How could he?"

"I don't know."

"Now what? He kidnapped Tiffany. The right move is to go to the police. But no one's listened to us so far, and all we have for proof is that he was printing articles on the shooting. The police won't buy that."

"Then we'll get something they will buy. We'll get proof."

Skye

Earlier, we texted Chris asking if he can meet up after school. He can't—he has to work and is on closing shift. We drive by the McDonald's to confirm he's there. His mother's car is, and I remember him saying she lets him borrow it when he gets off late. So his excuse is valid. But if he's at work all evening, and he's holding Tiffany captive, he'll need to stop and check on her later. We'll follow him after his shift.

That means we have time to kill, so I've suggested we make dinner for Jesse's parents. We used to do that sometimes—I thought it'd be nice for his parents to come home to a ready-made meal. Jesse tells me he still cooks for them when he doesn't have track, which goes to show that however much he may think he's changed, he hasn't really. Not the parts that matter.

We're making biryani when Mae texts. I sent her a message an hour ago to say I was having dinner at Jesse's and would be hanging out with him tonight. She hadn't answered, and I took that as an answer in itself—she wasn't happy.

When she texts, I figure she's had some time to prepare for battle.

Mae: I'm going to talk to Tiffany's stepmom.
Me: ???
Mae: I don't see anything in the news about the kidnapping, and I want Tiffany's family to know they should take this seriously.
Me: ok

A long pause, as if she's waiting for more. Waiting for me to understand the import of what she's saying—that's she on my side now.

Mae: I know her stepmom. Her company has done cleaning for me. I hired her after North Hampton. She'd lost some work because of it.
Me: ok

Another pause. She wants some acknowledgment that she did a nice thing, but I don't think that's the purpose of doing nice things.

Mae: I just wanted you to know.
Me: ok

I pause a moment, and then add:

Me: thanks
Me: should be home by dark, if not I'll text
Mae: I'd like you home by dark.

I don't respond. If I'm late, it won't be because I'm hanging out at the mall. I'm trying to save Tiffany.

I show Jesse the text stream.

"She's right about Tiffany's stepmom. She did lose a few clients. It was nice of Mae to hire her."

I sigh. "I should have said that, right?"

He leans against the counter. "I think she's trying, and I know why you don't want to cut her slack, but maybe, when you talk to her, you could say it was thoughtful. And it's good that she's talking to Mrs. Gold."

"I know, and I'd love to interpret this as meaning Mae's being supportive, but I can't help but wonder if she's also going there to get a feel for the situation. To see what Tiffany's family thinks, if they have evidence that she *hasn't* been kidnapped. I just . . . I don't trust Mae to be on my side."

Jesse moves forward and puts his hands on my waist. "She let you down. I'm just trying to give her the benefit of the doubt. You need more people on your side, and I don't understand how anyone can *not* be there."

I smile. "You may be biased."

"Only if knowing you makes me biased. Anyone who does would realize you couldn't do anything like this."

I put my arms around his neck. "I missed you."

"I know."

I laugh and duck my head, and when I come up again, he's right there, his lips going to mine. Or that's what he must intend. Instead, we collide, his nose hitting my mouth, his lips kissing my chin. We both laugh, a little embarrassed, and try again, only we overshoot and, yeah, still not quite right, and even when we do find each other's lips, it's . . .

I always read about perfect first kisses. This isn't it. We spend about two seconds trying to figure it out, and then both back away, fast, as if we can salvage the moment by pretending we weren't actually trying to kiss.

"Sorry," I say, as my cheeks blaze. "I, uh, I haven't . . . I don't have a lot of experience . . . Well, none, actually."

"Ditto."

I look up.

He shrugs. "No one was you."

"Ditto." I give a small chuckle. "So . . . we're kinda screwed, huh?"

"Nah, we just need practice. Lots of practice."

He puts his hands on my cheeks and lifts my face, and I keep it perfectly still, eyes half open, because apparently, whatever books and movies might suggest, this is not a maneuver to be attempted in the dark, at least not until a certain level of skill has been achieved.

He lowers his mouth to mine, and we kiss, and that's better—much better. I'm still careful not to move, though. Well, not to move anything except my lips. It takes a second, but we find a rhythm, and then . . .

And then there it is.

I'm kissing Jesse. I am finally kissing Jesse, and it's everything thirteen-year-old Skye imagined it would be. It's sweet and warm and gentle, and my head starts spinning like I really am thirteen, singing "He's kissing me!" over and over, and then . . .

Well, then I *don't* feel thirteen anymore, as I pull him closer and his arms tighten around me, the kiss deepening, igniting a spark that is definitely not for middle grade Skye, and inside, I'm not dancing and singing anymore. I'm grinning. Grinning and thinking I definitely want more practice at this, as much practice as I can get, and—

"Jasser?" The whoosh of the front door and his mother's voice.

We jump apart even faster than when the library volunteer caught us.

"Jasser?" she calls. "Do I smell something burning?"

We both look over at the stove . . . smoke curling from the pan. We start to run for it, collide and steady each other, grinning, and he calls, "We're in here!" as I race to the stove.

Skye

As we wait near the McDonald's, I think about Chris. He's been there for two years, rising to shift manager. Some kids take jobs for pocket money; Chris works to put food on the table. His dad is long gone and never paid child support.

Maybe hearing about someone like that should make me glad my dad pays. It doesn't. My dad pays because he has the money, and his professional rep has been tarnished enough by a school-shooter son. When Chris's father was around, he only did odd jobs and spent most of his time drinking and venting his drunken frustration on Chris's mom. I remember how Chris said that, matter-of-factly, when I commented on him needing to work most nights.

"I'd rather work than have him back," Chris said.

His mom's job at the supermarket doesn't support a family of four, so Chris chooses to hold down a part-time job and insists on buying the family's groceries. That's the kind of guy he is. Or the kind of guy I thought he was.

Now this . . . I can't comprehend this.

Is it misplaced revenge for his cousin? I didn't think they'd been close.

Or was that just an excuse?

He said he used to have a crush on me. Had I inadvertently led him on? Rejected him?

I can't see a misunderstanding between thirteen-year-olds being an explanation for what he's doing now. I can't see anyone having a good reason—ever—for doing this to someone. Which should seem to suggest it's not about me. But if it isn't, why is it aimed at me?

Maybe that's like trying to understand why Isaac would bring guns to school. Why he murdered three kids he didn't even know.

Jesse asked why Luka came out of that bathroom with a gun. Even hearing the question frustrated me. It can't be answered. It can't be understood. This is the same thing. Looking for a reason why anyone would do this to me is as futile as looking for a reason why my kind, gentle, *good* brother walked out of the boys' bathroom holding a gun.

We tail Chris from work.

"He's going straight home," I say. "His apartment's over there." I point at an old building in one of the city's worse neighborhoods.

Sure enough, Chris pulls into the lot. Jesse eases the car to the curb, lights off, as we watch Chris park. He gets out and looks around. Checks his watch. Glances at the building. Then he sends a quick text, pulls up the hood on his dark sweatshirt and lopes across the lot . . . heading *away* from his building.

I double-check the address I have for Chris. I'm squinting at the sign outside the apartment building when Jesse says, "No, that's his place. I did a project with him years ago. He's heading somewhere else."

We slip from the car. Chris scales a fence behind the parking lot. At the top, he crouches and looks around. Jesse and I both duck. Chris leaps down and the distant pound of his footfalls echoes through the falling night.

We loop around the lot, running on the grassy border so our footsteps don't give us away. When we reach the fence, Jesse boosts me. I peek over the top to see an auto-body shop. I have to read the sign backward—someone has turned it around, and there's a crack through the middle. Below the sign is a weathered FOR SALE one with a bright orange PRICE REDUCED sticker.

They might have more luck selling the place if they cleared the parking lot first. I count five junkers, four on blocks, all of them beyond the repair skill of any mechanic.

I'm looking at the surrounding buildings, trying to see where Chris went, when a light flickers behind an abandoned panel van. Metal clunks, like a rusted door opening, and I motion for Jesse to bring me down.

I explain what I saw and heard, and then say, "What if he has Tiffany in that van?"

"Then we wait for him to leave and go check."

Not what I was going to suggest, and he knows it, saying, "We're waiting, Skye. If he moves Tiffany, we'll hear it. Otherwise, there is absolutely no advantage to jumping him. Remember what happened the last time?" He nods at my arm.

He has a point. A very good one. It's just . . .

"Yes," he says. "My plan is very boring. Safe and boring."

"We need to place Chris at the scene," I say.

"I'm sure his fingerprints will do that."

"He'll wear gloves. He did last night."

"Skye, do not try to make this more exciting."

"I'm not—"

"Yep, totally are." He puts an arm around my waist and leans in as if to kiss me, and then stops. "Speaking of bad ideas . . ."

"Seems like a good one to me. Definitely more exciting than just standing around."

"But we're *standing around* to listen for him. Which means we can't get distracted by kissing."

"I hate it when you make sense."

"Only when it interferes with your grand adventures." He brushes his lips across mine, and then moves to the fence. He grabs the edge, hoists himself up and hangs there, peering over. A few moments later, he hops back down and says, "How about a compromise? We won't confront Chris, but considering all the trouble we've had convincing people, it'd be wise to get a photo of him near that van."

"Can you get that from here?"

"No, which is where you get your excitement. There's another fence right behind the van. That'll get us closer and give a better angle."

When we reach the fence, though, we see a problem—it's even higher, with wire along the top.

"If we go to the end and peek around, we'll be perfectly lined up for a photo," I say.

"Also perfectly lined up for Chris to see us."

"I'll keep my flash off. Just a quick peek and a snap."

"Yeah, and if that doesn't work, you'll creep closer and closer until you're right in front of him. We'll figure out something else."

We head along the fence. At the end, I see a car between us and the van. Jesse whispers a plan.

We creep to the car, and then I sneak along the back with my camera ready. Jesse heads around the front, where he'll toss pebbles, drawing Chris's attention while I get the picture.

It'd be a great plan . . . if Chris was anywhere to be seen.

When I get around the car, there's no sign of him. I catch an unexpected smell, though. One I recognize.

That's when I see Chris. He's sitting on the back bumper of the van, his phone in one hand, thumb zipping across the screen. In the other hand . . . well, that's where the smell comes from.

I take another two steps. My foot comes down, and I see something beneath it, but it's too late. I'm stepping on a crushed soda can. My foot catches the edge, sending it clinking away. Chris jumps up, dropping the joint, his sneaker coming down to put it out as he sees me.

"Skye?"

There's a clatter behind him. Running footfalls. Then a dark shape launches at Chris's back, knocking him down. His phone thumps to the ground.

"Jesse?" he says.

Jesse flips Chris over and pats him down.

"What the hell?" Chris says, looking confused.

Jesse empties Chris's pockets. Keys and a wallet.

"No knife," Jesse grunts as he double-checks.

"Knife?" Chris says, his voice rising.

I open the back door of the panel van. I know I'm not going to see Tiffany in there. Instead, I find exactly what I now expect—a small bag of weed, with rolling papers and a lighter. And a can of Axe body spray.

"I'd offer you guys some," Chris says. "But I get the feeling that's really not what you're here for."

"It isn't," I say. "I hate Axe."

He gives a strained chuckle. "It's cover-up. My mom wouldn't appreciate me coming home smelling like weed."

"I suspect she can still figure it out."

"Yeah, probably. I don't smoke much. Just . . . I had a rough night at work. But, again, I'm sure I'm not lying on the ground because you guys disapprove of my choice of stress relief. Any chance I can get up?"

"When you tell us where we'll find Tiffany," Jesse says.

"Tiffany Gold?"

"She's missing."

"What?"

Chris's shock looks genuine.

"You know I've been having trouble at school, right?" I say. "Someone harassing me and then framing me for it."

His eyes widen more. "Are you saying that was Tiffany? And now she's taken off?"

"No, but I think her disappearance is connected to what's happening to me. That whoever is harassing me might have taken her."

"*Kidnapped* her?"

"So you know nothing about that?"

"How could I . . . ?" His gaze travels from me to Jesse. "Wait, you're not accusing *me*—"

"I also mentioned that someone's been trying to get me to dig into the North Hampton shooting. Leaving notes. Dropping off articles and police report pages . . ."

He goes still. "Oh, hell." He exhales. "Okay, this looks bad."

I motion for Jesse to let Chris up. He does, but stays close, ready to put him down again.

"Yes, I put that stuff in your locker," Chris says.

"The articles and pages."

"Yes."

"The note saying *There's more to the story.*"

"Yes."

"The note shoved under the newspaper office door, saying *I know what you did.*"

"What? No. That wasn't me. Just the other one. And the pages." He shakes his head. "This looks so bad."

"Yeah, it kinda does," I say.

He looks around. "Can we go grab food and talk? I'm starving."

I point at the stubbed-out joint. "That'll do it."

He chuckles. "No, I didn't smoke that much. But I was trying to save money by eating when I got home. So I'm starving. I'm not trying to wiggle out of this." He points to the keys. "We can use my mom's car. You drive. Just be careful. Please."

"I don't have my license," I say. "Jesse brought his mom's car. We'll take that. I just need to call home and let my aunt know I won't be home before dark." I wave up at the blackened sky.

"I should tell my mom too," Chris says.

"Do you have a copy of the pages you gave me?" I ask.

His brow furrows. "Sure, up in our apartment."

"Jesse? Can you go with Chris and get those while he lets his mom know he's going out?"

Skye

On the drive, I take Chris's pages. I flip straight to the police report. I remember the detective slapping the file shut before I could read it, and my stomach has been hosting a butterfly convention ever since Chris handed them to me.

I read the report once. I read it twice. Chris wanted me to see something here that would make me proclaim Luka's innocence. But I don't. It's the opposite, in fact.

The pages are from the statement of the "witness" who told them Luka was involved. The report doesn't name Harley as the source, but it must be him. He's the only survivor. As the detective said, under the terms of his plea bargain, the details of his statement were secret, which is why he isn't named.

What I have are two pages that talk about Luka's involvement. Two pages clarifying, unequivocally, that my brother was part of the shooting. Isaac came up with the plan, but Luka was on board. He was angry with our dad and upset about our mother, and feeling like no one understood him.

Feeling like no one was paying attention to him.

Joining Isaac's plan to make them pay attention.

Exactly what Mr. Vaughn and Mae accused me of.

And now, maybe, I know why.

But this doesn't explain why Chris gave me these pages. Which is what I'm going to ask, obviously. I just want to hear his explanation first.

We go for pizza. I let Chris order, but when he adds bacon, I shake my head. He hesitates. Then his gaze shoots to Jesse, and he says, "Right. Forgot." Jesse says no, he's fine picking it off, but I'm glad when Chris amends the order. Making Jesse pick it off isn't right.

When the server leaves, Chris says, "I was trying to help. Which, obviously, is the polar opposite of what I did. In my defense, I had no idea the other stuff was happening."

He sips his Coke, and then says, "I never liked the official explanation. Luka as a shooter? He was my reading buddy in first grade. Did you know that?"

I shake my head.

"You and I were in different classes then, and it's not like you'd remember anyway. I wasn't having problems with other kids yet. Just trouble reading. Dyslexia."

"You're dyslexic?"

He nods. "Diagnosed two years ago, finally. It's helped me come up with strategies to make school easier, but mostly it just gave me more confidence, knowing I'm not stupid. Anyway, Luka was awesome. He was so patient with me. Years later, if he saw me anywhere, he'd stop to say hi, chat. How does a guy like that decide to go on a shooting spree?"

"It happens. Believe me, I've done the research."

"Maybe, but I couldn't see it. So I always had doubts. Then, last year, I went out with this girl from Southfield whose mom had worked the case. She's a detective with the RPD. Somehow the shooting came up—it was the anniversary or whatever—and she mentioned Luka. She overheard her mom once, talking to another detective about how she felt bad about Luka, always thought there was more to it. Not that the other cops covered anything up, but she felt like they missed something. I asked this girl to get me the police report. Which was totally wrong, I know. But I had to see it. And when I did, I knew there was a problem."

I'm about to say I don't understand, but he's still talking.

"I couldn't act on it," he says. "If my family discovered I was questioning the shooting? Suggesting one of the shooters wasn't guilty, when my own cousin died? Maybe I'm a coward, but I couldn't be the one to raise questions. It'd hurt my aunt and uncle too much. I was trying to figure out a way to do it anonymously. Then you came to RivCol, Skye, and I knew who I had to give those pages to—the person who could use them the most."

"To take a closer look at Luka's role."

"Right. If he wasn't guilty, then I'd like that cleared up. He deserves it. But the one who's suffering for it is you. You and your family. *My* family would like to see the case stay closed, and I need to respect that. They want to get past it. You can't. No one will let you. I see that now, and I'm really sorry if I made things worse."

Our pizza arrives, and I wait impatiently for the server to leave, and then say, "What was I supposed to see in that police report?"

"Did you read it?"

I admit that I just did now, in the car . . . and I tell him that the police found it in my locker.

"Damn." He squeezes his eyes shut. "I'm gonna have to warn Gayle. That's the girl who got it for me." He sends a quick text, and Jesse puts a slice of pizza on my plate as I continue waiting impatiently until Chris says, "She's not around. I'll talk to her when I can. Make my confession."

"So the report . . ." I prompt.

"You see the problem, right?"

"No, I don't. I read the pages a couple of times, but . . . nothing."

He takes the sheets from me. "Okay, so what Gayle got me were the witness accounts. These particular pages are the most important. You know who this is, right? It might say it's anonymous, but it's not."

"It's Harley."

"Right. Publicly, he said he didn't know Luka's role. That Isaac arranged everything and talked to Luka and Harley separately. Which is weird."

"Not if you knew Isaac," I say. "He always wanted to be in charge. Harley let him. Luka . . ." I shrug. "Luka thought friends didn't need a leader. They aren't a gang. If Isaac did something Luka didn't like, Luka called him on it. So to keep control of the situation, Isaac would definitely play it this way—not letting Harley talk to Luka about it, saying that was safer."

Jesse nods. "When, really, he just didn't want Harley to hear Luka questioning the plan."

"Yes," I say. "So Isaac tells Harley that Luka is all for it. Harley's not bright enough to question that. He's just relieved that Luka agrees. Luka was the one Harley went to for advice."

"The one whose opinion carried more weight," Chris says. "So, officially, all Harley will say is that Isaac told him Luka was in. Nothing more. Here, though, is where he gave the evidence that convicted Luka. In his so-called anonymous informant statement."

Chris runs his finger over the pertinent part of the report. "Harley says that he was in class with Luka when the school went on lockdown. Then Luka snuck out before the teacher got control of the situation."

"Snuck out and went to the bathroom," I say. "Then he came out with the gun. So this"—I point at the report—"actually proves Luka knew what he was doing. He knew the school was going into lockdown. He snuck out and hid in the bathroom with a gun. It's damning evidence."

"Except it's a lie," Chris says.

I look at him, confused, and he turns to Jesse and gets the same look from him.

"Where was Harley?" Chris prompts.

"What?" I say.

"At the time of the lockdown, where was Harley?"

"In . . ." I remember the image projected at NHH. "He was in gym class, wasn't he?"

"Right. Harley and Isaac were in gym when it all went down. That's how they got out of lockdown so easily. It was near the end of the period, and kids were going inside to change—no teacher around. So when Luka got shot, it was easy for Isaac to grab Harley and get the guns, which they had in their backpacks. The shooting started there, in the locker room."

"That's where Brandon Locklear died and another boy was injured."

Chris nods. "They walked out and shot Vicki Pryor—Owen's

cousin—as she was turning to run into the girls' locker room. She was shot in the back, which left her paralyzed. Then they continued into the hall and—" His gaze moves to Jesse. "And that's all the detail you guys need."

Because Jamil had been next.

"The point is where it started," Chris says.

"In the locker room," I say. "Isaac and Harley—" I stop. "Isaac and Harley were in gym. But in Harley's report"—I lift the file—"he said he saw Luka duck out when the lockdown was called. Luka was in English, though, not gym."

"Exactly," Chris says. "Harley's lying."

"That's a huge lie," I say. "And it's easy to see through. I can't believe no one's put that together."

"They probably have," Jesse says. "This is a statement, not an interrogation. It's what Harley claimed. It isn't what they proved."

"But if the police knew Harley was lying . . . ," I say.

"I have no idea what's going on," Chris said. "But if no one saw Luka duck out of English during the lockdown, he may have already *been* in the bathroom. He may not have known what was going on."

"But he still came out holding a gun," I say.

"Still, there has to be a reason Harley lied," Chris says. "And the only person who knows that is Harley. Who is alive and serving his sentence in a prison an hour away."

I go quiet.

"Do you still think I took Tiffany?" Chris asks.

I shake my head, and Jesse says, "But you can understand why we suspected you."

"Yeah, but now that you see it wasn't me, can I offer my help? Will you tell me what's going on?"

I explain as we eat.

A few times, Chris has to stop and say, "What? Are you serious?" and glances at Jesse, in case he's misunderstanding.

When I finish, Chris says, "That's *so* messed up. When you guys said you thought someone took Tiffany, I figured you were jumping to conclusions. Like maybe she just went away for the weekend. But someone really did take her—and sliced your arm." He looks at Jesse. "You're forgiven for jumping me in that parking lot."

We eat more pizza, and the server refills our sodas. When she leaves, Jesse says, "So the biggest clue is the hacking. That takes serious know-how. Way beyond me."

"The AV tech is midlevel," Chris says. "I could do it easily. I even know a local store that would sell the stuff, which might be a lead. So, yes, computer hacking at that level is rarer."

"You've been at RivCol longer than me," Jesse says. "Any idea who could pull this off?"

"The most I've heard of is a few kids who can access teachers' accounts, get tests and such. Which just means they've figured out the teacher's password. Not actual hacking. The last person at RivCol with mad skills like that was—"

He stops.

"Was who?" I ask.

"Vicki Pryor."

Skye

Vicki Pryor. Owen's cousin. The girl who was shot in the back. Confined to a wheelchair. She graduated from RivCol two years ago and is now studying computer science at MIT with a full scholarship. And the project that got her there? Telecommunications infiltration. In other words, hacking mobile devices.

"Hacking gets you into an Ivy League college?" I say. "I thought it'd get you a one-way ticket to jail." I glance at Jesse. "Sorry."

"I'm guessing her project was theoretical," Jesse said. "If you can show how a device or a system can be hacked, it helps companies build better security."

"Are you sure that's Vicki's specialty?" I ask Chris.

He taps his phone and turns it around. On the screen is a news article about Vicki's scholarship. It mentions that her project was on preventing tampering with mobile devices.

"It made the local paper?" I say.

"People are interested in survivors. It's a feel-good story. And

I've heard a lot about Vicki. Some of the victims' families stick together. For support." He sneaks a look at Jesse. "Not all of them do, understandably. For some it helps. For some it's a reminder."

"Like I said," Jesse says, "my parents *did* join a group. But after a while, yeah, it was just a reminder."

"I don't go to the group," Chris says. "Nella and I weren't close. But I hear the talk. Everyone's proud of Vicki. She liked tech before the shooting. Afterward, when she was recovering, she threw herself into it. I don't think anyone in her family has even been to college. A full ride at MIT is huge. But she's there—in Boston—not here."

"What about Owen?" I ask.

There's a long pause. Then Jesse nods. "Yeah, let's talk about Owen."

We spend the next twenty minutes doing just that. We go over everything that's happened, looking for things Owen couldn't have done.

We find nothing.

We presume Owen didn't have the know-how to hack, but Jesse says Vicki could hack the computers remotely. She also has the skills to monitor my phone and see those texts, saying I was meeting Tiffany in Fletcher Park.

The voices in the girls' bathroom could have been recorded, as Jesse suggested. Vicki records it with a friend and sends the file to Owen. Owen knows I'm in the bathroom, sticks the cleaning sign out front, comes in and plays the recording. Then he has it play in the halls, bouncing from speakers.

After I escaped from the office post-detention, Owen must

have taken the doorstop. He said Mr. Vaughn forgot kids in there all the time. He may have even distracted the VP to be sure he forgot me.

Sending that "anonymous" email to Vaughn from my account? Easy. Vicki hacks my log-in information, and Owen sends it while apparently cleaning a computer. Trapping me in the newspaper office? Owen would have the key, along with an excuse for being there late. Switching the newspaper articles? That'd be Vicki, having found a way to remotely access the files.

Finally, there's my attacker. A guy who was Owen's size.

"Where does Owen live?" I ask.

"He's renting a place in the country," Chris said. "I remember talking to him once, and he said he was moving there, glad to get out of the city."

"Which would be the perfect place to hold Tiffany."

"No," Jesse says.

"No, it's not?" Chris says.

Jesse looks at me. "I'm saying no to what Skye is about to suggest. She's going to point out that we need more to take this to the police. They haven't believed us so far. So we have to go and get a look at the house, see if we can find evidence of Tiffany being held there. Otherwise, the police are liable to tip Owen off by questioning him, which would be dangerous for Tiffany."

"Couldn't have explained it better myself," I say.

Jesse gives me a look.

"Well, is it wrong?" I say. "Any of it?"

He sighs. "No."

"Then I guess we're going to need to find out where Owen lives."

○○○

We're at Owen's rented house. Like Chris said, it's outside the city. It must have been a farmhouse at one time—with fields along either side and a forest in the back—but whoever owns the farm now rents the house and just works the fields.

It's the kind of place you might expect a twenty-year-old guy could afford to rent. It's big—two stories—but it's one building inspection away from being condemned. Several windows are boarded up. There's no front porch or any steps to get to the door.

Jesse pulls into a lane a quarter mile down, one that seems to be for farm equipment. We walk until we're standing behind trees at the property edge. My phone blips with an incoming text. I quickly turn it to silent and check the message.

Mae: It's after ten, Skye. When are you coming home?
Me: Soon.

I pocket my phone. The guys are surveying the dark house. There's not a single light on, and it's too early for Owen to have gone to bed. The driveway is empty, and I don't see any sign of a garage.

"He has a car, right?" I whisper.

Chris nods. "An old Honda."

"The lack of lights and a car doesn't prove he's gone," Jesse says. "It just very, very, *very* strongly suggests it."

"I'm going with Skye on this one," Chris says.

I turn to Jesse. "Chris agrees that we should sneak up to the house and see what's going on."

"Whoa," Chris says. "I never said—"

"If we cut through the field, we can come out in the forest. Come on."

Skye

Owen's "backyard" is mostly forest. By the time we're at the tree line, we're less than twenty feet from the house.

"We've seen the front from the road," I say. "We saw the east side as we were coming through the field, and now we're looking at the back. The house is dark. If you insist on checking the west side, we'll do that."

Naturally, Jesse insists. We walk as far in that direction as we can without leaving the cover of the forest.

"No car, no lights, no Owen," I say.

Jesse doesn't answer.

"If this really bugs you, we'll leave," I say.

"I just . . . I don't like it."

"You think it's a trap?" Chris says.

Jesse considers, and then shakes his head. "No one led us here. We figured it out on our own. Just stick together. If we see Owen—or *anyone* other than Tiffany—we're leaving, okay?"

"Agreed."

The moon is bright enough to lead the way. We're halfway to the back door when Jesse catches my arm. He's gone still as he squints at the house.

"You spotted something?" I whisper.

"A flicker of light. You didn't?"

Chris and I both shake our heads. I lean in to whisper, "If you really don't like this . . ."

He exhales. "I'm fine. I don't mean to be so jumpy." He rolls his shoulders and makes a face. "I just keep thinking about last night and . . ." His gaze falls to my arm.

"I know."

He leans closer, voice lowering as he says, "Just don't take off on me, okay? Please. I'm not trying to be a jerk."

"I made a mistake at the park. I won't do it again. I promise."

When we reach the house, we duck and sneak up. I'm peering over a window ledge when I see a flash of light. I duck fast.

Jesse whispers, "Passing car."

When I look again, I see that the window lines up with one in the front room, and through it I catch a glimpse of red taillights as a car passes.

"Must have been what I saw earlier," Jesse whispers.

I peek again. The window opens into the living room, and I can see the dining area beyond it. Both rooms are dark.

"I'm going to boost you," Jesse whispers.

He does, and I peer through at a better angle. There's enough moonlight for me to make out furnishings. An old sofa. An armchair with books substituting for one leg. As my gaze travels to the dining room doorway, I notice a large dark stain on the carpet. The moonlight catches it, and it glistens, still wet.

"I think I see blood," I whisper, and I try to get a better look. Jesse adjusts his grip and boosts me higher while Chris grabs the windowsill and hoists himself up to peer inside.

"Damn," Chris whispers. "That does seem like blood. A lot of it."

I'm about to tell Jesse to take a look when I notice something to the side of the wet patch. Just past the dining room doorway. Moonlight glints off an object on the floor.

A knife? I squint. It's an odd shape. And there's a second one like it a few inches away. Smaller pieces litter the linoleum and the carpet at the border between the rooms.

"Glass," I murmur.

"What?" Chris says.

"It's a broken tumbler," I say. "The pieces are there. That's what the stain's from."

"Oh, right. Now I see. It's not blood, then. Just Coke or something." Chris sounds disappointed.

Jesse lowers me to the ground. "So someone dropped a glass of liquid and left the whole mess—including the broken glass? I don't care how bad a housekeeper—no one does that. It's not safe, for one thing."

"And it doesn't seem like Owen is a bad housekeeper. The place is tidy otherwise."

"Maybe some of it *is* blood," Chris says. "Owen dropped a glass. Got cut. Took off to the hospital."

Jesse says nothing. He climbs onto the back deck and creeps toward the door. As he peers through the window, I resist the urge to join him. Someone should stand guard, and Chris is already slipping off to the next window.

Jesse comes back off the deck and whispers, "Just a mudroom and a couple of closed doors."

We follow Chris. He's boosted himself up to check through the other rear window. When Jesse lifts me, I see an empty room. Through it is the kitchen.

We tackle the basement windows next, but they're boarded up. There's no way of getting up to the second floor. Even the trees are too far to climb.

"So we've got a broken tumbler," I say. "That's it."

"But the house is empty," Chris says. "If we can get in, we should look around. That broken glass means *something.*"

I say nothing. I agree, but I don't want to make Jesse be the grown-up here. When I glance at Jesse, he's eyeing the house, considering.

"You two go," Chris says. "I've got guard duty."

"Thank you," I say. "Text us if you hear anything."

Skye

We break in the back door. That sounds far more badass than it is. While Chris and I hunt for a window to go through, Jesse demonstrates the advantage of being the levelheaded one. We're getting ready to smash through glass . . . and he's looking for a spare key. He finds one under a rock. It opens the back door.

The door leads into a mudroom. One pair of work boots sits on the mat. Above them hang the overalls Owen wears at school.

"So he came home today." I check the overall pockets and find a key ring. Jesse compares the keys to the spare and says, "No match. They don't look like car keys, either."

This set must be Owen's school keys. He keeps his car and house keys on another ring. I'm also guessing he has another pair of shoes for going out. Those aren't here either. More evidence that we won't find Owen inside.

Two doors lead off the mudroom. The first one opens into

the living room. The other goes to a dark basement. When I take a step down, Jesse catches my arm and whispers, "There's a lock."

He points at a keyhole.

"Right," I say. "And it's open."

"Exactly."

He's leaning in to explain when I whisper, "Oh," and he nods. If Owen was keeping Tiffany behind a locking basement door, he'd have secured it before he left.

"But—" I begin.

"She could still be down there," he whispers. "I know. She's not going anywhere, though. That sounds cruel. . . ."

He trails off, and I understand. We're reasonably certain Owen isn't here. That doesn't mean, however, that we should head straight into the basement when it'll only take a few minutes to confirm that the house really is empty.

We creep into the living room. As we approach the broken glass, I can see that the stain is still wet, but the liquid has soaked into the carpet. Spilled a while ago. I bend to inhale the caramel sweetness of cola.

Jesse's examining the broken glass. His gaze catches on one piece. Then he looks to the floor, his gaze skimming over the linoleum before rising to the wall. I move into the dining room and see what he sees.

There's blood on that one big piece of glass. None on the linoleum that I can see, but when I follow Jesse's gaze, I spot blood spatter on the wall. Not much, though.

"Dropped the glass, picked up a piece, cut his finger and shook it?" I say. "Spattering blood on the wall?"

"Maybe."

A board creaks overhead. Jesse grips my arm, as if I'm about to race for the stairs. I give him a look, and he eases off with a mouthed apology. We both strain to listen, but no other sounds come. Jesse takes a careful step toward the front of the house. One more step and—

A scrabbling noise sounds over our heads, and we both jump. As I turn, I can still hear it, seemingly coming from the wall beside us. The exterior wall.

I'm creeping toward the window when a high-pitched squeak has me falling back. A dark shape swoops past the window, and I startle-jump again. We both do. Then another shape follows and Jesse says, "Bats."

I move to the window. A third bat swoops down from the eaves and takes off into the night. The scrabbling in the walls has stopped.

I grumble under my breath, and we stand there, looking around, as if forgetting what we've been doing.

Jesse whispers, "All clear down here."

It does seem to be—if anyone was around, we'd have given ourselves away, jumping at the bats.

Jesse checks his watch. A hint that Owen won't be gone forever. I glance at the back door, thinking of the basement, but Jesse motions overhead. I nod.

We slip to the front hall. Through the kitchen doorway, I see dishes piled in the sink. Quite a few dishes, considering Owen seems a tidy homeowner. A sign that he's feeding a captive, too?

The smell of fried chicken hangs in the air, but I don't see take-out containers. There's a cast-iron pan in the sink.

Jesse taps my arm. Nothing to see here. Time to get upstairs.

We're almost to the second floor when a noise sounds from the attic. We both stop and look up.

No other sounds come.

I mouth, "Bats?"

Jesse shrugs. We continue on, slower now. Above us, on the second floor, we see four doors. Two are closed. We can see through the other two—a bedroom in one and a bath in the other.

Jesse's looking between the two closed doors. That's when something moves over his head, and I'm grabbing his shoulder to yank him back, and then I realize it's a dangling cord.

The cord hangs from a trapdoor in the ceiling. And it's swaying.

"Attic?" I mouth.

He nods.

I pantomime a bat and point at the cord, asking if he thought a bat might have set it swinging. He studies that cord for another moment. Then he motions for us to approach the trapdoor.

If it's not a bat, then something in the attic set the cord swaying, something moving about. Something that could be a girl bound and gagged, held prisoner right over our heads.

I'm right behind him. He's passing the railing at the top of the stairs. A thump sounds behind me, and I turn and—

A stifled cry of rage. A blur of motion. I'm spinning toward it, and I see an open door. An open door where there'd been a closed one.

A figure barrels straight for Jesse. I lunge. His hands rise to ward off the figure. It plows into him, battering like a ram, head lowered.

Jesse flies backward. He hits the railing. There's a crack. The old wood gives way, and he's falling, and I'm lunging to catch him, but it's too late. He's falling backward through the broken railing, arms windmilling.

A stifled scream. Not from Jesse. From the figure standing in the hall. It's Tiffany, her mouth gagged, hands bound, her eyes wide with horror as Jesse falls.

I'm already racing down the stairs, and then vaulting around the last few and stumbling to Jesse. He's flat on his back, heaving deep breaths.

I drop beside him. "Don't try to get up. Just stay there."

He motions to his chest.

"I know," I say. "I'm getting help."

I have my phone out, and I hear the back door slap open and the sound of running footfalls.

"Jesse? Skye?" Chris calls.

"In here!" I shout.

Jesse's trying to rise, and I put my hands out to stop him.

"Don't move," I say.

He shakes his head. "Just . . . wind. Wind knocked out." He gulps breaths. "I'm fine."

"You don't know that."

He keeps rising, brushing me off and wincing as he pushes to his feet. A thump sounds behind us, and I look to see Tiffany tumbling down the last few steps.

"Help her," Jesse says. "Chris, call the police. I . . . I just need . . . catch my breath."

Chris is already making the call, and I'm running to Tiffany. She's on one knee, tears rolling down her cheeks. I get the duct tape off her mouth, wincing as I do.

"I thought you were him," she says as I untie her hands.

"Owen. It's Owen." She looks at me. "Owen Pryor. He's the one—" She can't finish, choking on a sob. "I don't understand. I just don't understand."

"Where is he?" I ask.

"Gone. He—He left me here. Left me to—" She can't get out the rest, chest heaving. I finish untying her hands.

Chris says, "The police are on their way. Five minutes. They said if there's no sign of Owen, we should stay put. I'll watch the front."

I lead Tiffany to a chair in the dining room. Her gaze keeps flitting to the front door, and her mouth opens, and I know she wants to go, just go. But the police are right. If there's no sign of Owen, we shouldn't run.

I'm not sure Tiffany and Jesse *could* even run. Jesse's on his feet, helping me with Tiffany, and he's breathing hard through clenched teeth, clearly in pain.

Tiffany glances at the door again.

"We're fine here," I say. "We didn't see any sign of him, and his car's gone."

"I know. I just . . ." She straightens. "I'm fine. I'll *be* fine. It was just . . ."

She looks up at me. "He *left* me here. He came home from work, and I could hear him making dinner, and then he took a call. From Vicki, I think. He started swearing and he said they were done, that he couldn't finish it. When he got off the phone, he threw something. A plate or . . ." She sees the broken glass on the floor. "That. It must have been that. I heard it smash, and then he came upstairs, and he never said a word to me. Never opened my door. I heard him in his room, drawers opening and shutting, like he was packing a bag. Then he left. Left *me* bound and gagged and locked in." She meets my gaze again. "How could someone do that?"

I shake my head. "I don't know."

I really don't.

Skye

The police arrive with an ambulance for Jesse and Tiffany. Jesse's parents are right behind them, whipping along at the same speed. Mae follows a few moments after, as does Chris's mom. Jesse gets taken to the hospital right away, leaving me only time to say a quick goodbye as Dr. Mandal assures me she'll text as soon as she has news.

I give my statement, and then I hear Tiffany's voice rising, as if in panic, and I jog over there as Mae talks to the police.

"I just want to go home," Tiffany is saying to the paramedics. "Please. I don't need the hospital. I'm okay, and I just want to go home."

"You need to be checked out. Your parents—"

"I'm eighteen. And there's no sign of my parents, is there?"

I catch a note of bitterness in her voice, but then she says, evenly, "I told my parents there's no reason for them to come. If someone can drop me off at home, I'll be fine. Really, I will."

The paramedics insist. She is the victim of a crime; the police will require a full report from the hospital.

"Can I come along?" I ask the paramedics. I look over at Tiffany with a wry smile. "I'll keep you company while you wait for a doctor. That always seems to take forever."

"Hanging out in a hospital is the last thing you need tonight," she says. "I'm sorry. I don't mean to be whining."

"You've earned it."

"I'm just tired and . . ." Her gaze goes to Chris's mom, who is hovering over him, her face drawn in worry.

"Maybe you should tell your parents to come—" I begin.

"No." She tears her gaze away. "There's no need."

"You were *kidnapped.*" *And they should have come running, no matter what you said.*

"I'm fine. My stepmom works nights, and my stepbrother is only five, so Dad needs to stay home with him."

Whatever my family issues, I cannot imagine I could *keep* Mom or Gran—or even Aunt Mae—away if I said I'd been kidnapped. Tiffany keeps glancing down the road, as if hoping to see headlights. But the road stays dark.

"Can I come with her?" I ask the paramedics again.

One nods, and I hurry to tell Mae.

Mae follows the ambulance to the hospital, but she's going to stay in the waiting room unless I need her. They take Tiffany into a room where, yes, she has to wait for the doctor. I sit with her. We don't talk much, but it's a comfortable silence, as if we both know that any small talk right now would be awkward.

When a man shouts in the hall, she jumps, but it's just a drunk guy, and he's quickly shuffled off.

"You're safe now," I say.

"Am I?" She rubs her hands over her face. "Owen's still out there."

I speak carefully when I say, "I don't think he'll come for you. He'll know you've already given a statement and identified him. I'm not sure why he kidnapped you, but this wasn't . . . it wasn't about . . ." I swallow. "This was my fault. He was after me. You just made the mistake of being nice to me, trying to help. I'm sorry. I'm really, really sorry."

She moves beside me and puts an arm around my shoulders. "You didn't do anything wrong, Skye. Your coming back to Riverside just set him off. He was . . ." She inhales. "Unhinged, I guess that's the word for it. He acted normal, at school, but the guy who kidnapped me was a different person. Like Jekyll and Hyde. He kept ranting about how you shouldn't have come back, how it was an insult to the families, how he had to make you leave."

"So why abduct you?"

"His cousin—Vicki—hacked into your cell phone. He could see all your texts, including the ones I sent. That's how he knew you'd be at Fletcher Park. He planned to grab you there, but then Jesse showed up with you. Owen was leaving—running out—when he saw me. And I saw him. I recognized him. I asked what he was doing there . . . and then I spotted the knife. He came at me so fast I couldn't . . . I tried to . . ."

She blurts the rest. "He knocked me out. He was panicked because I recognized him, and he remembered the texts—the ones where I said I knew something about the newspaper hack. I woke up with a knife to my throat, and Owen demanding to know what I found out about the newspaper."

She gives a sharp laugh. "Do you know what it was? My important information? I remembered that the newspaper computer had a cloud-drive backup, and I found the files you saved. That proved someone tampered with the newspaper and deleted the hard-drive backups. That's it. That's all I had."

I put my hands on hers, and she squeezes them.

"I think, after that, he realized what he'd done," she says. "He'd stabbed you. He'd kidnapped me. Those are serious crimes. Really serious. I heard him arguing with Vicki on the phone this evening. He said he was through. That's when he left. Left me . . ." Her voice wavers. "He left me to die, Skye. He just walked out and left me to die."

I put my arms around her and hug her as tightly as I can.

I'm outside the hospital room. They've given me a chair, and I appreciate that, so I don't want to seem ungrateful by wandering off. But I can hear through the examination room door, and that's really awkward.

A nurse is trying to convince Tiffany to let them perform a procedure, and I haven't heard what it is, but I catch the words "test" and "police," and I know what they're asking. Tiffany says she doesn't need it, and she's trying to stay calm, but she's freaking out a little. I wish I could go in and be there for her, but I also know she wouldn't even want me overhearing this conversation. So, yeah, really awkward.

When the nurse comes out, I rise to go back inside, but she says, "Sorry, hon. Tiffany needs to see the doctor first."

"Is she okay?"

"All things considered, yes. Poor thing. I can't imagine what she went through, and I'm glad someone's here for her. Thank you."

I nod.

The nurse looks back toward the room. "She did that for kids after the shooting. I'm not sure if you knew that. If *anyone* knew that."

"I didn't."

"Tiffany didn't want to make a big deal of it. Especially given the circumstances. But I was here when they brought her in. They'd barely finished treating her before she wanted to help. She wanted to sit with any of the kids whose parents hadn't arrived. They all had, though. No one was alone except . . ." She clears her throat. "The other boy."

It takes a moment to realize who she means. "Harley Stewart."

"Yes. She knew his family wouldn't be quick to come. He was under guard, of course, but she wanted to sit with him. I guess she thought even someone like him shouldn't be alone. I always remember that. She has a good heart. A really good heart."

"She does."

The nurse pats my arm, smiles, and leaves me to take my chair again.

Skye

We drive Tiffany home. Mae tries to walk her to the door—I think she plans to make a point about Tiffany's father not coming to the hospital—but Tiffany doesn't want that. I don't blame her. No one needs the drama right now. So we watch Tiffany go inside. Then Mae takes me to see Jesse.

Dr. Mandal texted me earlier, saying Jesse only has a couple of cracked ribs and a bump on his head. He was released before we left with Tiffany. His mother invited us to stop by on our way home—Jesse would like to see me, make sure I was okay.

I expected Mae to say it was too late for social visits, but I think she knew how badly I wanted to see Jesse. In the hospital, I wanted to be a good friend to Tiffany, but it took all my willpower not to run off and check on him.

Dr. Mandal tells me Jesse is in the living room, and she takes Mae to the kitchen for tea.

I hurry into the living room . . . and he's asleep on the couch.

I squelch my disappointment. Of course he's asleep—it's been a long night and he's probably on painkillers. I tiptoe alongside the couch.

He's sleeping on his side, his face toward me. I bend over and press my lips to his cheek—

Jesse grabs me. His hands wrap around my waist, and he tosses me down beside him . . . and then lets out a sharp hiss of pain.

"Yep," I say as I sit up. "Cracked ribs, remember?"

"Oww."

I chuckle. He reaches over and pulls me down into a kiss.

"Another bad idea," I say.

"You're right. Better close the door."

"That wasn't what I meant." I shake my head. "They gave you something for the pain, didn't they?"

"Possibly." He pulls me into a kiss that leaves even me gasping, and my ribs are perfectly fine.

"I think we're getting better at this," I say when I back up.

He grins. "Much better."

"Which is not to imply we don't need more practice . . ."

"Not at all."

We kiss again. And again. Possibly again, though at some point, I lose track of where one kiss ends and the next begins. It just feels good. So amazingly good.

Whatever else is going on, at this moment I am happy. Happier than I have been in so long. Happier than I thought I'd ever be again.

We're cuddling and kissing and whispering when the sound of footsteps in the hall makes us both jump. We pull apart then, and wait as his father passes. Then we sit together, my head on his shoulder, his arm around me.

"How are you doing?" he asks.

"Better now."

He smiles. "Ditto. And Tiffany?"

I tell him about the hospital visit.

"I don't care if she's eighteen," he says. "Her parents should have been there."

"I know. I felt bad for her. Especially after what the nurse said. I never knew she was injured in the shooting."

"Twisted her ankle, I think. She was running and fell, and then she hid and wasn't found until the final sweep of the school. I always thought about that—even though she must have known the shooter was her boyfriend, she still hid. I can't imagine what that would be like—knowing you aren't safe even from your own boyfriend."

"Sometimes it's your own boyfriend that's the danger, even when he's not a school shooter."

"True. I guess I can't imagine that, either."

We're quiet for a minute. Then I say, "You know what I can't imagine? Offering to sit with Harley after what happened. I like to think I'm a good person—"

"You are."

I make a face. "I can be, but that's a whole other level of goodness. Of forgiveness. I don't hate Harley the way I hate Isaac, but I'm not looking forward to sitting across from him in a prison visiting room, either."

"Are you thinking of asking Tiffany to come along?"

I shake my head vehemently. "Never. I'm just . . ." I pause, as wisps of thoughts flit past, too ethereal to grasp. Another shake of my head. "I don't know what I'm thinking."

"That you'd like to kiss me again?"

I smile. "Right. Yes. I'm pretty sure that was it." I lean toward him. "Thank you."

"You're welcome."

I can't sleep. I'll start to drift off, and then bolt awake, heart pounding, with the urgent sense that I'm forgetting something. I lie there, going through all the things that could be keeping me awake. It's not a short list. On a few of the items, my mind slows and circles, like smelling something familiar and thinking, *Is it butterscotch? Kind of, but not exactly.*

Something to do with visiting Harley Stewart? Kind of, but not exactly. I do keep thinking of Tiffany sitting with him in the hospital, and I'm not sure why—I guess it's like I told Jesse, that I can't imagine being that forgiving and I wonder if that's wrong of me.

Whatever's bothering me is connected to Harley, but there's more to it.

Something to do with Jesse? No. Chris. No. Tiffany? Kind of, but not exactly. I feel terrible about what happened to her. But I can't fix that, and *this* feels like something I can fix. Or, more accurately, something I can figure out. Before it's too late.

Owen? Yes, it has to do with Owen. Am I worried he'll come after me? Yes, but Mae is changing the locks tomorrow, and for now, she has the alarm system armed.

I'm not freaking out over Owen, but my anxiety circles around him.

Owen and Harley.

Owen and the shooting.

Is there a connection? Not that I can see, beyond Vicki.

Owen didn't go to North Hampton. At the time of the shooting, he was a senior at Southfield. But could he still have been connected to it? A seventeen-year-old can easily slip into a different high school.

But if Owen was somehow part of the shooting, why would he come after me? He certainly wouldn't encourage me to investigate. That'd be his biggest fear—that I'd start asking questions.

Wait. No. He *hadn't* been the one who'd encouraged me to dig deeper. That was Chris.

Owen only wanted me gone. Wanted me gone so I *wouldn't* dig?

Could he have only been faking outrage over having me in Riverside to get Vicki's help?

When I close my eyes, I keep seeing Owen's house. The broken glass. The kitchen sink.

Why am I thinking of broken glass and a pile of dishes?

I shake it off and focus on Chris and the file. That police report. Why would Harley tell a lie that could be so easily disproven? Where he'd been at the time of the lockdown would be a matter of record. He could not have been in English class—

I bolt upright.

I sit there a moment as I work it all through. Then I grab my phone and text Jesse.

Jesse

Jesse wakes, gulping breath, heart pounding so hard he winces as his bruised ribs ache. He wipes sweat from his eyes and checks the clock on his phone. Three a.m. He groans. Barely an hour of sleep, and he's already had three nightmares.

He's just about to close his eyes when his mother raps at the door.

"My name is Jasser Devesh Mandal," he calls. "I'm sixteen. I live at 324 Spruce Grove Lane. And you're holding up three fingers."

"Two," she says through the closed door.

"Well, that's good. Otherwise, the fall might have given me x-ray vision. Which would be weird. Cool, but weird."

She chuckles, and he says, "Open the door. Make sure I'm okay."

She opens it but stays in the hall. "How's your head?"

"Fine. Ribs hurt, but otherwise, apparently, I land like a cat."

"Cats land on their feet."

"I don't have to. I'm bionic. All those steroids."

She makes a face, like she doesn't appreciate the joke, but she finds a smile for him.

"I'm okay, Mom. I'll *be* okay."

She leans against the doorjamb. "You seem happy."

"For a guy who tried rescuing a kidnapped girl and got knocked through a railing for his trouble? Sure, all things considered, I'm pretty happy."

"Is it Skye?"

He groans and thumps back on his pillow.

"I have to ask," she says.

Yes, she does and that's a discussion they'll need to have, but he really doesn't want to deal with it now. He props himself up again. "I'm happy because I came clean about the dope. I'm happy because I've resolved to get my act together in school. I'm *very* happy because Skye's back, and she's made me see where I'd gone wrong and realize I want to fix it. Now, good night, Mom."

She leaves, closing the door, and Jesse lies on his back and thinks of Skye. The problem is *how* he's thinking of her. He wants to pull up memories of her being here, of her kissing him, the look in her eyes, the feel of her lips on his. Instead, he keeps thinking of the nightmares. First, he dreamed of Owen attacking Mae and Skye in the parking lot. He double-checked his phone, reminding himself that she'd texted to say good night once she was in the condo. *Safely* in the condo. In the second nightmare, she got inside and texted him . . . and then was attacked by Owen. Check the phone again. Confirm that she texted a final good night from bed. And that brought nightmare number three: Owen attacking Skye in her room.

Jesse picks up his phone. Definitely no messages after that one.

Uh, yeah. Because she went to sleep. Like she said.

His stomach still twists as he stares at the message. Maybe he should—

Wake her up to see if she's safely asleep? Here, you want to focus on something? Check out that kiss emoji she sent with her last message. There? You like that?

He smiles. Then he reads his own last message to her.

Jesse: Sleep tight.

Sleep tight? What was he, her grandfather?

He thumbs through his emojis. Yeah, no. He's going to need more. He flips over to the browser, and as he does, a text pops up.

Skye: Jesse?

He fumbles to send back: here

Skye: Can we switch to laptops?
Him: Right. That's safer.

As soon as his is open, she's calling, and he hits Connect, and there she is. She's in bed, on her stomach, laptop in front of her. She's wearing a T-shirt with her hair tumbling down around her face. She's looking intently at the screen, frowning slightly. Then he must appear on her screen, because she grins, and it lights up her face, like he's just pulled a Hershey bar from behind his back, and that grin makes him feel . . .

Lucky. It makes him feel lucky. As if everything he's screwed up in the last three years has been wiped away, the universe presenting him with this reward for getting through it, a reward he isn't sure he deserves, but he'll take it anyway. He'll definitely take it.

Skye presses her thumb to the screen, and he presses his to it, and she grins again, and he thinks *I want to see you. Right now. I'm freaking out over Owen, and yeah, maybe that just makes a good excuse, but I really want to see you.*

"You weren't sleeping, were you?" she asks.

"Nah. Mom just did her first concussion check. Then I was looking up emojis."

Her brows arch.

"You sent me an emoji in your text," he says, "and I realized my phone doesn't have enough, so I was looking for one to send you."

She laughs softly, and her head bends over her keyboard, hair falling forward as she types. The text bar appears with the smiling-pile-of-poo emoji.

He chokes on a laugh. "Not exactly."

Her lips part, eyes dancing, like she's ready to continue the conversation, but then she hesitates and straightens, her expression sobering. "I was actually calling because I need to talk to you about something."

"Sure."

"It's—" She stops short and looks over her shoulder, and every muscle in his body tenses.

He's there. Owen is there.

"What'd you hear?" he asks as casually as he can.

She shakes her head. "Just paranoid. I think I've figured out something. A connection I missed before. If I'm right . . ." She nibbles her lip.

"I'll come over. You can tell me in person."

Another head shake, her hair swaying. "Mae would freak. And you shouldn't be driving in your condition."

"I don't have a condition. I cracked a couple of ribs. My head's fine; Mom's just being careful."

"For good reason. It can wait until morning." Her gaze moves up, as if to the top of the screen. "It'll be daylight in a few hours. I'll grab a taxi, pick up breakfast and come to your place. We can talk then. Okay?"

No, it's not. He's worried, and he wants to see her. *Now.* But that's his problem.

"I'll text you at seven," she says. "You can ask your parents if it's okay for me to come over that early."

"It will be."

Skye

I told Mae earlier that I've been smart about this so far. I have to continue being smart—*smarter,* if possible, more cautious, more careful. Also more respectful. I don't want to encourage Jesse to sneak over when he's been hurt. And I don't want Mae waking up and finding me gone. That'd be a slap in the face after what I said earlier about wishing I didn't need to sneak out.

I do want a better relationship with Mae. I also want to maintain my good relationship with the Mandals. And, let's be honest, even without those things, if I did let Jesse drive over, I'd panic, worrying he'd pass out from an undetected concussion.

I'll see him in a few hours. What I have to say will wait.

That does not, however, mean I can sleep. My theory keeps swirling in my brain. I try making notes to get it out of my head. That doesn't help. I decide to email those notes to my own account, and I tell myself that's just for backup, but I'll admit, part of it is so there will be a record, in case anything happens to me before I can tell Jesse. Clearly I've watched too many movies.

When I try to send the email, though, it doesn't go through. The Wi-Fi is down. Middle-of-the-night service work, I guess. I save it as a draft and resume staring at the ceiling.

A floorboard creaks, and I jump up . . . only to hear the soft click of Mae's bedroom door, as she goes back to bed after a bathroom visit. I did the same thing when Jesse was on the phone, jumping at some random noise.

Time to admit I'm not getting any more sleep tonight. I'll go grab a snack and read.

I head into the hall. As I'm passing Mae's bedroom, I hear a clack inside, as if she's checked her phone and then set it on the nightstand.

Could I talk to Mae about my theory? I'd like to. Give her a chance, and if she brushes it off as my wild imagination, then I'll know where I stand.

I tap on her door. "Mae?"

When she doesn't answer, I put my hand on the knob. Then I hesitate. If she didn't answer my rap and call, that might be a hint that she just wants to go back to sleep. And do I really *want* to run this theory past her? What if she *does* believe me and notifies the police, and it turns out I'm wrong? How will that look—to her, to the police . . . and to the person I'm accusing?

No, Jesse's the one who needs to hear this. The guy I can trust to listen and give a thoughtful, levelheaded response. I'll speak to Mae after I've told Jesse what I've figured out.

What I've figured out . . .

I want to be wrong. I really want to be wrong. Just another case of Skye's wild imagination. But my imagination has always been bound by that part of my brain that loves math and science. The logical part. The problem-solving part.

I've worked through the evidence and come to the correct conclusion. I know I have, as painful as it might be.

I release the doorknob and walk to the kitchen. I open the cupboard and . . .

There's food.

Well, technically it passes for food, though a dietitian might argue. The cupboard is stuffed with junk food. Cookies, chips, candies, and those granola bar things that pretend to be healthy but we all know better.

I check the freezer. Pizza. Pizza pockets. Pizza rollups. Yep, every variation on frozen pizza ever invented.

I'm not sure whether to laugh or sigh. Maybe even cry a little, because this is proof that Mae really is trying. Trying so hard. I complain about her hipster selection of food, and what does she do? Fills the cupboard and freezer for me. Except she doesn't know what I eat, so she just buys everything that teens consume in movies.

We'll figure this out. And if "figuring it out" for Mae means "finding someone else to care for this alien creature," then I'll deal with that, as I've dealt with everything else in my life.

I open the cupboard again and take out a bag of Oreos. I'm putting it on the table when a light flickers in the front hall.

I peer down the hall to see a tiny green light on the wall. It's solid now, and the "flicker" had just been me moving. But now that I've seen it, I find myself staring.

Why am I staring at a green light?

When I realize the answer, my gut goes cold.

The security panel light is green, just as it has been since I arrived, because Mae hasn't been using it.

Except tonight, after we got home, I watched her set it. She gave me the code and made me write it down. Then she had me disarm it and rearm it.

I must have screwed up when I armed it.

No, we both saw the green light turn to a flashing red one.

Then I must have done something wrong. Something that disarmed the system after we turned away. Or Mae took out the garbage and forgot to rearm it.

And am I just going to presume that?

I walk into the front hall. With every step, I pause to listen, but the only sound I hear is the hum of the circulation fan.

I reach the panel and peer at it, as if from up close, that solid green light might reveal itself to be a blinking red one in disguise. Of course it's not. The panel is closed, no sign of tampering.

I step to the front door. The lower lock is engaged, the dead bolt still in place.

I'm freaking out over nothing.

The door is still locked. The alarm hasn't been tampered with. Mae must have turned it off. I heard her get up. Maybe that's what she did.

Why would she do that? It doesn't make sense.

I check the locks again. Both engaged, as they were last night. A thump sounds from another room, and I spin.

The apartment is silent.

I look into the kitchen. At the butcher's block of knives.

Just take one.

That's silly. Dangerous, even.

Take one.

I step forward. The kitchen light goes out.

All the kitchen lights go out—the overhead one and the one on the microwave and the one on the fridge. The green light of the security panel stays on, though. Okay, a fuse blew in the kitchen. That's all.

I reach for the hall switch. Flick it up.

The hall stays dark, lit only by the glow of the security panel.

I try the other light, for the entryway.

Nothing.

The power has been cut.

Skye

No, the power can't have been cut. The alarm is still—

Battery backup. Otherwise, someone could just cut the power and break in.

No electricity. No Wi-Fi.

I put my back against the wall and reach into my pocket for my cell . . .

I'm wearing pj pants. My phone is in my bedroom.

I blink hard, trying to adjust to the nearly nonexistent light. As I do, I listen for something, anything. But the apartment is completely silent now, with the power out. No hum of the fridge or the fan.

Absolute silence.

I swallow, and I swear the sound echoes along the hall.

I could throw open the door and run. But where? To a neighbor, bang on the door in my pj's . . . only to discover that everyone's power is off, that it's just a blackout, and the Wi-Fi was only the first sign of trouble.

I could glance out a window to check, but I'm nowhere near one. I could open the door and see if the hallway is lit, but if someone's in here, they'll hear me turning the bolt.

Do I really think someone's in here?

There's no sign of it.

Except that green light. Showing that the alarm system is off.

I rub my forehead. *Think, think, think.*

To get inside the condo, someone would need to have keys and the code, and Mae wouldn't just hand those out.

But someone did get past the locks last Saturday. Came in and left my boots and the chocolate bar and Luka's shirt. However much I've tried to deny it, I know someone broke in.

I remember when my family had an alarm. It only lasted a few months, because I could never remember to disarm—or arm—it. I was always racing in and out, my mind elsewhere, and after a half dozen false calls to the security company, my parents left it disarmed. But outside the family, no one had that code.

Wait. Someone had. Someone who needed regular access to our house when my parents were at work and Luka and I were at school.

I remember something Mae said. It doesn't exactly explain this. It could, though. With a slight stretch. And if it does, it's yet further proof that my theory is correct.

I look up and down the hall.

Be smart.

Be careful, and be smart.

So many options, enough to make my pulse race and my head throb. Look out the door. Get a knife first. Get my phone first. Shout for Mae. Run to Mae.

Careful. Smart.

Forget pride. Forget the possible humiliation of treating a power outage like a murderous intruder.

Act like it's the worst-case scenario.

I slide toward the kitchen, my bare feet making no sound on the hardwood. I slide a knife from the block. Not the biggest or the smallest, but a knife I can hold in one hand. Wield with one hand. Then back to the front door. I hesitate there. Bend and peer under, hoping to see a hall light. Nothing. Which might only mean the door is well sealed.

I rise and continue sliding along the hall to my bedroom. The door is open, just as I left it. I creep inside.

A click.

I spin toward my closet as I remember the jingle of the hangers. Is that what I heard? I don't know. It was just one click.

The door is cracked open. Did I leave it open?

I can't remember.

I inhale as deeply as I can without making noise. My heart's thumping so hard I can barely breathe.

I ease toward my bed. The phone is there. Right there where I left it. I snatch it up in my free hand, and then wheel on the closet.

Nothing. All I hear is the sound of my breathing.

I lift the phone, keeping one eye on that closet door.

Call Jesse.

Call 911.

Jesse.

911.

I squeeze my eyes shut for a split second. *Just call someone.*

I make sure the sound is off, and then I text Jesse.

You up?

Really? That's what I'm going to say? Why not add a smiley face, too?

I just want to make contact. Make contact and reassure myself that someone is there.

I'm scared, Jesse.

I think there might be someone in the condo.

That's what I want to say, and I'm ready to type it as soon as he responds.

A red exclamation mark appears beside my message, saying it couldn't be delivered.

I glance at the top of the screen.

No signal.

How can there be no signal? It's easy to disconnect our Wi-Fi, but you can't just disconnect a cell tower.

No, but you can block the signal with a jammer. A piece of technology you could probably pick up at the same store where you bought your remote speakers and projectors.

I hurry into the hall.

Get out.

Run and get—

I look at Mae's bedroom door.

No way am I running without warning her.

I creep to her door and turn the knob. Then I push. The hinges creak, and I jump, nearly dropping my knife. I clutch it tighter and throw open the door.

Mae's bedroom is pitch-dark. She has blackout blinds, and

they're drawn shut with heavy curtains pulled over the top, as if a single point of escaped light might keep her awake.

I turn my flashlight app on low, and I can see her form in bed. She can't be too soundly asleep. I heard her no more than ten minutes ago.

No, I heard *something.*

Footsteps in the hall. A clack in her room.

I swallow and grip my knife. It's just a few steps to Mae, yet I can't seem to cross them.

I'm scared.

No, I'm terrified.

I'm afraid there's a reason Mae didn't wake when I knocked on her door. When I called her name. When I stepped into her room.

I'm afraid if I go to her bed and find . . .

If I find that anything has happened to her, I'll break down and lose my chance to escape.

But I have to check, don't I?

I swallow, and I adjust my grip on the knife and the phone, and with the light guiding my way and my ears tuned for the slightest sound, I cross those few steps. My knees bump her bed.

"Mae?" I whisper.

Why whisper? If someone's here, they know exactly where I am. Every move I make must echo through the silent apartment.

I walk around the bed. There's a shape in it. I reach out and feel my aunt's hip. Then I'm at the top of the bed, and I see her dark-blond hair fanning over the pillow.

"Mae?"

I take her shoulder.

"Mae?"

I shake her, lightly at first, and then harder and—

She flops onto her back, and I let out a yelp, and I drop the phone and knife as my hands go to her neck, desperately searching for—

I find a pulse. Or I think I do. I can't hear her breathing. I'm right here, and the room is silent, and I don't hear her breathing. I lean in, my ear going to her lips. Then I catch it, but it's as faint as her pulse.

When I shake her harder, she flops like a rag doll.

She's sedated. Heavily sedated. *Too* heavily sedated. I know that, and all I can think about was the time I came home with Gran, a month after the shooting, after we went out to lunch, and Mom stayed behind, and I went into Mom's room and . . .

She'd overdosed on sleeping pills. She tried later to say it'd been a mistake and she'd miscounted, but I knew it hadn't been. I'd run in, and I'd found her just like this.

My heart slams against my ribs as I shake Mae, saying, "Wake up. Please, Mae. Just wake—"

A board creaks in the hall. I stop. There's a soft thump, like a stockinged foot coming down. Then silence.

I take a deep breath. Pick up the knife. Grip it tight. And then . . .

I start to call Owen's name. But I know it's not Owen. I know who it is, and yet I still want to say his name, pray I am mistaken.

I take a deep breath.

"Tiffany?" I call.

No answer.

I start to again say "Owen," as if silence is proof that my theory is wrong. But I know better.

My heart's pounding so hard it takes a second for me to get the words out.

"Tiffany? I know it's you."

Knife ready, I start toward the door, letting my feet fall hard, my footsteps clear.

Run, Tiffany. Just run. Please. You have time. Run, and let me get help for Mae and take care of her, and the police can go after you.

Just run. Please, please, please . . .

A figure fills the doorway.

Skye

It's Tiffany. I knew it would be, but I still hoped. I hoped with all my heart that I was wrong.

"Why?" I say.

She snorts a laugh, and rage fills me. I remember how horrible I felt about her being kidnapped. I remember sitting at her side in the hospital, consumed by guilt, tripping over myself to apologize, while she was so understanding.

I think of the nurse, telling me that Tiffany has such a good heart, and of myself thinking, *Yes, yes, she does. So good. So brave. So strong.*

Such a liar. A hateful, twisted liar.

I grip the knife and—

She raises her hand and points a gun at me.

"You should see your face, Skye," she says. "You're like a little kid asking why somebody was mean to you. A little girl asking why her big brother wanted to shoot up his school."

"Luka didn't want to shoot anyone."

"You just keep telling yourself that, little girl."

"Luka hid the gun in the bathroom. That's why he went in there."

"Exactly. To get the gun and shoot—"

"And shoot who? The school was on lockdown. Luka was the one who *put* the school on lockdown. He's the one who called the police. Isaac gave Luka a gun, and he put it in the bathroom."

"Why would he—?"

"Because he's Luka." My eyes start to tear up, but I blink it back fast. "He hated guns. Wouldn't even go target shooting with our dad. Isaac told him the plan and gave him a gun, and he couldn't bring himself to carry it around. So he hid it in the bathroom, stole a girl's cell phone and called the police."

"Nice story, but—"

"You're the one who told the police Luka was in class when the lockdown was called. You lied, and then you gave yourself away."

"Gave myself away?"

"The performance art at the school, the show you put on for me. You're in the images in the English class. You were in Luka's class. You, not Harley. You're the one who gave that statement to the police, saying Luka snuck out after the lockdown was called. Instead, he was in the bathroom waiting to hand over the gun. Which was a really dumb, clumsy mistake. But that's all Luka did wrong. He made a mistake."

"Your darling brother planned—"

"No, he didn't. You did. You and Isaac. I don't know how much Luka knew. But he never agreed to that shooting."

"And the part about me being involved? When there's no proof that I had anything to do with it?"

"But there is. Whoever gave that report to the police knew the basics of the plan, but no details. That's why we presumed it was Harley. You told the police that you only knew Isaac was up to something with Luka and Harley. You said that Luka definitely knew what was happening. In other words, you lied."

"I remember how much you liked to tell stories, Skye. This isn't one of your best."

"It's all theory, of course. The details, that is. The heart of it, though—that you were part of the plan—is proven fact."

"Proven how?"

"By the fact that you're standing here, holding a gun on me. You'd gotten away with it. You successfully set yourself up as yet another victim: the poor girl whose boyfriend turned out to be a psychopathic school shooter. Then I showed up. The one person who had a reason to dig deeper. Especially if I started hanging around with Chris and Jesse. You knew Chris had doubts, didn't you?"

"Chris Landry is a—"

"I'm sure you figured out he questioned the official story. He wasn't digging, though. But if I came back? That might change his mind. So you counseled me to stay away from him. Stay away from Jesse, too. Bad, bad boys. Dangerous boys."

"You're crazy."

"No, but you tried to drive me there, and when that failed, well, making me *look* crazy should do the job just as well. Between you, Owen and Vicki, you covered all the bases."

"Owen? Owen kidnapped me—"

"The fried chicken says otherwise."

Her face screws up. "What?"

"You said Owen came home in a panic. And then he made fried chicken?"

"I had to *eat*."

"Nice that he cooked for you. I saw the plates in the sink. Two full settings. Lunch dishes, too, which is odd, since he'd have been at school."

"He came home."

"And he let you eat off the china? All you had to do was break a plate and attack him. But there *was* broken glass, wasn't there? In the living room. Glass with blood spray on the wall. According to you, he threw that tumbler in a rage. And then picked up a few pieces, cut himself, and then *stormed* out? Weird."

"I don't know what you're implying—"

"I'm guessing it was a fight. A falling-out between partners in crime. *Were* you just partners in crime? You said he had a crush on you."

"It doesn't matter—"

"So you guys were a couple. Okay. He came home for dinner and said he wanted to quit your crazy plan. You fought, and he ran."

"You found me tied up—"

"*Partially* tied up. Not that well, either. I bet it's really hard to bind your own hands behind your back. Luckily, I was too freaked out about Jesse's fall to notice. You were staging your escape, and then we showed up. Do you know what's the worst of it, Tiffany? If you hadn't launched your campaign to drive me off, I'd never have investigated the shooting."

"That's bullshit. You can't leave well enough alone. Just like your brother. Always have to be the hero. Always have to do the right thing."

"Which Luka did, when he tried to foil your plan."

"He didn't even know what the plan *was*, the idiot. I told Isaac to keep Luka out of it, but he gave him a gun. Gave it to him and didn't tell him why—just 'Hey, here's a gun'—in case he decided to join the shooting on his own. And what does Luka do? Calls the police to turn over the weapon. If Luka had any balls, he'd have refused to take the weapon. But no . . ."

That rage sparks again. I listen to her mocking my brother, and I realize—really understand—that she was behind it all. That she is the reason my brother is dead, and it takes everything I have to swallow my fury and give a measured response. I must stay calm. I must survive this so I can tell the truth. So I can clear my brother's name.

So I say, "Luka took the gun because he knew it was safer in his hands. And he probably suspected something else was going on. That's why he called the police. So what *was* the plan? You shoot up the school and go down in a blaze of glory?"

Her lip curls. "I wasn't going down. *Ever.* We were going to be legends. Kill as many kids as we could, and then run to Mexico."

"What movie did you swipe that plot from?"

"I got Isaac out of the school. Did you know that? I *rescued* him. And then what does he do? Panics. Loses his nerve and loses his mind. Starts saying that the only *real* way out is to kill ourselves. Kill myself? I hadn't *done* anything. I was not putting a gun to my head."

"But you agreed to, didn't you?"

"Of course I did. He would have turned on me the first chance he got. I just let him go first. The moron."

"Then, after he was dead, you went back to the school, where you hid and faked hurting your ankle. They found you in the final sweep and took you to the hospital. What did you say to Harley while you were 'sitting' with him? No, you didn't say anything, did you? You wanted to see if he'd say anything to you. If he knew you'd been behind it all. He didn't, so—"

"Enough. You've done a very good job of stalling, Skye, but it's time to kill your aunt."

"Wh-what?"

She laughs. "Did you think this was a nice girl-to-girl chat? Air our differences and go our separate ways, having come to a better understanding of each other?"

"I can't prove anything. No one has believed me so far. Just go. Run, like you planned to before."

"I'm no longer the dumb fifteen-year-old who thought life on the run with her boyfriend would be *so* romantic. Why do you think I didn't take off with Owen? I'm not running; I'm fixing this."

"How is *this* fixing it?"

"Because once you kill your aunt, you're free to tell the cops any story you want. They won't believe you. You'll be the bad seed who snapped. Murdered your aunt. Started ranting that the girl who befriended you—who got kidnapped because she tried to help you—is actually the mastermind behind the North Hampton shooting."

"They'll investigate—"

"Based on what? The smell of fried chicken? There's no sign I was ever here. The security system wasn't tampered with. The locks weren't picked."

"Your stepmom has the keys and the code from when she cleaned the condo for my aunt. And you came along to help."

The look on Tiffany's face tells me I've guessed right.

I lift my phone. "Mae and I were talking about you by text, and she mentioned you used to clean with your stepmom." I hit buttons on the phone. "Here, let me show you."

"That doesn't prove—"

"No, but your confession does."

"Confession?"

I waggle the phone. "The audio file I just emailed to Jesse."

She snorts a laugh. "Nice try. Check that phone again. The Wi-Fi is off and the cell signal is blocked."

"You mean *our* Wi-Fi. You disconnected the router. Which didn't stop me from connecting to our neighbor's unsecured one."

I look at my phone. "Yep, the file has been sent. Jesse will—No, strike that. Jesse just got it. He must not be able to sleep. In pain from that fall, I bet. Well, he has the audio, so forget about getting away with it."

"You lying bitch."

"Don't believe me?" I hold out the phone. "He's downloading the audio now. See?"

"Give me that."

"Hell, no. I'm not handing you my phone. You can see it from there. Just look. Downloaded thirty percent. Forty—"

She lunges for the phone. I throw it at her. Throw it in her face and slash my knife down on the hand holding the gun, but she dodges.

I don't expect that. I slash again, but it's wide, panicked. I kick, too. My foot makes contact. The gun rises, and I grab for her wrist. I drop my knife to grab her. She doesn't expect *that*. The gun falls as she wrenches back. I kick the gun aside and dive at her.

She scoops up the knife and strikes. It catches me in the sleeve, but only snags, and I punch, my fist slamming into her side.

She hits the wall with a thud and the knife falls. She lunges for it. I stomp on her hand, and she lets out a screech of rage and pain. I grab her by the wrist. She yanks back before I get a grip. Then she's gone, out the bedroom door, racing down the hall.

I'm about to go after her. Then I remember the gun and make a split-second decision to let Tiffany have a head start. There's something I need to do first.

When I catch up, she's at the front door, fumbling with the dead bolt.

A knock sounds at the door. She freezes.

"Skye?" Jesse calls. He knocks again. "Ms. Benassi? I'm sorry for coming by, but I thought of something I need to tell Skye, and she isn't answering her phone, and I got worried."

Tiffany turns to me. Slowly turns.

"That recording never went through," she says.

"Not the first time—I wanted you to come closer. But once you ran, I connected and sent it. It's in his inbox. He'll get it eventually. So step away from the door—"

She charges. I slash the knife. It slices into her. Blood sprays. But she doesn't care—is beyond caring. She shoves me as hard as she can and runs back toward the bedroom. Back to Mae.

"Jesse!" I shout. "Call the police!"

"Open the door!" he shouts.

"I can't." I'm racing after Tiffany. "Please. Get the police!"

Tiffany slides into Mae's room and slams the door behind her. I grab the handle, but there's blood on my hands, and I can't turn the knob. I grasp it with my shirt and twist and throw it open—

Tiffany is standing beside the bed, and she's retrieved the gun. The barrel points at Mae's head.

"Hand me your phone," she says.

When I hesitate, she waggles the gun. I retrieve my phone from the floor, pass it to her. She looks at the screen and snorts.

"No Wi-Fi," she says. "You're such a liar." She shoves my phone into her back pocket. "If it's any consolation, you should be glad you couldn't send that recording. Otherwise, I'd have had to make you kill Jesse, too. Now I just need to hide until the cops break down the door and find you beside your aunt's dead body. Bring that knife here. You have work to do, Skye."

"No."

"That wasn't a suggestion." She turns the gun on me. "Step over here—"

"No."

"I don't know what new trick you think you have up your sleeve, Skye. Or are you just stalling until Jesse gets help? I'm not going to give you that much time. You have thirty seconds—"

"Shoot me."

"If you're calling my bluff, that's a very stupid move."

"Is it?" I step toward her. "There's no one here to pull that trigger for you."

"What are you talking about?"

"You. The great Oz. The mastermind behind the screen. That's what you think you are. Do you know what you *really* are?" Another step. "A coward."

"Are you actually insulting me when I have a gun in my hand?"

"You don't pull triggers, Tiffany. You make other people do it.

You have no idea what it's like to kill someone. You sneer at Isaac for shooting himself. You sneer at Owen for running away. Yes, they broke . . . because you broke them. You made them do what you couldn't do yourself, and then you sneered when they couldn't hack it. That is the worst kind of coward."

"Do you really think this is a good idea, Skye? Goading me—"

"Fire the gun."

"You have ten seconds—"

"Stop talking. Pull the trigger."

Her finger twitches.

She glares at me. "Five—"

"Pull it, you psychotic bitch."

Her finger twitches. But that's all it does. It twitches, and her jaw sets, as if she's struggling to pull that trigger.

"Oh, come on," I say. "It's not that hard. Isaac did it. Over and over he did it. For you."

She grits her teeth, and she closes her eyes, and then she pulls the trigger.

The gun clicks. She pulls it again, but I'm already leaping at her. I drive the knife into her, just enough to make her drop the weapon and try to grab me, but I have her by the wrist, and I'm wrenching her around, and two seconds later, I have her on her knees, arm pinned behind her head.

"You emptied the gun," she manages to snarl through clenched teeth.

"Duh. You knew I didn't stay behind to send that recording. What did you think I was actually doing? I guess I'll have to actually thank my dad for teaching me to how to load them. Now get on your stomach and put your hands behind your back."

Skye

I haul Tiffany into the bathroom. Even if she's tied up, I'm not leaving her with Mae. I open the front door, and Jesse's there, and the police follow, and for once, there's no need to explain. Like Jesse, the police had already begun to suspect Tiffany's "kidnapping" story. Come morning, they would have been questioning her again. I just bumped up the timeline.

Mae regains consciousness at the hospital. By the time we leave, the police have found Owen, hiding in a motel twenty miles away. I was right about the argument. He hadn't planned to stab me. He only bought the knife to scare me. The plan had been to knock me out, "kidnap" Tiffany and blame Jesse and me for it. That's why the police had been called about Jesse having bomb-making materials—so they'd search and find evidence that he'd helped abduct Tiffany. Except Owen planted the evidence in his locker—easy for a custodian to do—and the police hadn't checked that. They hadn't even believed Tiffany had been kidnapped.

That's when Owen had enough. After school, he came home and told her he was done. They fought, and he took off.

Owen and Tiffany had been dating for months. They'd been hiding their relationship until she graduated, so he wouldn't lose his job. Then I came along, and they found something new to bond over.

As for Vicki, she'd known nothing of Tiffany's involvement. To her, Owen was just trying to get me out of town, and she'd supplied the tech.

And the three seniors who'd hassled Jesse and me? They had nothing to do with any of it. They were just part of life—everyday assholes with no goal larger than stirring up trouble.

In light of Tiffany's testimony, the investigation into the shooting will be reopened. Will that prove, beyond a doubt, that Luka was innocent? No. Nothing can.

With Tiffany's prior statement invalidated—and her confession on my phone—we only lose proof that Luka *was* involved in the shooting. The police will make a statement. Yes, that means they shot an innocent teenage boy, but under the circumstances, even I can't blame them. They were expecting a kid with a gun. Luka was a kid with a gun. He failed to put it down fast enough—confused or surprised or just slow to react. A tragic mistake.

The blame, ultimately, lies with Tiffany. She set the shooting in motion. She is responsible for my brother's death, as certainly as if she shot him herself. I will make sure she goes to jail for it. I will take the stand against her. I will sit in that courtroom every day of her trial. She will pay for what she did to Luka. To all of the victims.

My brother can never be truly vindicated. Some people will

still believe he intended to join Isaac and Harley in the North Hampton shooting. I accept that. What matters is that I have *my* answers, and I know they're the truth because I know my brother.

Three weeks later, Jesse is leading me someplace. I have no idea where. I'm blindfolded. It doesn't smell good—I can say that much. It stinks of moldy carpet and body odor and rancid butter and an industrial-strength cleaner that still can't get rid of the rest.

When he finally removes my blindfold . . .

"A movie theater?" I say, looking around.

I'm standing at the front of an auditorium. An empty one—not surprising given that it's ten o'clock on a Saturday morning.

"Private screening," he says.

"Of what?"

He waves to someone in a projection booth. The lights dim. The screen jiggles to life, showing an image of an empty room. Then a guy walks in.

"Oh my God!" I say. "Is that Duncan? From All-Time Five? Well, I mean, he *was* with ATF, until he left the group to—"

Jesse lifts a finger to his mouth. Duncan turns to the camera and says, "Hey, Skye," and I squeal. An honest-to-God tween-girl squeal that has Jesse choking on a laugh as I slug him in the arm with, "It's Duncan! He said my name!"

On the screen, Duncan continues. "Jesse tells me you guys were supposed to go to our concert three years ago, on your first date. I'm sorry you missed it, but I hear you two finally reconnected, which is awesome. And since you didn't make the concert, he's bringing it to you."

The screen goes dark, and then it lights up again, the first strains of music drowned out by the screaming of the crowd.

The screaming swells as the band walks onto the stage. I grab Jesse's arm. "It's the *concert*. And *Duncan*. How did you get him to do that?"

"Seems his solo career isn't doing so hot. I hired him. Pretty cheap, actually—"

I slap my hand over his mouth. "Ack, no!"

He tugs my hand away. "Sorry. Uh, I . . . I contacted him and told him our story, and he happily agreed. Refused to accept payment. He wanted to do it for you."

I grin. "Much better." Then I throw my arms around his neck and kiss him, and I keep kissing him until the music begins and I can't help glancing at the screen. Jesse chuckles and pulls away, saying, "More of that later. This is for you."

"For *us*. But you do realize I remember every word to every song, right? I'm going to scream them all, at the top of my lungs."

"Good." He takes my hand, squeezing it as he turns me to face the screen. "I've been waiting for that, for a very long time."

I'm hanging a photo in our living room. Our new living room. It's been barely a month since that night with Tiffany, but when Mae puts her mind to something, it happens. Fast.

She's bought a house. A four-bedroom one just a few blocks from Jesse. Gran and Mom arrived yesterday. They're moving in, and Mae has hired a full-time caregiver to help.

Yes, I'm staying in Riverside. This is my home, and I'm taking it back.

Mae might have gone about it the wrong way, but ultimately, she was right—I needed to face this. It was the only way to find myself again.

Mom and I are hanging an old photo of Gran and Grandpa over the fireplace. Gran stands in the middle of the room, directing us to shift it up, down, left, right . . . With each new move, Mom rolls her eyes at me.

Finally, I say, "There, perfect."

Gran motions for us to lift the picture up a bit. I ignore her and pound in the nail while Mom holds the photo. When we're done, Mom rumples my hair, like she used to, and gives me a quick hug. Before she pulls away, she whispers, "We'll be okay, baby."

I think we will be. On the sofa is a college brochure Mom picked up after announcing her intention to take a few courses, in hopes of honing her rusty graphic design skills. That's a good sign. Really good. I know, though, that finding out the truth about Luka won't fix her depression. There is no insta-cure. There's a continuum between sickness and wellness, and my hope—all of our hopes—is that this will push her closer to the "well" end.

Mom had depression, but the shooting nearly destroyed her. I'm not sure if I truly realized that. I think there was always a part of me that wanted to tug her sleeve and say, "You've still got one kid, Mom. Don't forget about me." And, yes, maybe I resented her a little, when she couldn't be there for me.

I understand better now, after what I've been through. I understand how she blamed herself for what happened with Luka. Dad certainly blamed her. So did others, as I heard at RivCol. Luka's mom was "crazy." Either he inherited some gene or her neglect pushed him to vent his frustration by joining a school shooting.

Now, like me, she knows we didn't miss something in Luka. We didn't fail him. As important as that is to me, it means more to her. It is the lifting of a dark veil, and when I look at her now, I see my mom again. She even woke me up this morning with one of her god-awful songs.

After the photo is hung, I realize Mae is holding a book and a shoe box. She hands the book to Mom and the shoe box to me. I open it. Inside . . .

My breath catches when I see what's inside.

"Luka's sketches," I whisper.

Mae nods. "I took them off your bedroom walls after you left. I knew you'd want them again someday. I hoped you would, anyway."

I hug her. She doesn't expect that, and it's kinda like hugging a statue, but she doesn't resist. When I pull back, she plants an awkward kiss on my forehead.

I hear a noise and look over to see Mom crying. My gut seizes, as if in the course of three seconds, she's plunged into the pit of depression again. Then Gran sits beside her and puts an arm around her shoulders, and together they open the book Mae gave her. It's our family photo album.

Mom looks up at Mae and says, "I thought this was gone forever."

"Never," Mae says.

I slip out then. I walk to my new room, and I sit on the bed, and I go through Luka's sketches, and I cry. I can do that now.

Cry. Grieve. Mourn.

It hurts so much, and there are days when I almost want to go back to thinking Luka was a monster, so I don't have to feel this.

But that only lasts a moment. I have my brother again, and that's what I wanted, more than anything.

I tack up a sketch of the two of us, dressed as goofy superheroes.

Make me a hero, Skye.

I kiss my finger and tap it to his forehead. *You are, Luka. To me, you always were. Now you always will be.*

ACKNOWLEDGMENTS

First, a huge thank-you to S. K. Ali for her feedback on the portrayal of Jesse and his family. S.K., thank you for making this such an easy and positive process. I cannot tell you how much I appreciated that.

Also, to my editors Phoebe Yeh at Crown US, Lynne Missen at Doubleday Canada and Antonia Hodgson at Little Brown UK, and my agent Sarah Heller, thanks for all your help whipping this one into shape!

ABOUT THE AUTHOR

Kelley Armstrong is the #1 *New York Times* bestselling author of the Darkest Powers (*The Summoning, The Awakening,* and *The Reckoning*), Darkness Rising (*The Gathering, The Calling,* and *The Rising*) and Age of Legends (*Sea of Shadows, Empire of Night,* and *Forest of Ruin*) trilogies for teens, and several thriller and fantasy series for adults. Her two most recent YA thrillers both received starred reviews, with *Publishers Weekly* saying *The Masked Truth* is "overflowing with twists," and *VOYA* praising *Missing* as "a compelling thriller that keeps the reader hooked until the end." Visit Kelley online at kelleyarmstrong.com.